Every Man a King

Every Man
a King

A King Oliver Novel

Walter Mosley

MULHOLLAND BOOKS

Little, Brown and Company

New York Boston London

Copyright © 2023 by Thing Itself, Inc.

Hachette Book Group supports the right to free expression and the value of copyright. The purpose of copyright is to encourage writers and artists to produce the creative works that enrich our culture.

The scanning, uploading, and distribution of this book without permission is a theft of the author's intellectual property. If you would like permission to use material from the book (other than for review purposes), please contact permissions@hbgusa.com. Thank you for your support of the author's rights.

Mulholland Books / Little, Brown and Company
Hachette Book Group
1290 Avenue of the Americas, New York, NY 10104
mulhollandbooks.com

First Edition: February 2023

Mulholland Books is an imprint of Little, Brown and Company, a division of Hachette Book Group, Inc. The Mulholland Books name and logo are trademarks of Hachette Book Group, Inc.

The publisher is not responsible for websites (or their content) that are not owned by the publisher.

The Hachette Speakers Bureau provides a wide range of authors for speaking events. To find out more, go to hachettespeakersbureau.com or call (866) 376-6591.

ISBN 978-0-316-46021-7 (hardcover); 978-0-316-47421-4 (large print)
LCCN 2022943379

10 9 8 7 6 5 4 3 2 1

MRQ-T

Printed in Canada

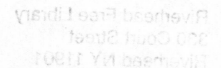

Every Man a King

1.

I DROVE MY tiny cream-colored Bianchina up the FDR to Seventy-First, crossed the park, passing the Strawberry Fields memorial, and then made my way up West End a few blocks until turning left, finally arriving at an imposing gate in the Great Wall—the only entrance to a sprawling estate overlooking the West Side Highway and the Hudson.

I stopped at the thick crisscrossed stainless steel bars and waited. Across a broad, two-hundred-foot-deep lawn could be seen the four-story white stone home. The structure itself occupied half a Manhattan city block.

The owner of this impressive example of opulence was multibillionaire Roger Ferris, called King Silver by international society pages, jealous competitors, and those who liked catchy nicknames that had the ring of truth.

The not-so-reclusive Ferris had moved out of Stonemason's Rest Home to take up residence in the heavily guarded hall because he was in serious *negotiations* with his son and daughter over control of MDLT (Mains dans la Terre) Inc. Roger's children, Alexander Ferris and Cassandra

Ferris-Brathwaite, had filed suit claiming that their father was no longer competent, arguing that the board of directors of MDLT and the state of New York, among others, were legally bound to appoint them his trustees. If they were successful, they would become executor and executrix of an international conglomerate estimated to be worth north of eight hundred billion dollars.

Sitting in my minuscule Italian car, I considered the siblings' claim against their father. He was ninety-one years old, an advanced age for a captain of industry. The *kids* were both past retirement age themselves. The argument that he, Roger, was too feeble to run an international conglomerate made sense except for the fact that anyone who spent more than five minutes talking to the man knew that he was vibrant, vital, and vigilant. He played a mean game of chess, and before the recent pandemic and legal troubles, he still danced every day. I knew of his gamboling because his regular dance partner was my grandmother—Brenda Naples.

Brenda was ninety-three, sharp as a whip, and black as a moonless night on an ancient sea. She met Roger at Stonemason's and they quickly became three-quarters of an item.

It was an unexpected coupling. Roger had been rich since the moment of his conception, whereas Brenda was born of sharecroppers, the issue of earlier sharecroppers, who were, in turn, born from three centuries of enslavement.

"Hey, King," intoned a voice I knew quite well.

"Forth," I replied, turning my head to gaze out the driver's window at the huge white man who seemed to have materialized from nowhere.

Forthright Jorgensen was six foot five with more muscle than most athletes. His hair was tawny and his eyes a color blue that almost seemed synthetic, it was so bright.

Forthright's father, Anders Jorgensen, was an anarcho-syndicalist who only believed in The Struggle; one might have said that this was his religion. Forthright became an old-school libertarian and started organizing unions. When he gave up on the American brand of labor coalitions, he published a notice in the *Western Worker* magazine saying, "I am abrogating my membership in the unions I belong to because of their inability to inspire political change and to fully eradicate sexism and racism from their ranks, and their failure to comprehend the underlying fascist tendencies of modern-day capitalism."

"You here to see Brenda?" Forth asked me.

"She's here today?"

"Been all week."

"Well then, I'll be happy to say hey."

"If it ain't her, then what brings you up here?" Forth was close enough that he could give my small auto a cursory once-over. He was, after all, in charge of security for the mansion and everyone in it.

"Roger said he wanted to see me about something. You know he won't talk about anything serious over the phone."

The security guard lifted his head, looking at the sky, and said, "You get that?"

He was talking into a microphone secreted somewhere on his person. There were a dozen security guards sprinkled around the grounds and one in a communications center where pertinent information was transferred to Roger.

When I heard that Forthright had given up on unions because of his stringent beliefs, I told him about the job Ferris had and he took it because in MDLT's recent incarnation, Roger had instituted a profit-sharing program in which 40 percent of real profit—those monies made before taxes, reinvestment, bonuses, and perks—was divvied up among all employees who had worked three years or more for the company.

"You think you'll get rain before a hail of lead?" I asked the security chief, killing time while we waited for a reply from on high about my status as visitor.

"It's no joke, Joe. The kids are really serious about fleecing the old man. They know he wants to turn MDLT over to the employees…and I'm not just talkin' about the dudes and dudettes in monkey suits. He wants everybody, including the foreign mining staff, to share in ownership. I'm absolutely sure that his kids would kill Roger if they could."

I felt the chill of fear pass over my shoulders. My grandmother would be in danger if assassins came in to eradicate Roger. I wanted to keep her safe but knew that she wouldn't have any of that.

I'm over twenty-one, Black, and free, I imagined her misquote. *Ain't nobody gonna make me scared. Nobody but the Lord.*

"Go right in," Forth said over my worries.

The stainless steel gate lifted, and I drove about twenty feet until reaching seven granite buttresses that blocked my way. After the gate lowered behind me, the stone ramparts sank seamlessly into the ground.

I was free now to approach the manor.

*   *   *

Dozens of yellow rosebushes lined the road up to the house. The paved lane formed a semicircle up past the front door. I exited my minicar, leaving the keys in the ignition so one of the security staff could park it somewhere underground.

Up close, the white walls of the house showed underlying veins of faint primary colors. I'd been told that the manor was constructed from the most valuable stone extant.

The front doors occupied an area twelve feet wide and fifteen high. The door to the left was made from pink ivory wood filigreed with gold wire in the shapes of various sinuous flowers. The right-hand door was ebony wood, carved with a bas-relief of dozens of laborers in the process of building a great but undefined edifice.

There was no knocker or doorbell, but that wasn't necessary, as every visitor was announced well before they reached the threshold.

My grandmother opened the door maybe two and a half minutes after I got there.

"Baby," she said, and then pulled me down by the lapels of my powder-blue sports jacket in order to kiss my lips—a greeting that was our custom.

Behind her was a vast foyer with five doors. This lobby was painted buttery yellow and sported a vase at the center of each intermittent wall. Each urn contained two dozen roses of either the primary or secondary colors.

"What you doin' here on a Sunday when you should be in church?" my grandmother asked with feigned suspicion.

Brenda told everyone that she was four eleven, but I was sure that she'd fudged an inch or two. She hadn't topped a hundred pounds in the decades I'd known her.

"Roger asked me to drop by," I replied to her semiserious query.

Brenda's face got a look that I recognized as stern. She let her head dip to the side, then clasped her hands in front of the bright scarlet kimono she wore.

I understood her trepidation but didn't want to feed that worry, and so said, "You're looking pretty spry, Grandma."

"All that dancin', I suppose."

"You still go out dancing? I thought Roger was worried about gettin' shot?"

"He hired a quartet to play Tuesdays, Thursdays, and every other Friday. Got me so I can take a walk around the property every mornin' 'fore five."

"He wake up that early too?" I asked.

"You know I don't sleep in that white man's bed, King."

"I don't know," I protested with a smile. "It's been a while, and he's got you up on your toes."

"He's a fine man, okay? But a woman cain't be rushed."

I wondered what a rush to sex felt like at ninety-plus years of age.

"You have any idea why your friend called me?" I asked, wondering when she was going to invite me inside.

"No. But you don't want to get too deep into anything with a man like that."

"Because he's white?"

"Because he's rich and spoiled and don't give a goddamn about little people like you and me."

"But he's your boyfriend."

"That don't matter. One time, back down in Mississippi, I had a beau name of Rooster, his given name. He ran a juke in the Delta and killed four men and one woman—that I know of. I loved that man like okra loves rain, but you better believe I knew what he could do."

"You gonna let me in, Grandma?"

While she pondered that question, the sound of hard-soled footsteps came from one of the five halls leading into the deep yellow foyer.

"Joseph!" Roger Ferris hailed from a doorway to my left.

My grandmother winced.

"Roger," I intoned.

"Come join me in the office, young man."

I did not take umbrage, because forty-four compared with ninety-one actually was young.

"Lead the way."

Considering the general lavishness of the manor, Roger's den was an anomaly, as it was small and unadorned. The walls, ceiling, and floor were all somewhere around eighteen feet in width and length. The floor was sealed pine, and the desk pressboard lined with lime-colored linoleum. Slatted folding chairs were the only seats. There wasn't even a window.

He went to stand behind the zombie desk.

"You don't have a bookcase?" I asked, lowering into my seat.

"This is the room I do business in," he said. "No comfort, no distractions."

Roger was six feet tall and weighed maybe forty pounds more than my grandmother. He sat, exhibiting both gravity and elegance. Then he took out a pair of glasses with semitransparent red frames and donned them. Staring at me through those lenses, he was reminiscent of a predatory

9

bird from thousands of years before humans dominated the Americas.

Having been told that this utility closet of an office was only about business, I asked, "This got to do with your kids?"

"Not at all."

"Huh."

"There's a man named Alfred Xavier Quiller," Roger began.

I'd heard the name. The natural-born genius Quiller was a poster boy for the Men of Action and other like-minded alt-right organizations. I knew the name, though at that moment I couldn't recall his shtick.

"Mr. Quiller has been detained by an as-yet-unidentified branch of the government. That or maybe an independent agency representing them."

"An independent agency? How does that work?"

Roger sat back in his folding chair, evaluating the question.

"There are times," he said, "when legitimate federal institutions are not allowed to take action. At these times they often use independent agencies to obviate the law."

"I see," said the blind man.

"Quiller is being investigated for tax evasion," Roger continued, "of involvement in the murder of a US citizen on foreign soil, and for the sale of sensitive information to the Russians."

"That's a full dance card."

"I don't like him. He's a misogynist, a racist, a thief, and an elitist of the highest order. I'd be happy to see him shot by a firing squad, hanged by the neck, or stoned in the town square. But the government may very well be railroading him, and the betrayal of our civil rights is a crime worse than any he's being held for."

"So the stoning has to wait for a constitutional review?"

"Excuse me, Joe, I . . . This issue is important to me."

His plaintive response was a surprise. Ferris was an easygoing boss man—most of the time. That and he usually laughed at my jokes.

"Sorry," I said.

King Silver squinted hard and then lowered his head. He had to reach up to keep the red glasses from sliding off his nose. After a few seconds, he looked up again.

"Quiller got a note to me. He said that he was innocent of the crimes he was blamed for, that he was extradited from France only after being kidnapped from a dacha he owns in Little Peach. That's an exurb of Minsk in Belarus. He says that the government has been holding him without due process."

"When did this all happen?" I asked. "I mean, usually something like that is twenty-four-hour news fodder."

"I'm not sure. Maybe the government is afraid of what might come out. That'd be a good reason to hold him without a judicial review. Fucking Patriot Act."

"If he's being held unofficially, how did he manage to reach out to you?"

"He bribed a guard. Gave him a, you know, um, a token I'd know was his and a note explaining his situation."

Roger looked into my eyes, nearly beseeching me, though I could not tell for what.

"They have him in a private cell on Rikers Island," he added.

"Rikers." I uttered the word with hardly a tremor.

The cold went through my shoulders all the way down to my fingertips. I'd spent time as a prisoner at Rikers. They gave me a private room too; it was called solitary confinement and nearly broke me.

"Yes," Roger concurred. "They're holding him there illegally while getting their ducks in a row."

"What does that have to do with you?"

The billionaire let out a silent sigh, then hesitated.

"He knows that my weak spot is human rights."

It didn't sound like much of a reason, but I kept that opinion to myself.

"I want you to go to Quiller," Roger went on. "Question him and then look into his claims. Find out if he really was kidnapped. Identify the dead man. Decide if he was murdered, and if he was, was the killing justified."

"Guilt or innocence is why you have a trial," I countered.

"A trial would be meaningless in this case. I've reached out to the so-called authorities, and they have turned a cold shoulder."

I smiled, thinking about my own joints.

"Something funny?" Roger wanted to know.

"Calm down, man. You asked me to come, and I'm here. You wanted me to hear you out, and I'm listenin'."

Roger nodded and leaned back in his uncomfortable chair.

"I know, Joe. Thank you for coming."

"So what if you believe this man is not getting a fair shake? I could point at ten thousand young, and old, men and women around the country in the same situation. What's special about Quiller? Or, in other words, what's he got on you?"

My question had a definite impact on Roger's face. It was the look of haggard determination.

"I have committed no crime," he said.

"But are you innocent?" I shouldn't have asked, but I just couldn't help it.

"I've done my share of wrong in this long life," he acknowledged. "I've cheated and stolen. Some might even say that I've been the cause of a few deaths. You're right, I owe a debt to Quiller, but not because of any culpability on my part."

It was a delicately constructed claim. A slight breeze could have blown it over. But that was true of most of my clients.

"Is that all?" I asked the brooding billionaire.

"Will you do it?"

"I'll start and see where it goes."

"That's all I can ask," he said, and then paused. "Brunch is served soon. Let's go over the particulars and then have something to eat."

2.

ROGER AND I spent the next three-quarters of an hour going over the details of what he'd been told and what he'd found out on his own, how much I'd charge, and, finally, what resources he could make available to me.

"Let's wait till I ask around," I said, "before you call out the cavalry." I stood up from the folding chair and added, "After all, this is intelligence gathering, not war."

He nodded, but my estimation of the job caused a sour twist in the rich man's lips. He was used to bullying his way through the world.

I was used to clapping bullies into cuffs.

"I have something for you," he said, reaching into a pocket.

"Hi, Daddy," Aja, my daughter, hailed as I stepped out of the cube room into the wide, blue-carpeted hallway.

"What are you doing here, honey?"

"Grandma B invited me to brunch."

Aja was a couple of inches shorter than I with dark brown skin and bright eyes. Valedictorian of her high school class, she swam competitively and loved playing in basket-ball pickup games around Manhattan. There were very few women allowed in those games, but the city basketeers knew that she left it all on the court.

"I thought you were going to write that paper today."

"And that I wouldn't even eat?"

I smiled and she kissed my cheek, the scarred side. She was the closest person in my life and I thanked the God I didn't believe in every day for her.

"Aja-Denise," Roger greeted, coming out after me.

"Hello, Mr. Ferris," she said. "How are you?"

"Even if I fall dead after our meal, this would have still been a pretty good day."

My daughter giggled at his over-the-top words and the three of us made our way toward the afternoon dining room.

Everywhere was a trek at Silbrig Haus, Roger's name for his humble abode. We walked down the long hall, through a painting gallery, across a sitting room, and finally into a room that sported a twenty-foot-long hickory table set next to a bulletproof wall of a window that looked across the Hudson into New Jersey.

Everything Roger had or did, lived in or thought, was immoderate and excessive.

Seated at the north end of the dining table were my grand-mother and her grandnephew, my watered-down cousin, Richard "Rags" Naples.

"Rags," I said, holding out a hand as he rose to his feet.

"King," he rejoined.

I felt the strength in that grip. Rags was a rough-and-tumble ex-soldier, ex-mercenary, ex-bodyguard who now worked as a *specialist in delicate extractions*. Ten years my junior, he didn't look dangerous but that's what made him so good at his job. His hands were not only powerful but roughened from extreme exertions. His face was...wizened; not wrinkled, but rather etched with extremely fine lines. He was acorn brown and the same height as my daughter.

"How's extractions?" I asked.

"Keepin' me on my toes, all eight of 'em."

Everyone got to their feet to exchange kisses, hugs, and handclasps. My grandmother's place was at the head of the table for all daylight meals. Roger took that position for dinner.

After Forthright came to join the get-together, we all sat.

The meal consisted of buckwheat waffles, wild rice and citrus salad, smoked salmon for my daughter, who'd given up mammal-red meat, and thick bacon for the rest of us. The serving staff brought out the trays containing the meal and then left us on our own to divvy up the largesse.

"So," Roger said a while after we'd started eating, "Aja-Denise, how's school going?"

"Okay. They have us studying world history from the Industrial Revolution up through the later nineteenth century."

"That's an interesting period," Roger said. "A lot happened then to shape the world—for better and for worse."

"That's what they say in almost every lecture," Aja agreed.

"What college is it?" Rags asked.

"Beckton University."

"Never heard of it," our cousin stated.

"It's in Detroit, been around for nearly fifty years."

"You moved to Michigan?"

"Beckton is a low-residency school," Forthright put in. "They offer what one might call a radical arts education."

"So what do you study there?" Rags asked anyone who wanted to answer.

"They have all kinds of degrees," Aja responded. "You can study architecture for the twenty-first century, Chinese medicine, footprint ecology, and about fifty other subjects."

"And what's your major?" Rags asked.

"I'm getting a degree in knowledge, which is also called a PhD in liberal arts."

"PhD? Don't you have to get a BA first?"

"It's a six- or seven-year course of study," my patient daughter explained. "You pick up the lower degrees along the way."

That conversation went on for a while. As it meandered, my mind drifted to the job Roger wanted me to do. There was little involved that I liked or felt drawn to. To begin with, there was the nightmare called Rikers Island.

Most of the literature I've read on psychotherapy says that all humans' true psychological natures were developed before the age of six; what you experienced combined with the structure of your DNA bespoke who you would be from then on. You could make conscious changes to your mind, but you had to work at it all the time because the person you were born to be was always ready to come out and play, and play hard.

I believe in that psychological rule of thumb even though my experience has seemingly been the exception.

While Aja explained the ins and outs of her extremist education, I was remembering the twelve weeks I endured becoming a new man under the pressure of Rikers. When I was incarcerated I was still a New York City cop, a detective working his way up the ladder. Then I was framed, arrested, beaten, doused with piss, and threatened from the time I woke up, through my tedious and dangerous day, until falling back into nightmare, only to wake up in terror again.

I'd been in the hole three weeks when guards took me to the *shower room* to wash off the crud. I was already permanently scarred by a con named Julee, who wielded a jagged tomato can lid. I'd already been told that I'd spend the rest of my life in stir.

The shower was an empty room made of concrete and cinder blocks. When we got there the guards made me strip. Then they brought out a hose designed to put out fires. They blasted me for maybe two minutes, but it felt like forever. I could still feel the bruises at that rich man's table.

When the hose was shut off I was too stunned to get to my feet. Freezing, I could hardly breathe. One of the guards was yelling something, but the words failed to convey meaning—at first.

"He said get your ass up or we gonna clean out your butt-hole with this here hose!" one of my tormentors shouted.

Biding for time I said, "Why you doin' this shit to me, man?"

"For knockin' out Jimbo's tooth," another guard replied.

There were four guards in all. That was the usual count for badasses, and by that time I was one of the most dangerous convicts in stir. Jimbo was a huge Black guard who thought he didn't need any help transferring me to the meeting with my lawyer. Despite hunger, thirst, and fifteen pounds' worth of chains, I whipped around and hit Jimbo so hard that the blood was gushing from his mouth.

My surprise was that he only lost one tooth.

"... right, Daddy?" Aja said.

"What?"

"Richard says that maybe a degree from a school like Beckton might not be good for getting a job, and I told him that I could, probably."

I was still in that torture room, looking at the meal through a chink in the cinder block wall.

"What kinda diploma you got for your work, Rags?" I asked my cousin.

At first he riled, no doubt thinking that I was somehow insulting him. But when Rags went over the words in his mind he smiled and then nodded at my challenge.

"Yeah, yeah," he agreed. "It's the man you hire, not the diploma."

The meal went on after that. Outside the cell of my mind people laughed and conversed, ate and shared their ideas. I wanted to join in, but once I'd begun remembering Rikers and the man I no longer am, I couldn't change tracks. I went into jail a guardian of the peace and came out lawless, or, at least, unbound.

"Baby?" my grandmother cooed.

"Yeah?"

"You wanna come help me with the dishes?"

"We have people who wash dishes for a living," Roger pointed out to Brenda for probably the hundredth time.

"Every man got to clean up his own mess," she replied.

"But why does Joseph have to help? Washing dishes is women's work." Roger was rich enough not to have to bend to social expectations. He said whatever he felt.

"Women's work is keepin' fools like you in line," Brenda Naples informed the billionaire.

"What's wrong, Joe?" my grandmother asked while we worked our way through the dishes.

The sink was restaurant-size. There were two dishwashers, one for breakables and the other for pots and pans, and enough staff that if each one cleaned only three dishes the job would be done. But Brenda put liquid soap in hot water, donned her own personal rubber gloves, and washed each piece of tableware by hand. I rinsed and dried, a job I'd done since I was five years old visiting my grandparents' cold-water shack in Jackson, Mississippi.

"Nothing, Grandma," I said.

"You know a child is never s'posed to lie while doin' his chores."

"So I could lie any other time?"

"Answer my question, King."

When she called me King in that tone, it meant playtime was over.

"Why you invite Rags to brunch?" I wasn't going to spill my guts that easily.

"He's a trustworthy soldier."

"Doesn't Roger have enough security with Forthright and all?"

"I called Richard for you."

"Me?"

"Roger didn't tell me that he was callin' on you. That means he's tryin' to protect me from some danger he's puttin' you in. That's why I called your cousin, so you'd see him and remember him if you get in too deep."

"You know I'm forty-four," I reminded her.

"Ain't none of us could make it on our own, child."

I'd been receiving pearls of wisdom like that from my father's mother for all my years. That was probably the reason I didn't embark on a life of crime like my dad and his brothers. I knew for a fact that it was from her words that I found strength in the bowels of Rikers.

"I love you, Grandma."

We were all out on the driveway that went past the front doors of Silbrig Haus. Forthright's people brought my Bianchina and Rags' sand-colored CJ-5 Willys Jeep. The militaristic vehicle was a small and sturdy version of its World War II counterpart—and a perfect automobile for Rags.

Before climbing in he handed me a business card. It had been blank but Richard had jotted down his initials, two phone numbers, and an e-mail address.

"Granny B told me that you might be wanting my help with something," he said as I read the scant markings.

"She worries too much."

"That is an existential impossibility," the self-educated mercenary said.

I smiled and clapped his shoulder.

*　　*　　*

Aja bundled in next to me in the tiny car.

We made it over to Park Avenue and toured down toward Lower Manhattan in no particular rush.

"You gonna work for Mr. Ferris?" she asked when we were crossing Fifty-Seventh.

"That what your great-grandmother said?"

"No. She asked me when I was gonna have a baby."

"She did?"

"Yeah. Her sister Lottie has two great-great-grandchildren and Grandma B doesn't want her getting that far ahead."

"Granny B has six great-grands as it is," I argued against the woman not there.

"Yeah, but I'm her favorite. She knows that my kids won't come askin' her for money."

At that time Aja lived, with four other girls, in a fourth-floor walk-up on Bowery Street not far from Delancey. I stopped in front of her building and leaned over to hug her good-bye.

"See you in the morning?" I asked. She worked in my office, pretty much ran my life.

"I want to take the morning to finish my essay on Fanon."

"*Wretched of the Earth*?"

"*Black Skin, White Masks.*"

"Never read that one."

"You mean there's a book you haven't read?"

"I love you too, honey."

She jumped out and ran up the stairs of her overpriced tenement. I sat in the car in front of her door a good five minutes before pulling away from the curb.

3.

IN ORDER TO get to Rikers Island, a part of the Bronx, you have to go through the borough of Queens. So, at 10:00 the next morning I was driving across the Francis R. Buono Memorial Bridge. Mingus played on the boom box. His smoother jazz compositions provided calm when my heart refused to slow down. And that morning it felt as if the blood pump wanted to jump out of its cavity.

I had a good deal to be worried about. Alfred Xavier Quiller, an icon of the alt-right, was being held without legal accord, by some shadowy authority, in New York City's very own prison—the last place in the world I'd volunteer to visit. Roger had assured me that he'd greased the way for me to get to Quiller, but what if he was wrong? What if I was swallowed by shadow when I made my visitor's request?

At the Rikers Island Visitor Center, uniformed minders took my name, looked it up on an old desktop, had a little discussion among themselves, and then sent me to a special waiting room not much bigger than Roger Ferris's work cube. The walls were dirty gray. The blue linoleum floor was scuffed and gritty underfoot. There were three chairs and the mild scent of tobacco smoke on the air. The fluorescent lighting put me on edge, but at least it was quiet in there.

There'd been no body search, no camera monitoring my behavior. No one looked in on me. The closed door to the waiting room wasn't even locked. These nonevents were strange for an island dedicated to the submission of its residents, their visitors, and the very concept of freedom. I could have had a weapon. I could be smuggling contraband. They didn't know.

When the door finally opened, my watch, given me by a man named after the devil, said it was 11:07.

Two guards came in, one white and the other Black. Their uniforms were reminiscent of the NYPD. This bothered me because I was once a cop, still liked things about that job, but I hated everything about Rikers.

"Joe Oliver?" the Black guard asked.

"Yeah?"

Neither man appreciated my lack of respect.

"Come with us."

I considered a moment and then stood.

"Where to?"

"Just follow us," the white guard sniped as he turned to go back out the door.

They led me to a sickly green metal door, worked the locks with three keys, and then ushered me down a steep stairwell that descended the height of at least three floors to an underground tunnel. The passway was wide and well lit. We passed a door now and then, but there were no other denizens.

"How come you guys didn't make me go through the metal detector?"

"You want us to give you a cavity search down here?" the Black guard asked.

It was the wrong thing to say. From that point on I started coming up with plans of how to disarm, disable, and kill my official chaperones. Rikers Island had made me a murderer even if I had not yet fulfilled that potential.

Before my fantasies could work their way into the real, we came to an iron door that was no more than six feet high and only about a yard in width. The door's age was evocative of a medieval knight that might at any moment come to life, reinvigorated by some ancient incantation of evil.

The white guard worked a key in the lock, then pushed the door inward. I expected a horrendous whine of metal sparking against stone, but the portal's moving parts were well oiled.

My left hand was shaking slightly and my feet felt as if they were growing toe roots. I took a deep breath.

A strong and warm yellow light flowed out from the inner chamber. The room was large and well appointed; it seemed more like a hunting lodge than a prison cell.

"Go on in," one of the guards said.

I wanted to step forward but my feet wouldn't hear of it.

The other guard pushed hard, making me stumble across the threshold. The sweating started when the iron door slammed shut. I closed my eyes.

This was the nightmare that had plagued me for many

years: being thrown in a cell on Rikers Island with the door banging behind.

A few seconds passed before I could force myself to look. The extra-large cell was luxurious compared to anything I'd ever seen in that prison. A couple of oil paintings in frames on the wall, a real bed, and throw carpets here and there. The centerpiece was a grand oak desk behind which sat a high-backed chair, its back turned toward the entrance.

There was someone sitting in the chair. I could see his head and shoulders.

"Mr. Quiller."

From the chair rose a very tall, gaunt, and quite palpably clean-shaven man with a long, coarse brown mane. He wore walnut-colored wool trousers, a dark brown waistcoat sewn with golden threads, and a long-sleeved yellow shirt that veered close to the buttery hue of a Dutch tulip.

The man turned the chair and sat again, placing his hands flat on the desktop. Tattooed on the back of his left hand were the words *neque receptus, non deditio*—never give up, never surrender.

"Are you?" he asked as if it were a complete question.

"Am I what?" A singing and dancing seven-year-old Shirley Temple couldn't have lightened my mood.

The inmate was just as frightened.

"Why are you here?" he asked.

"Roger Ferris sent me."

"What?" Fear turned to fury on the gaunt man's face. "He dares to send a Black man in here after I ask him for help? Doesn't he know what I could do to him?"

"You mind if I sit down?"

There was a three-legged stool set before the master's desk.

"You're not staying," he said.

I lowered onto the stool.

"Get your ass up and go tell your master to try again," he commanded.

"Fuck you."

A note of surprise shone on Quiller's face.

"I don't know who you are—" he began.

"Joe Oliver," I said, cutting him off. "Here to hear your story."

I could tell by the surprise in his eyes that he didn't know how to respond. For a long moment he considered.

And then, finally, he speechified, "I'm a patriot; a white man in a white land where, one might say, too many shades clutter the landscape."

Amazingly, I was beginning to enjoy myself in the bowels of Rikers prison.

"That's a bastardization of Ezra Pound," I said on a smile. "He was likely a genius but more crazy than smart."

My captive host now took a moment to review his expectations of me.

While he considered, I noticed a huge gutter cockroach making its way along the wall to my left. The creature's carapace was broken, letting one wing flare out behind. It moved slowly, dragging its big body forward on three bent legs rather than walking upright on all six. I had more sympathy for that bug than for most inmates I'd come across in prison.

"Where were you educated?" Quiller asked, turning my attention from the dying thing.

"Two years at City College," I said, "and the rest right here in Rikers."

There was heat underneath the gray of his eyes, hot coals still alive under the ashes.

"I haven't had a conversation of substance with a Black man in a dozen years," he said.

I wondered how much substance he had shared with Black women.

"Think of me as a potential lifeline thrown from the shadows above," I suggested.

"I've reason to be suspicious of men in shadow."

One of the reasons Quiller was despised in so many communities was that he had said, publicly and on many occasions, that *niggers, redskins, chinks, slits, and beaners should only be counted as three-fifths of a person, and their votes should be tallied thusly.*

"Look, man. Like I said, I'm here on behalf of Roger Ferris. He has asked me to find out if you're being set up and, if you are, to prove it. You asked him for help. Here I am."

"Show me."

It was in my shirt pocket. I'd warned Ferris that they'd take it away from me when I passed through the metal detector at the visitor center.

"I doubt that," Roger had replied.

"Have you ever been there?"

"No. But I know the game."

The token was to prove that I did come from Ferris. It weighed about an ounce and was an inch and a half in diameter. I fished the medallion out of its pocket and tossed it on the desktop.

Quiller picked up the old coin and smiled.

"The one time we ever met, Roger showed me this. Did he tell you what it was?" His question had the tone of a man who was just about to lay down a royal flush in a high-stakes game of poker.

"No, but I know how to look things up."

"And you still brought it here to me?"

"I know," I said. "It's old, worth five million dollars on the open market. But I wouldn't steal it anyway. A handshake from Roger Ferris is worth more than that, even on an off day."

Quiller nodded, then flipped the Brasher Doubloon back to me. I caught the proof with my left hand and bundled it away.

That was the turning point. Quiller stared at me, equal parts hope and despair. He brought a hand to his mouth and started crying, silently.

A white man weeping over a gold coin. If it wasn't the tragic history of the modern world it would have been funny.

It took maybe three minutes for the silent sobbing to come to an end. In that time the dying roach pressed forward about an inch and a half.

Quiller composed himself, rubbed his nose with an open hand, and said, "They want me on my knees because of the truth."

"Who does?"

He looked down at the desk.

I waited again. After the roach crawled another inch or so I said, "Mr. Quiller."

Still looking at the desk, he said, "I killed a man who was an agent of the Deep State. It was midnight and he was standing in the kitchen putting something in my butter-milk. Later analysis revealed that the carton was laced with enough poison to kill a hundred men."

"What kind?"

"Excuse me?"

"What kind of poison?"

"Ricin."

"Who examined the milk?"

"You're not going to sit here and interrogate me," Quiller said.

"I am if you want my help."

We experienced another spate of silence. Quiller's hot gray eyes moved around furiously, trying to get the upper hand in his mind.

Finally he said, "I have an advanced chemical lab in a town called Peanut in southern Kentucky."

When I didn't say more Quiller started up again.

"I drink buttermilk every day. I have it here in the cell."

"Did you know the man?"

"No, but the wallet he carried said that his name was Holiday, Curt with a *C* Holiday. The man who grabbed me out of Belarus told me that his name was Thad Longerman, another agent of the fucking Deep State."

"He told you his name?" I was incredulous.

"He told me *a* name."

"Where did this conversation take place?"

"It was in some kind of house on the outskirts of Paris. They were waiting to get all the ruse in play before deposit-ing me in the pensione."

"And how did that work?"

"They drugged me. Just when the drug was wearing off

the French police arrested me and turned me over to agents of the United States."

"No extradition process?"

Quiller sneered.

"So you killed Curt Holiday in Belarus?" I asked.

"No. Togo."

"And then you fled to Belarus?"

"First I went to Cape Verde. I went to Europe later."

"How'd you kill Holiday?"

"Why?"

"Details are important," I said. "You never know when some small fact might rear its head."

Quiller nodded almost imperceptibly.

"I shot him with a Walther PDP."

I asked some more questions. He answered without much feeling.

He gave general descriptions of the man he murdered and the one who kidnapped him, nothing I'd recognize or remember.

After a while he ran out of details.

I asked, "Is there anything you need from me?"

"Like what?"

"I don't know. Something I can bring to Ferris or do to get you out of here?"

Quiller's gaunt face seemed almost to fold in on itself. I'd seen that helplessness many times before. As a cop I'd chased down and arrested many a man and woman who saw in me the worst fate they could imagine. They knew it was the end for them.

"Is there anyone you want me to talk to?" I asked. "Any message you want me to deliver?"

There was, but he still wasn't sure if I could be trusted. The muscles in his face bunched up and his eyes became slits.

Finally his visage relaxed and he said, "My wife has an assistant. Her name is Minta Kraft. Her number is listed under the name Gloriana Q, just Q, the letter. She's out on eastern Long Island. I don't want you bothering my wife, but Minta will pass along any information and provide answers to questions you might have."

"Minta Kraft, aka Gloriana Q," I said.

"Yes. If she asks you for some kind of proof, tell her I said that you are the eclipse."

"The eclipse," I repeated. "Is there anything you want Ms. Kraft to tell your wife?"

Quiller's face hardened, to hold back another round of tears, I believed.

"She," he said and then stopped. "She has to stay strong, stay strong."

I let those words fade before saying, "I'll tell her. I will."

He nodded and I stood up from the stool.

There was a question in the white man among white men's eyes. I stopped moving and waited to see if his gaze would don words.

"Is that all?" he asked at last.

"For now."

"Isn't there anything else?"

"You want the coin?"

Again I had become a conundrum in the prisoner's gaze.

"I have a memory device that contains many thousands of gigabytes detailing damning information about political leaders, military analysts, public figures... and the rich. The reason the government hates me so is because I can bring the world down around their heads."

"So what?"

"The name Ferris appears on that device."

"I don't know a thing about that."

Quiller didn't know whether to believe the claim, but that didn't matter. For me it was time to go.

4.

I BANGED ON the iron door with my fist but there was no response. After waiting nearly two seconds, I got the milking stool and used it to pound heavily on the barrier.

"Take it easy!" the Black guard shouted through iron. "We have to get the key."

"Let me out of here!" was my reply.

It felt like years had passed between the time I crossed the bridge of the damned to Rikers and when I was safe in my Bianchina again. My violent outburst against the cell door frightened the salt and pepper guards. They knew an out-of-control con when they saw one. They knew the malice harbored in my heart.

I made it to the Montague Street office a few minutes before 1:00.

I considered going to my third-floor apartment first, but there was a lot of work to do, a lot of fearful energy to work off.

"Hi, Daddy."

Aja was sitting behind the reception desk working on something that took both the computer and a few stacks of paper to deal with.

"What's all this mess?" I asked.

"I was just trying to get your quarterly statements together to send to the accountant. Some of these expense checks make no sense at all."

"Like what?"

"Like this one here," she said, taking a crumpled piece of paper from the open pencil drawer. "It says that you paid for a dinner with somebody named the letter *B* for six hundred dollars at a restaurant called Butts and Things."

"So?" I said, perching on the edge of the desk. "That sounds pretty straightforward."

"A six-hundred-dollar dinner at a strip club in Newark? And the bill, no details, just a total of six hundred three dollars and forty-eight cents."

"Well, um," I uttered. "You see, ah, the waitress was an informant. You know?"

"Your snitch," Aja said, unable to hide her smirk.

"Yeah. I paid her six hundred for an address of a guy, another informant."

"What about the three forty-eight?"

"I had a Coke."

"Why not just say you paid six hundred dollars for information?"

"Because then I'd need to file a ten ninety-nine and Boomba would have to pay taxes, only she wouldn't, pay taxes that is, and I'd end up spending a thousand dollars for an address that the subject had vacated three weeks before."

"Boomba? What kind of name is that?"

"The kind of name that an informant who works in a strip club might have."

"Okay," she sighed.

"You don't have to do this, sweetie. I usually just send Maxie a box with all the papers and he makes sense out of them."

"How am I ever gonna be your partner in the business if I don't know how the business works?"

"You're not gonna be my partner," I said pointedly. "You're gonna be a doctor of liberal arts in California selling art to billionaire deep-sea colonists and married to a nonbinary polymer surgeon whose specialty will be increasing the human potential."

"It was almost a year ago I said that."

"Really? Seems like only six months."

"You know everything isn't a joke."

"No," I agreed. "Did you finish that paper?"

"Fanon is hard." Aja-Denise's eyes knitted into something like worry.

"To understand?"

"No. Just his talk about how Black people have given up their identities because of what white culture has done to us."

I love my daughter.

"I gotta work on this job your great-grandmother's boyfriend gave me. Unless somebody really important calls, can you just take a message?"

"Sure. What's the job?"

I told her about Quiller, my visit with him in hell, and that we'd get paid enough for this one job to take it easy for the rest of the next quarter.

36

"Maybe we could take a vacation with a couple of your girlfriends." I made the offer because I could see how serious she became while listening to me.

In my office I turned my swivel chair to stare through the window down on Montague. Pedestrians strolled along talking broadly with friends or silently passing alone. Some talked on their phones while others studied the small screens. If there is such a thing as passive ecstasy, I was feeling it right then. I had walked into the lion's den and come out again—more or less whole. That was a joy unequaled in my dreams.

"Daddy?" the intercom blurted.

"Yeah?"

"I need to talk to you."

"Okay. Come on in. Make sure the front door is locked."

She was wearing a floral dress of blues and reds with a white background and a choke chain comprised of deep red beads, each carved into the form of a rose. The hem of the dress flared out at the knee. All that beauty, and yet she strode in like a prosecuting attorney ready to seek the death penalty.

She took a chair before the desk and I gave a smile that had not the slightest hope.

"What's up?" I asked.

"Quiller is a killer," she rhymed. "Maybe he hasn't shot anybody, but his words are deadlier than a fully loaded assault rifle."

"Are we forgetting the freedom of speech?"

"He's still a killer."

"So am I." That was the first time I made such a confession to my daughter. She knew, of course, that I often went armed in the world. She even knew that I'd been in gun battles where people had died. But I'd never been so blasé as to admit to my culpability with a shrug.

A.D. looked as if she wanted to spit on the ground at my feet.

"He's a murderer," she said.

"You have, I suppose, heard of the burden of proof?" If she was going to prosecute, I was going to show that I could lawyer too.

"How can you sit there and defend him like that? He spews poison in his books and on TV appearances and, and, and he shits on our rights."

Aja knew how much I hated it when she cursed. I was old-school. In my heart I held women to what used to be called a higher standard. But the world had changed and if I wanted a relationship with the new order I had to at least be aware of its expectations.

"Sure," I said. "All that's true. But Roger asked me to do a job and I work for a living."

"But Quiller," she sputtered and then was lost for a second or two. "He's a racist."

"So am I and just about every other dark-skinned person that lives in America. This whole country got the poison of racism in its marrow. You know that."

"But he hates Black people, Daddy. He hates you and me and Mom and everybody like us. If you help him you'll be helping what he believes in."

It was a day of many deep breaths.

I gazed into the anger of my daughter's eyes, feeling

pride for what she was saying. I was happy that she was still pure in her mind, absolute in her expectation of what was right.

"Do you hate anybody, honey? I mean without a good reason—a damn good reason."

Aja was smarter than I and quicker too. She saw where my argument would lead and so slowed her accusatorial roll.

"Mr. Ferris could hire somebody else to take this case," she offered.

"Sure he could. But he asked me."

"You've turned down potential clients before."

"Roger's more than a client."

"Yeah, he's rich."

"No. It's not that. He makes your great-grandmother very happy. Happier than she's been since your great-grandfather died. And one time, when he didn't have to, he helped a client of mine, a Black man, escape the injustice of the criminal courts."

She knew what I was talking about.

"But Quiller has said such terrible things and, and he preaches that everyone who is not a white male is less than human."

"Forty percent less," I added.

"How can you laugh at this?"

"I'm not laughing, Aja. I'm trying to prove to you that I know what I'm doing. And I'm not working for Quiller. I'd never take his money. But I owe Roger. I'm going to look into the case, and if I find that the forty percenter is being railroaded I'll turn that information over to the man who hired me. If I find out that Quiller is guilty...I'll just walk away."

Aja's eyes gauged my worth. It looked as if she found me lacking. That's a moment that all fathers have to face.

After her interminable silence Aja said, "I'm going back to my desk."

She stood up and walked out. If someone had asked me at that moment to explain my emotional state I would have said, *Everything good and everything bad that makes me human.*

5.

THE VACUUM AJA left in the office and in my chest did not feel good. She was right about Quiller, but even though I agreed with her politics, I was bound to take his case, so it felt right to feel bad about what had to be done.

Alfred Xavier Quiller enrolled at MIT at the age of fourteen. He graduated in twenty-one months and then designed a car engine that ran on oil derived from the seeds of a weed that grows mostly in Utah. He'd begun plausible research on a Malaysian spider that lives and works with others of its kind. He'd made a theoretical model that would increase the tensile strength of the webs of this species and proposed to farm them for a viable alternative to steel. Before he came up on the government's bad list he'd begun work on a cannon that could, literally, shoot a spaceship to the moon and beyond.

Quiller was a landscape painter and a passable poet. He served as an intelligence interpreter in the army for three years before receiving an honorable discharge. He'd also been a freehand rock climber of some renown among the advocates of that sport.

On the other hand, Quiller had started the three-fifths movement when he was only fifteen, positing that so-called white men had proven throughout history that they were at least 40 percent more productive and therefore more valuable to the human species than any other group or gender. Because of this *truth,* he said that all the colored races and white women should be limited to 60 percent of full voting rights unless they took a test proving their *equivalence,* or, as some have said, their *whiteness.* Because of an extremely long, and yet still bogus, statistical equation white men would not be required to take this test. Quiller proved to himself that he wasn't a misogynist because he believed in the evolution of the hyena, which made the female the superior.

The race-baiter continually misinterpreted Darwin, like so many others have, by replacing the word *fittest* with *strongest* in the survival dictum of that great thinker.

In short—he was a man of towering intelligence fueled by a zealot's ignorance.

Recently, while on the run from the Justice Department, Quiller stopped long enough to create an hour-long Quiller-Talk explaining further ruminations on the place of women in the modern polity. He claimed, vehemently, that even though women were inferior to white men in the political realm, they were actually more important as citizens. Further research, he revealed, had discovered that women were 79 percent more influential in child-rearing than men. Because of this lopsided social advantage, Quiller felt it necessary to apologize for his deprecatory diatribes on femininity in the past and also to say that women should always be given the benefit of the doubt in any constitutional question that didn't concern the vote.

I found myself wondering about the reasons behind this public apology and ultimate rejiggering of his political beliefs. It came as a surprise that I was beginning to have empathy for the man whom I'd started out hating as much as my daughter did.

What intrigued me about his movement in the alt-right world of race-baiting was that there was no group I could find that he identified with—beyond the nebulous concept of whiteness that he used as a template for history. He was happy to include Black people, for instance, in the American polity as long as each individual had only a 60 percent share of a single vote. And if a Black or brown person proved that they were as good as white by passing his test, then Quiller had no problem with allowing them to be equal.

I could see why Aja hated him. The arrogance left a bad taste.

And Aja was right about his obsession, not only with whiteness but also with being a man. Even white women had to take the *voting rights equivalency test.*

He was forty-eight years old, a staunch supporter of animal rights, a vegetarian who ate shellfish now and then, and an extraordinarily prolific writer. Alfred did not sleep much—two hours every night with a one-hour nap sometime in the day. He had written and self-published a fifty-eight-volume collection concerning his political beliefs. This collection was titled *Testimony.* He claimed that it was his proof of the superiority of certain groups within a species.

Testimony had gone out of print four years before and there were precious few editions available.

Two years before Roger hired me, Quiller left the country under a cloud of suspicion from the federal government. It seemed as if, through his space cannon research, he'd come across a plan that some nut had to shoot bombs into space that would be hidden from foreign tracking. Somehow this doomsday construction would be useful when the Chinese or the Russians tried to invade Faneuil Hall.

A document detailing this plan had made it to Space Cannon headquarters and from there it may have been delivered to the Russians. It was clear that Quiller had seen the documents but less so that he distributed them.

At any rate, the forty percenter left the U.S. and made his way to and through those nations that did not have extradition treaties with America.

When I executed a search for the name Curt Holiday I came up with a murder investigation in Togo. Quiller was named as a person of interest (however you say that in Togolese) in the murder of Holiday in Quiller's waterfront apartment. Holiday had been shot six times. After the slaying, Quiller flew to Cape Verde. A week later a Togolese representative was invited to question Quiller. After this interrogation the charges were dropped.

The State Department was not happy that one of its citizens could be murdered and forgotten so easily and issued an international warrant for Quiller's arrest. Sometime after that Quiller moved to Little Peach in Belarus.

The best word I can use to describe my research is *sordid.* Quiller's mother, Visalia Rill, put him up for adoption at the age of four. She said that his father was a one-night stand and that the only thing she knew about him was that his name was Quiller. Her son, she said, had been an unruly child from the moment he could sit up straight.

The articles I read about the boy Alfred said nothing about his behavior, but it might say something that he was never adopted.

Years later when Visalia realized how successful her son had become, she tried to get in touch with him. She was living six miles deep on the wrong side of the tracks in Gary, Indiana, and hoped that he would take her in.

He did not, and after seven months of trying to have a personal audience with her son, she ate poison and died.

I tried to understand what it would feel like to be Mr. Quiller. It seemed that all he had to rely on was his mind. He couldn't trust anybody and nobody loved him enough to include him in their lives. His mother neglected him and when he returned the treatment she committed suicide.

The phone rang while I was considering the subject of my investigation. I could tell by the light that it was an interoffice call.

"Yes, honey," I said using the speaker mode.

"I'm sorry, Daddy. I didn't mean to get on you so bad."

"You don't have to apologize. I'm proud of you being so passionate about us. And you're right—this guy's a piece of work."

"That's not you."

"No. But I have to make sure that I don't end up support-ing his crazy agenda."

We talked for a while about my research and how I felt about it.

After that I asked, "Anything else?"

"Uh-huh. Mom's on line two."

6.

"HEY, MONICA," I said on the exhalation of a breath that felt as if it had been drawn almost two decades before.

"Hi, King," she said.

The utterance of the word *King* was a relic of our long and tumultuous relationship. When we were still married she would sometimes call me King when I'd come home from a long day of being a cop. Back then my middle name meant that I was going to get lucky if I could keep my eyes open.

"So, uh, what's up?" I asked.

"I was reading the *Daily News* today about Lillian Lawler. I don't know why but I didn't know that you were involved with that case."

I was trying to get a bead on the topic of our discussion. Monica did not like me, much less care about what I did. When I went to Rikers the first time, she refused to pay my bail. That because an overzealous investigator showed her a picture of me and a woman in flagrante delicto. Now that we were divorced and she was married to a very successful

47

investment banker, she still bled me for whatever she was legally entitled to. She once even tried to botch a case I was on by warning the man I had been hired to follow.

"I just had a small part in the investigation," I said. "Ms. Lawler hired me when the prosecutor and the police said that there were no other suspects being considered."

"That's not what it looks like to me. There was a picture of you standing behind her and the article said that a private detective uncovered the evidence that...what did it say? That a private detective came up with the evidence that torpedoed the state's case."

Lawler was a New York blueblood who married a nouveau riche nobody named Constantine Psomas—aka the can man. Psomas had made it rich selling canned goods on-line to individuals and groups throughout South America and Africa. Lillian's family owned supermarkets all over the United States and so the two met and, sadly for both of them, married.

Constantine was a dog, though not in the Darwinian sense. He played fast and loose with other women and Lillian's inherited fortune. When she filed divorce papers he penned a tell-all memoir about the sleazy secrets of the Lawler clan. When she hired another detective to scrutinize his business and tax history, that man, John Merrill, was murdered in the supposed commission of a mugging.

Six weeks later, Lillian says that she came downstairs in their Sutton Place mansion to find a bloody Constantine lying within the vestibule between the outside door and the entrance to the house. His throat was cut and his eyes were gouged out.

The prosecutor, a lovely woman named Paloma Alvarez, had a bug up her ass for Lillian. I think the prosecutor's antipathy was due to the fact that Lawler made no secret of the fact that she considered herself superior to the hoi polloi that crowded the streets of our fair city. Alvarez felt that she and her brethren were treated as less than and therefore Lillian must have murdered her Greek husband.

I gave the socialite a pass because I was pretty sure that she thought everyone—white, Black, or brown—was beneath her. And, to be clear, Lillian Lawler would have never been found guilty of her husband's murder. She had a whole raft of lawyers to protect her and it just wasn't possible for her to inflict Constantine's wounds on her own.

The problem was open court. If Ms. Alvarez could bring Lillian to trial she could produce the unpublished memoir as damning evidence. That would have caused great embarrassment for Lillian and her kin. My job was to prove that there were others in the world that might have wanted the can man gone.

So, I compiled a sixty-eight-page document showing that Constantine had cheated and stolen from so many people, including some affiliated with organized crime, that the prosecutor's office was forced to quell the case against his wife.

"I didn't prove that she was innocent," I said to my ex. "All I did was show that the police and the prosecutor hadn't done a good enough job looking for other suspects."

"Well, at least you stood up for a woman in a legal system dominated by men."

When she said that I knew that she was going to ask for a

favor—a big one. I knew this because she saw me not only as her enemy but also as the nemesis of all womankind.

I sighed.

"What?" she asked.

"Yes," I agreed, "what?"

"I don't understand."

"You called me King, you complimented my work, and you haven't even blamed me for not siding with you over Aja's refusal to accept Harvard's offer of that physics scholarship."

"A degree from Harvard would make her career," Monica said, trying hard to hold back her anger at our daughter's choices and my part in them.

"We'll see."

"Yes, we will."

"Okay. You've been civil and even-tempered. Now...what do you want?"

After a long pause Monica said, "Coleman's been arrested."

Coleman Tesserat. Just the mention of his name has been known to cause me to rattle off a whole dissertation of spite and bad wishes. The banker and my ex-wife lived in a bougie neighborhood and ate exclusively at the fanciest restaurants. When he deigned to suffer the company of other Black people Coleman only associated with the talented tenth and Jacks and Jills of the American Black social order. Coleman still used the word *Negro* and was having an extramarital affair with at least one woman.

"Arrested? What for?" I asked, trying not to let my grin bend the shape of the words.

"It's not funny."

"I'm not laughing," I lied.

"He was arrested on some kind of made-up charges, something about heating oil."

"Okay. Have you seen him?"

"No."

"Why not? Somebody show you a picture of him naked in some other woman's house?"

"Be civil or I'll hang up."

"It's your nickel, Mon. I don't care if you never call me again."

I wasn't kind because Monica had nearly gotten me killed not bailing me out of Rikers and, I learned later, Coleman had advised her to let me languish in there for three months.

"The government," Monica said and stalled. "They aren't letting anyone see him."

"Not even his lawyer?"

"He doesn't have one."

"Why not?" It was the day for me to care about people I'd rather see dead.

"We're broke."

"Broke? I thought he had millions."

"The government has frozen all our assets. Everything."

"The federal government?"

"Yes."

"They gotta offer him bail. You could put up your house."

"It's mostly mortgage debt." You could hear in her voice the humiliation she felt.

"He's sequestered and you're broke. That's some bad acid there."

"I don't know what to do, Joe. I called the bank. They wouldn't even put me through to his boss."

"Damn."

Monica might have thought that I was making a comment on the severity of the problems she was having. But that was not the case. What disturbed me was that I was actually concerned. I cared about my ex-wife's distress over a man who helped her nearly kill me.

What was wrong with me?

"And why are you calling me?" I asked.

"We need help."

"How much is his bail?"

"One point five million."

"One... point... five."

"Yes."

For nearly fifteen years I'd been a cop. I made a decent living, bought a house, and paid the bills. Monica never worked much and it felt good taking care of her and Aja. I was proud of my salary, but just hearing "one point five million" made me the quarterback target of the whole defensive line.

"Joe?"

"Yeah?"

"We need help."

"I could recommend a lawyer. I know a congressman or two."

"I have to get him out of jail. He'll go crazy in there."

"I don't have anywhere near a hundred and fifty thousand."

"They told me that he has to come up with the full amount."

"Why?"

"He's a flight risk, that's what they said. Isn't there some way you could borrow it?"

"From who? J.P. Morgan?"

"That man your grandmother's been seeing."

That was the first inkling I had of just how much Monica loved her dog of a husband.

"Damn," I said again.

"Stop saying that."

"Monica, are you really asking me to put myself into a lifetime of debt over Coleman?"

"I'm not asking for him. I'm asking for me."

"When I tried to call you from Rikers you wouldn't answer."

"I was wrong."

Three words. *I was wrong.* She was wrong and so I should tie myself up in knots and jump off the nearest skyscraper.

"Yes, you were," I said.

"I need this, Joe."

"You're not calling me King anymore," I pointed out. She knew what I meant.

"I can do that."

I wasn't trying to get together with her. Her humiliation and broken heart made me almost feel bad. I asked her about my middle name to make sure I was right about the extent of her bald conviction.

"You know that if Coleman ran he'd never pay me back. I'd spend the rest of my life paying his debt."

Her silence told me that if Coleman got out and asked her to run—she would have done it.

"This is crazy, Monica. Insane. Look, I'll try to see what's going on with your man. If I can help him, I will. But I'm not going to borrow a dime."

"Okay," she said in a voice so mild she might have been a child.

"Where are they holding him?"

"Somewhere in Manhattan. A place they call the Metro-politan Correctional Center. Something like that."

"Okay. I'll call back when I've done a little research on my own."

After we got off the phone I sat at my desk suffering psycho-logical symptoms that could best be described as a fugue state. There were thoughts in my head but I couldn't grab on to them. The ideas were…fugitive in my mind, furtively trying to keep away from close scrutiny. I didn't love my ex-wife anymore but…but something.

The intercom buzzed and I hit the answer button.

"Yeah, Aje?"

"What did she want?"

"Are you ever gonna get married, honey?" was my reply.

"What?"

"Your mother said that Harvard would have made your career."

"What career?"

"Exactly."

"Hello?" She answered on the third ring.

"I looked up the number for Gloriana Q so I guess you must be Minta Kraft."

"And to whom am I speaking?"

"My name is Joe Oliver. I'm a private detective."

"I haven't asked for the services of a detective, Mr. Oliver."

"Someone else has hired me."

"Who is that?"

"I can't say, but what he asked me to do is to look into the case of Alfred Xavier Quiller."

"What has that got to do with me?"

"I went to see Mr. Quiller on Rikers Island and he suggested that if I had any questions for his wife that I might pose them to you."

Ms. Kraft sat on that for a moment, then asked, "Did Mr. Quiller have anything you were to say to me?"

"That he wanted me to tell his wife to be strong."

After a beat she asked, "Anything else?"

"That I was the eclipse."

Another hesitation and then: "I'm going to put you on hold for a moment."

I loved my daughter. Just when I thought I was about to lose my mind she called me back to bedrock. Now I was doing my job, working for a living and momentarily safe from harm.

Seven minutes later the fog had cleared and Minta Kraft's voice came back on the line.

"I'll have to reach out to Ms. Prim before I can answer any questions, Mr. Oliver," she said in a friendly enough tone.

"Ms. Prim?"

"Mathilda Prim—Mr. Quiller's wife."

"Does she know Lillian Lawler?"

"I don't think so. Why?"

"I don't know. The name, I guess. You want my number?"

"Is it the one you're calling me from?"

"No," I said and proceeded to give her my current cell number.

7.

THE METROPOLITAN CORRECTIONAL Center is located on Park Row behind the Thurgood Marshall U.S. Courthouse on Foley Square. It's a big building that doesn't look much like a jail from the outside, but once they let you in, it's a cold sweat on a hot day.

"Mr. Oliver?" a man in an awkwardly designed dark tan and light blue suit asked.

I was in the fifth-floor waiting room, sitting among lawyers, sad and disgruntled family members, and a few nondescript male individuals who were, no doubt, thugs.

"Yes," I said, standing and holding out a hand.

"Agent Raoul Davies," he said without returning the gesture.

We stood there a moment being watched by a dozen pairs of eyes in the locked-door antechamber. I let my hand go down and waited.

"Why don't you come with me?" Davies suggested.

The eyes followed us until we went through a pink and gray door.

*   *   *

Davies guided me down a slender hall to a squat door, also pink and gray, which opened onto a small chamber about three times the size of a janitor's hopper room. What was surprising about this room was that it was empty—there wasn't even a chair to sit on.

Turning to me, Davies asked, "How do you know Art Tomey?"

"His daughter went missing a few years ago and he asked me to find her."

"Did you?"

"If I hadn't he wouldn't have called you."

Art Tomey was a high-profile criminal lawyer who took federal cases, mainly. He had clout and owed me. That's the bread and butter of a private detective's life, deep debt that comes out of shadow and pain.

The federal agent was my height with twenty extra pounds of flesh and sinew distributed evenly around the frame.

"You're a walk-in," he said.

"I don't understand. Art called you, right?"

"Yes, of course. What I mean to say is that our facility's surveillance team didn't see you in a car anywhere around here."

"Oh. Yeah. My office is on Montague Street over in Brooklyn. I walked across the bridge to get here."

"I see. What's your interest in Mr. Tesserat?"

"He's married to my ex-wife. Didn't your surveillance team tell you that?"

"No one likes a smartass," he advised.

I took it. He was in charge and the MCC reminded me of Rikers.

He watched me. He was a professional watcher.

"Why are you here?" he asked.

"To see Coleman. Monica, his wife, told me that he has no lawyer and that you won't let her see him."

"So you try to put pressure on us through Tomey?"

"Is it working?"

Davies did something with his tongue in his cheek, looking like he had a piece of food lodged in there somewhere.

"We're debriefing Mr. Tesserat," Davies said, giving up on the blockage. "As soon as that's done he'll be allowed visitors."

"I walked all the way over here, man. At least you could let me shout at him a minute or two."

The agent's eyebrows went up about half an inch, making it look as if an idea had occurred.

"Do you know Tava Burkel?" he asked.

"Never heard of him. It's a him, right?"

"Why are you here, Mr. Oliver?"

"To see Coleman Tesserat."

"You're not a lawyer."

"And you're not a snake," I said, feeding nonsense with its kin.

The federal agent snorted and turned.

"Follow me."

The hallway was reminiscent of an upscale mental hospital where the patients were kept behind pastel gray closed and knobless doors. The air felt cloying, but that was probably my aversion to lockups of any kind. The hall turned twice before we came to a room that had a man in a black suit slouching against the wall next to it.

This sentinel came to attention when Davies rolled up.

"He there?" Agent Raoul asked.

"Not yet," the man in black said. He was about five eight and had the stance of a wily boxer. It was something about the way he managed both weight and balance.

"Let him in," the boss told his minion, tossing his head in my direction.

While the sentry worked an imposing-looking key on the door, I fought down the urge to run.

The room was small and bare, tan from ceiling to floor, furnished with two folding chairs and a small table that was bolted down. There was a thick and very dark scuff mark to the right of the chair I sat in. I couldn't imagine what had made that smudge, but it gave the impression of a violent action.

There was another door opposite the one I came through. It too had no knob.

Sitting there I was thinking of how much I didn't like the incarceration trend I was going in. Too many locked doors and institutional settings. Too many dismissive guardians.

The door before me came open and Coleman walked through. The uniform he wore was dark blue with big yellow checks in unexpected places. His shoes seemed to be made of paper and he was bound with manacles, hands to feet.

Good-looking Coleman was my height, but unlike me he was light-skinned. Ten years my ex-wife's junior, he usually had an arrogant sneer when seeing me. Not that day, however.

He shambled over to the chair on the other side of the table.

"Can't shake hands" were his first words.

He managed to push the chair out and when he finally sat we looked at each other a moment or two.

"I always thought I'd be seeing you in the jailhouse." His voice was softer than usual but the arrogance the same. "But not like this."

"Why they got you in here, Coleman?"

"That shit doesn't concern you."

"Oh yes, it does. I don't care about Monica, but she's Aja's mother and you have to have a bull's-eye on your back for this here."

I was having way too good a time lording it over Tesserat. He was a dog but I was the same breed. He'd been seeing my wife when we were still together, but I'd been seeing half a dozen women around the same time.

"They're sayin' I had something to do with a heating oil scheme," Coleman said reluctantly.

"You mean buying heating oil at a deep discount and then selling it as diesel fuel?"

Coleman sat up straight and angrily.

"Come on, man," I said. "Everybody knows that they're just about the same. That what they say you been doin'?"

"I don't know what they're talkin' 'bout."

I was sure that we were being watched and recorded, so I couldn't ask questions that might give the watchers fuel for their case.

"Who's this Tava Burkel?" I asked.

Coleman's eyes widened. "Look, asshole, just raise the money and get me outta here. Add an extra ten thousand and I know a lawyer I can retain."

"I already got you a lawyer."

"What? Who?"

"Art Tomey."

"He's, he's one of the best criminal lawyers in New York." For a moment Coleman forgot his predicament. "How'd you get to him?"

"Do you know Burkel?"

"No. Why you askin'?"

"I want to make a report to your wife and to Art. I mean, he's already filed with the federal authorities. He'll have all the dirt on you. I just need to know what to expect."

"I told you," he said, desperately trying to take control of the visit. "This shit is too much for you. Just do what Monica asked and stand back."

I took a moment to be quiet. Tesserat was frightened, but I couldn't blame him. There's nothing in the world more terrifying than no way out. A prison door, a coffin lid—it was all the same.

"What?" he demanded.

A beat or three more and I said, "We don't like each other, Coleman. That's the way it should be. Monica asked me to come and I'm here. She wants you out and I'm tryin' to help. But you, motherfucker, you will not order me around or tell me what to do. I don't like you and you know if somebody calls to tell me you're dead I won't shed a goddamned tear."

No way out. That's a feeling that needs to be underscored now and then.

Coleman bit the inside of his left cheek and let his head come down about a quarter inch.

"I felt somethin' on my chest last night," he said. "And when I sat up a dyin' rat fell off me. My cellmate is whiter than toothpaste but only speaks some kinda Middle East babble. He prays five times a day and he's always watchin' me. And, and... if I don't testify against this guy I was workin' with I get twenty-five years."

"So talk," I said as flippantly as I could.

Coleman raised his head to look me in the eye. If someone asked me the color of those orbs anytime before that moment I would have said brown. But looking at him across that table, breathing the same air, I saw that they were dark ocher, like ancient amber wrapped around secrets of the past.

I felt a tightening in my gut. Empathy for my enemies was not a good fit.

"Look, man," I said. "I know they're listenin', but if you want my help you got to give me somethin'. Who is it they say you been workin' with?"

He looked left and right before saying, "You right about what the feds blamin' me for. They say I'm workin' with a Russian mob buys heating oil with one corporation and then sells it as diesel fuel with another one. They say I been brokering the sales."

"You been dealin' with the Russian mob and livin' in the house with Monica? Havin' Aja come in there to eat with you when you doin' something so serious as to have Raoul Davies outside vetting who you talk to?"

Coleman got my meaning. He knew he fucked up.

"Yeah," he said. "Yeah."

"You know somethin', Coleman?"

"What's that?"

"You are a special human being."

"What you mean?"

"Used to be a Black man had to be Malcolm X or Martin Luther King Jr. to be under investigation by the feds. Back in the day, and the day before that, they just killed niggers. Shot us down. Hung us in the deep woods. But now look at you. They got you in here with suspected terrorists and dyin' rats."

"I need your help," he said, and meant it.

"You got it."

8.

IT USED TO be that pedestrians walking across the Brooklyn Bridge had to share their lanes with bicyclers. It was an uncomfortable fit with a lot of jostling and abridged (excuse the pun) rights. But then the city pushed the bicycle lane out to share with cars. Suddenly it was an easy and comfortable stroll to the other side.

I liked it. Parents with their kids, people jogging, lovers walking side by side. It almost felt normal, like there was no such thing as prison and racists, ex-wives and gouged-out eyes.

Midway across the span I stopped to gaze over the side toward Ellis Island and the Statue of Liberty. The water had the look of creped pea-green fabric and the sky was a washed-out blue.

My phone chirped. The little screen told me that the caller was unknown.

"Hello."

"Mr. Oliver?" Minta Kraft asked.

"Ms. Kraft. How are you?"

"I'm calling to tell you that I have time to meet with you this afternoon if you can get here by three."

"We could just talk on the phone," I suggested.

"No. I never discuss my employer's business electronically."

"What's the address?"

When I got to the office, Aja was at her post amid dozens of crumpled slips of paper, a ledger, and, of course, the computer screen.

"Hi, Daddy," she said.

"I got to go out to Long Island."

"How come?"

"To speak to Quiller's wife's assistant. She won't talk on the phone."

"Is it safe?"

"Is anything?"

"Daddy, you need to change jobs."

"I thought you wanted to be my partner. Now you say I should change professions?"

"Not professions. I've been reading up on all the jobs that private investigators do. You could work for some corporation making sure their properties are safe or keep people from stealing. The kind of work you're doing is just too stressful."

"I don't feel stressed."

"You should. I was reading more about that man Quiller. He has meetings with the Klan and Nazis and all kinds of bad people. They love him."

"That sounds like a good learning curve."

"What's that supposed to mean?"

"Well, they love him and I might very well be trying

to save him from getting railroaded by the government. By connection they should love me."

"I don't think it works like that."

"Well, anyway, I love you, shorty."

Southampton is a long ride from Brooklyn. Lots of cars and a countryside that is flat and fertile. For some reason I wasn't worried about Quiller and Russian mobsters there in my car listening to Keith Jarrett live at Köln. The concert was at once rousing and calming.

I was half the way through a second hearing when my GPS spokesperson told me that I was in Southampton and to turn right.

There I was driving down long blocks where most of the hedges were so high you rarely saw a house. And when a dwelling was visible you knew better than to call it a house. It would have been like calling a saber-toothed tiger a calico kitten.

I followed the grand boulevard until finally getting to a block before the ocean. There the nice GPS lady told me to turn left and that I had reached my destination: a rambling mansion the back end of which stood on stilts above quiet waters. The front of the three-story house was even with the ground and I was able to drive up to within a few feet of the front door.

Exiting my tiny car, I wondered why there wasn't some kind of security there to assess my level of threat.

I pressed the doorbell but didn't hear anything. It was a big house.

A man opened the door maybe thirty seconds after I rang; a white man. He wore comfortable and yet presentable clothes—dark trousers and a short-sleeved white shirt that wanted to be blue. He didn't like me but held any outsize antipathy in check.

I waited for some kind of greeting.

"Hello. Mr. Oliver?" a woman's voice came from behind the man.

Popping around the side of the sentry, she appeared. A healthy specimen in a one-piece teal-green dress that partially muted a powerful figure.

"Ms. Kraft?"

"Minta," she said.

Behind her were two more white-man guards, also dressed presentably down. Thirty or forty feet farther on was a floor-to-ceiling set of windows that looked out on the sea.

"Come," she bade me. "Let's go sit where we can see the water."

The three guardians moved aside for me and the private secretary.

On our walk toward the windows I wondered if I should have heeded my daughter's warning.

"We don't get visitors very often around here," Minta Kraft told me. "Sometimes a representative from the town council comes asking for support. This morning there was a Girl Scout selling cookies."

"Did you buy any?"

Minta stopped to smile at me. She was fair-skinned with raven hair and eyes that shifted around the blue-green range. She was certainly a white woman, around thirty, but somewhere in her genetic lineage there had been a few lingering strands of Mongolian DNA.

"The peanut butter sandwiches," she said. "I love how tiny they are."

We had reached the far window overlooking the deck, which hovered above a calm sea.

"Don't you love them?" Minta asked.

"Love what?"

"Girl Scout cookies."

"No." My tone was abrupt, brusque even. It had already been a rough road.

"Oh. Excuse me. Have a seat?"

The lanky chairs were cast iron. Strength behind apparent weakness has always attracted me.

"Tea?" she asked once we were seated.

"Coffee'd be good."

"Rudolph?" she said.

One of the guardsmen ambled over.

"Mr. Oliver would like coffee," she said to him. And then to me: "Milk?"

"Black," I said, looking Rudolph in his dead eyes.

He went away and I found myself hankering for a peanut butter cookie.

"I never get tired of the ocean," Minta was saying. "I was born and raised in Cleveland, but the first time I saw the Pacific I knew my place was at the shore."

"This is the Atlantic."

"As long as I can look out and not see the other side," she assured me. "That's all that matters."

"What you do in California?"

"L.A. I went to USC for economics."

"That prepared you to be a rich woman's assistant?" On edge, I wanted company.

"Here you go." The guard placed a steaming blue mug down before me.

"Thank you." I was full of dishonesties and deceits.

Minta, who was no longer smiling, waited for Rudolph to get beyond earshot.

"Ms. Prim told me that she was ready to answer your questions," she said.

"So how does it work? You write down what I need to know and then pass it on to her?"

"Um, well, first I need to know what you're planning to do. I mean for Mr. Quiller."

"I don't know yet. But when I find out I'll be telling him."

"What does Mr. Quiller say?"

"That in order to get to his wife I have to talk to you."

Kraft wasn't easily thrown off. She sniffed at the air and continued. "He's very worried about Ms. Prim being exposed to stress. She loves him and wants to get him out of that place."

"I imagine she does."

"Do you want the same thing?"

"I have a very particular job."

"And what is that?"

"To find out the government's involvement in Mr. Quiller's arrest and to see if the charges hold water."

"And how do you plan to do all that?"

"Ms. Kraft. Minta, I'm not here to answer your questions. I'm here to investigate the circumstances that brought Quiller to Rikers," I said and then took a breath. "Quiller pays your salary, doesn't he?"

"I can't see where that's any of your business."

Many thoughts, retorts, and curses sprang to mind, but I decided that standing would be my best reply. When I turned to leave, two of the mercenary-like guards were standing there—maybe eight feet away. Belatedly I appreciated how brilliant my grandmother was. She and Aja too.

The two men stood in such a way as to block my passage.

I was unarmed and pretty sure that they had backup somewhere.

Now and then Death rears her head in everyone's life. That was my first true peekaboo of her elegant manifestation in what I came to call the Quiller Case.

"Mr. King Oliver," a woman's voice sounded from off to my right.

The words held more than mere content. They also conveyed musicality, depth. But as much information as it held, the voice also hid meaning.

When I turned my head I did not expect to see a gorgeous Black woman. Tall, she was maybe thirty-three looking twenty-six, dark-skinned with a face that was the shape of an inverted egg. Mathilda Prim's figure was reminiscent of a Playboy bunny of the late sixties—opulent, impossible.

"Ms. Prim?"

"You and Adam can leave, Rudolph," she said, looking me in the eye.

"Yes, ma'am," Rudolph replied.

His words contained real civility. That was a surprise.

The muscle left. When I turned back I saw that Minta had also gone.

"Joe would be fine, ma'am," I said to the lady.

"Yes," she said. "Of course."

She glided over to the chair that Minta had abandoned and sat. It was all so terribly elegant.

"Won't you join me?" she offered.

Back in my chair, I took my first sip of coffee. It was pretty good.

"I was told your given name but I prefer King Oliver, the cornetist who mentored Louis Armstrong."

She didn't smile, but there was no tension or hostility to her expression either. She was the mistress of what she surveyed—the deep blue sea and me.

"It's our true history," I said after a scant lull.

"What is?"

"Jazz."

There was the hint of a smile on just her lips.

"Yes," she agreed. "People here, in this country I mean, give short shrift to the contents of their hearts."

"Unknown loves that guide their every step." It felt like I was completing a quote that had never been uttered.

"That's why they hate themselves," she continued, gazing toward the interior of the house.

"Are you foreign-born?"

"No, but . . . it feels like that sometimes."

For some reason that made me look out on the water. There was a solitary black-sailed boat out there—drifting.

"Do you drink, Mr. King Oliver?"

"I'd take bourbon if you got it."

I'm not sure what you would have called the room we were in. It was very large and mostly unfurnished, with the exception of the two cast-iron chairs, a small cherrywood card table, and a squat maple cabinet flush against the wall behind me.

Mathilda Prim went to the wall-hugging breakfront cabinet and threw open its curved doors, revealing that it was a bar of sorts. She took out a ceramic decanter with two glasses and poured.

"You don't take ice, do you?" she asked when placing the two double shots down.

"That little bar of yours doesn't seem to belong in a big fancy house like this. You'd think there'd be a whole alcove dedicated to hooch."

"That's right," she averred. "You're a detective, aren't you?"

I took a drink.

"So what information can I give you, Mr. King Oliver?"

A simple question, and the right one to ask, but it made me hesitate. The black sail was still on the water. Minta Kraft was probably on some upper floor practicing yoga.

"I'm here trying to find a reason, an excuse, to want to help your husband. I mean, you are his wife, right?"

That reply was the cause for her first full smile, actually a grin.

"How can I help?" she asked.

"Explain to me how his stance in the world jibes with you . . . being here."

Ms. Prim performed a one-shoulder shrug that seemed to render my question meaningless.

"He hates Black people," I pressed.

"He doesn't hate me."

"Do you love him?" I asked, knowing that the question had nothing to do with my job.

She paused, considered, looked into my eyes, and said, "Yes, yes, I do."

"Do you hate your mother, your children, yourself?"

My question didn't seem to disturb her. She put away the smile and watched me for a moment, two. Then she rose and went to the door in the window-wall and walked out on the deck.

At first I thought that in this way she was ending the interview. But because she left the door ajar I finally decided to follow.

The deck was at least forty feet wide. I caught up with Quiller's wife at the four-foot-high weathered pine fence at the far end.

I stood there next to her waiting for some retort to my accusations.

After a long while she said, "When I met Alfie he was all up in his head. He was giving a talk at Syracuse University and the Black Students Union was there giving him shit." She smiled at the memory. "I didn't say anything. Al held his own and all the kids got mad.

"Later that night I was working my job as a cocktail waitress at the Copper Hen in DeWitt. He came in and recognized me. When I asked him if he wanted a drink, he asked me why I didn't have anything to say at the talk. I told him that he and the students were just flexing and not in any way trying to work the arguments through. While we were talking, this big white guy walked up and asked Al if I was bothering him. He said no and when the big guy walked away Al asked me what I would have asked."

"What did you say?" I wanted to know.

"I asked him if he believed in a pure white race, a bloodline that contained no other racial identifiers. I don't know what it was, what that question sparked in him, but we had a talk after that, that lasted for three days."

"You think it might have been because you're so attractive?"

"Maybe," she said with a flip of her hand. "On the second day he asked me to marry him. I told him, 'Hell no.' On the third day I said yes."

Water was lapping against the pylons that held up the outer deck and half the house. It sounded like alien whispers about things I will never understand.

"So," I asked, "did he change?"

"He...learned something, I think. Something about so-called equality."

"What?"

"I had his child. He played with Claxton Akim all the time. His blood in a Black boy made him, I don't know, understand."

"That's pretty hard to swallow," I admitted. "I mean, he's still associated with some pretty awful folks."

"Look deeper, Mr. King Oliver. See what you find."

9.

I FINISHED THE whiskey, Blanton's I think, while trying to get Ms. Prim to tell me what more there was to learn about her husband. She probably had little light to shed, but Mathilda Prim was a force of nature the way those calm waters were—extraordinary power at rest. I found myself wanting to sit above the Southampton sand and sea working out the muddled logic of her foot in the bear trap of that life.

After a while she said, "I have some things to see about, Mr. King Oliver. Is there anything else?"

"When I came here I was under the impression that Ms. Kraft would be the go-between, that I wasn't to meet you."

"Yes. That was the intention."

"And yet, here we are."

She smiled and said, "It was very nice to meet you."

It was the friendliest dismissal I'd ever experienced.

The four mercenaries that made up at least part of the manor's security force were standing around my car when I exited the rambling mansion. I actually considered running, but four hundred years of truly public education stopped me.

I walked toward the car door but found Rudolph standing in the way.

"We're giving you a ride," he stated.

"What about my car?"

"Give Adam your keys."

As a private detective I rarely experienced intimacy with the subjects of my investigations. I was on the other end of a monocular, on the other side of the wall, or listening in on phone calls—illegally. Maybe I was on the World Wide Web sifting through bits and bytes for precious clues. The closest I got to most people like Rudolph was through a telephoto lens. But the cases I was becoming steeped in, the tragic study of Alfred Quiller and the stupidity of my ex-wife's husband, brought me up uncomfortably close with the subjects.

For instance, Rudolph's depthless eyes were a flat tan and he had an odor neither sweet nor savory. He smelled like a lunch-bucket worker in wood scented by varnishes and wax, sawdust and powerful soaps.

I handed the man named after the worst sinner my key chain.

"Where we goin'?" I asked Rudolph.

At that moment a large van, painted darkest blue, drove up. The sides had no windows.

"Get in," Rudolph said.

The four custodians and I huddled into the van. The seating was laid out like the back of a stretch limo: a long banquette on the driver's side with a love seat across, where I was installed. The only window in the vehicle was the windshield and it was mostly occluded by a jury-rigged barrier constructed of panel wood and painted a garish red.

There was no talk in the car. No communication whatsoever.

I suppose one might see my predicament as dire. After all, I was a Black man bunged into a windowless van surrounded by the acolytes of a rabid racist sect. But that wasn't nearly as frightening to me as was Rikers or the MCC. I could fight back against those racists with at least a whisper of a chance of success on my side. There I had a shot, but you learned on the street that you would always lose against the system. The men and women who ran the institutions of incarceration had the right to kill me, whereas the men in that van had to have the will—and even then I stood a chance.

Instead of worrying, I thought about Mathilda. Her dark skin and unwillingness to adhere to any kind of expected norm intrigued me. Thinking about her brought me, of course, to her husband. Was she his prisoner, his dirty secret, or maybe a human doorway to a new man?

The ride lasted for just about an hour. The last fifteen minutes were tempered by the stop-and-go of street traffic. I imagined station wagons and stop signs. From the front of the van came hints of soft rock music and flashes of light.

At one point a man's voice from the wheel said, "A cop's behind us."

One of the nameless sentinels pulled out an automatic. I gauged my odds of disarming him and shooting another. I might have tried it if Rudolph wasn't studying my face.

A tense minute later the driver said, "They're gone."

A few minutes more, by my devil-spawn watch, and we

came to a stop where the engine cut off. When the side door to the van slid open I saw that we were parked in a closed garage. I was feeling optimistic about my chances at survival because my escorts hadn't felt it necessary to restrain or brutalize me.

It was an attached one-and-a-half-car garage used by a vehicle that had bled a copious amount of oil. There was a closed blue door that led into the house. Rudolph used a key to get this door open.

"Go on in," he said.

The garage door led first to a very domestic laundry room the size of a janitor's storage closet. There a small and boxy washing machine was set directly underneath a dryer of the same size. A largish utility sink took up the remaining free space. The doorway leading into the house proper opened on a dark hallway that was only three paces long. Beyond this was a lighted space that turned out to be a modest kitchen lit by a quartet of electric bulbs shining inside a rose-colored glass bowl that was screwed into the ceiling.

I stopped in the kitchen to reevaluate my predicament.

Sitting in the car, surrounded by young and hale zealots, I was like a swaddled infant, unable to make my own moves. But in the kitchen I might be able to arm myself, find another exit or hiding place.

"In here," a man's tenor voice called.

I followed the words through another doorless doorway, into another cramped hall, then through to a small living room decorated with an inadequate sofa, an old-time TV tuned to a newscast, Fox I think, on at a very low volume, and a recliner chair where sat a smallish, balding white man in a green suit. The shoeless man wore light blue socks festooned with dark blue diamonds.

"Mr. Oliver," the tenor greeted behind a perfectly welcoming smile.

"Mr. Cormody."

The beaming lips morphed into the expression of a bad taste.

"Did one of the men tell you my name?"

"It's my job to know potential players in any investigation. You're the so-called war secretary for the Men of Action."

Relaxing, Rembert Cormody sat farther back, bringing the big knuckle of the pointer finger of his left hand to his lower lip.

"I'm impressed," he said.

I shrugged and, without invitation, sat on the less-than-ideal couch.

"You're investigating Alfred Xavier Quiller?" Cormody asked.

"If you say so."

"No benefit being coy, son. I'm alone right now, but them that brought you here are watching; be sure of that. This is what you would call a serious meeting."

"If you hired me to do a job I'd tell anyone asking about that job the same thing."

"And who hired you?"

"My clients expect anonymity."

"Good for them. But I'm not sure how it is for you."

"What am I doing here, Mr. War Secretary?"

Cormody, a small and slight man, sat up in the recliner without engaging the mechanism, looking like a wrinkled green chick in its nest.

"We feel that Mr. Quiller and his family should be protected from unwanted scrutiny," he said.

"Has somebody complained that I've made them feel unsafe?"

"We have eyes."

"And mouths too. Maybe you should use those to ask Al or his wife if they feel they're being harassed by me."

"You're right," he said. "I'm the one asking the questions. You are the one standing on the gallows with the rope around your neck."

Even if Rembert was an expert in some Eastern exercise system I believed I would have been able to incapacitate him before he could stop me. I suspected that he had a weapon secreted in the folds of the mechanical chair. I could snap his neck and come up with the probable firearm before the other white men ran in to be slaughtered.

I could taste their blood. It was this tang that calmed me.

"Look, man," I said. "I'm not gonna give you anything. Okay?"

"Do you have anyone that might speak for you?"

I understood the question but asked, "Meaning?"

"Is there anyone that might sway us from disciplining you?"

In order to be a cop, or a PI who takes on criminal cases, you have to live just a little bit outside of the normal fear responses of the average Joe. My body had made the decision to kill Rembert. The only thing holding back my hands was a thought, a memory of the man I once was; the man who colored inside the lines for so very long.

"My uncle," I said, "but he's in prison for some kind of crime so convoluted that the prosecutors had to fudge the evidence at his trial. If he was a white man they would have found him not guilty."

Cormody gave that non sequitur answer serious consideration. He even laced his fingers trying to work out the informational knot of my reply.

I smiled mercifully and said, "Melquarth Frost."

Cormody's head pulled back and then swiveled from one side to the other, making sure that there was no one else in the room. Melquarth, even just his name, had that effect on certain people.

Having made sure of temporary safety, Cormody looked back at me. This time his eyes doing God's honest research.

After maybe two and a half minutes of this fruitless investigation, Cormody said, "Excuse me a moment."

He hopped up from the nest of the reclining chair and moved quickly from the room.

Sitting on the hard-cushioned couch I reviewed my assets. I didn't have a weapon or any way to make a call. My wallet was of little use. I wanted to kill somebody, I truly did, but there was no profit in that. I might have made it outside, and once there, I might have found some foliage in which to hide. It all seemed a little much. There was already a plan in motion. Might as well have confidence in myself.

Seeking distraction from the deadly situation, I began to wonder again about Mathilda Prim.

I couldn't imagine what she was doing with Quiller or, for that matter, what connection there was between the odd couple and the extremists who had taken me. Prim was a lover, Quiller a thinker, and the MoA a people who, at least, coveted violent action.

Having these thoughts, I was preoccupied when Cormody

came back to the room. He was climbing into his recliner when I became aware of his return.

"Mr. Frost says that you are a good friend and associate," he said.

I smiled, sure that my sociopath buddy had said a lot more than I was all right—though he probably used fewer words.

"What's your interest in Quiller?" I asked the secretary of war of the MoA.

"This meeting is for your interrogation," he said pointedly. I noticed that he didn't call me *son* this time.

"I need to go," I said. "I have appointments to keep."

"Look, Mr. Oliver, we are a valid, benevolent society that's only trying to make sure that the government doesn't try to suppress a great man's theoretical work. You know, the government is the enemy of all freethinking men."

I was nigger-no-doubt when I entered the house, but now I was a fellow freethinker with a common enemy to boot.

"We don't like each other, Mr. Cormody, we both have that right. But I'm not trying to hurt, subvert, or expose anything about your great thinker. I'm working for a third party who merely wants information."

"What information?" The war secretary was nervous.

"I'm not gonna tell you that."

"How do you know Frost?"

"If you asked him that question he'd tell you I was a scarlet bird. I'd say that despite his whiteness, he is my darkest sin."

The little white man with the big aspirations evaluated me again, this time for about a minute.

"You can go out the way you came," he told me. "Nobody'll mess with you."

10.

MY MIDGET CAR was parked in the garage, hiding the huge oil stain on the concrete floor. The keys were in the ignition and I had yet to spill one drop of blood over my exertions. If I walked away from the jobs Ferris and Monica had given me I'd almost definitely survive the season.

Night traffic back to Manhattan was moderately heavy. I elected not to play music because the melodies might have colored my thoughts about the steps I was either to take or to vacate.

Years ago, when they sent me to Rikers, I felt as if I'd never leave. The problem with receiving a life sentence, even if that judgment is reversed a mere three months later, is that you have been bereft of hope and freed from the fear of consequence. When there's no more need to cower, a certain kind of personality begins to take needless chances.

If you've already paid the ultimate price in your mind,

then resistance against superior forces is—almost—all you have left.

But even lifers have extenuating circumstances: lovers, mothers, children, and, now and again, for some, God.

The Supreme Being wasn't in my arsenal but Aja-Denise was.

"Yeah," I said aloud to no one in particular, answering a question no one had asked.

At that moment my phone sounded.

"Hello."

"I was getting ready to go out on a hunting expedition for moa snakes."

"Hey, Mel. Thanks for the endorsement."

"How you get mixed up with Cormody and his fools?" asked the man named for Satan's uncle.

After a few minutes of shorthand explanation I said, "I think I got it covered, though. You scared the shit outta their boss."

"The Far Right and the Russian mob and you got it covered?"

"Maybe I might need your help up the line, but for right now I'm okay."

"I'll keep the phone open for you, Joe."

Advice is best given in interrogative form. That way the work is done by the student rather than the teacher, who should already know the answers. Mel's inquiries about my predicaments caused me to make a call.

"Daddy?" she said over a din of music, laughter, muffled conversations, and shouts.

"Where are you?"

"Pluto's."

"How can you stand all that noise?"

"What do you want, Daddy?" my daughter asked with loving exasperation.

"I think you were right about this case."

"Hold on a second, I'll go outside."

She moved down a corridor of lessening sound until there was silence.

Then she asked, quite seriously, "What's wrong?"

"I need you to call your grandma B and tell her that I want you and your mother to stay behind the Great Wall for a few days."

"Why?"

"Because when you kick a hornets' nest you're likely to get stung."

"Are you safe?"

"I can take care of myself in situations like this, but I got people coming at me from Roger's case and also from the thing I'm doin' for your mother and Coleman."

"What thing you doin' for Mom?"

"Coleman got in Dutch with the feds and Monica is all worried."

"You don't have to do anything for that fool," Aja said indignantly.

"I'm not asking for you to take Coleman there. As a matter of fact you should tell your great-grandmother that he is definitely not invited. But your safety comes first and part of that is protecting your mom."

"Okay. I'll call. But do I have to go right now? Milla's gonna have a surprise birthday cake in a couple of hours. I'd like to be here for that."

"I can't tell you what to do, honey. But this is really LAD."

LAD is our family's private acronym standing for *life and death*.

"Okay," Aja said. "I'll go now. You be careful too."

I was home around midnight. My apartment is on the third floor of the office building. You could climb a rope ladder up through the ceiling of my office, but that night I used the stairs to get there. By 12:30 I was sitting cross-legged on the bed thinking about the cases I should drop.

Quiller was the rock and Coleman the hard place. And there I was, not nearly as frightened as I should have been.

The sun was on my face in the morning. I didn't remember lying down, much less falling asleep.

"Hi, Daddy," Aja said when I called. "We're here and we're safe."

"Tell your mother I'll be in touch as soon as I know something."

"Where are you?"

"At the office."

"You gonna get Mr. Frost or Uncle Rags there with you?"

"When and if I need them."

Thad Longerman. I couldn't find him anywhere. Not on the net, on the dark web, or in the phone book. He wasn't registered on the part of the NYPD database that I could access, and the program I had to read past articles from fifty-two American newspapers had no inkling of him.

The most likely Curt Holiday ran a company called Personalized Services. His partner in that business was a buxom redhead named Tex Bradford. A weight lifter, Tex had a seventy-five-inch chest with hands the size of medium shovels. The company he and Curt ran was small but laid claim to elegance. Headquartered in Culver City, California, they did no work in that state, nor on the West Coast at all. They had a presence on the dark web as well as the WWW. Among their dozens of digital testimonials, one individual named was d'Artagnan Aramois—a self-defined *free-wheeling capitalist*. D'Artagnan ran a small export business out of Manhattan called Safe Haven. His product was a brand of casket built from a cheap synthetic material that promised to keep its passenger whole for centuries. Personalized Services worked with d'Artagnan doing a *hands-on* service. A few testimonials talked about working with Curt or Tex soon after making a deal with Safe Haven. Taking that information and a few other tidbits, I set out to do some honest-to-God investigating.

D'Artagnan Aramois's Safe Haven was housed on the seventy-third floor of the Empire State Building. There was a light on behind the frosted window that took up the upper half of the door.

When I knocked a man's voice called out, "Come on in."

The office was small and notably without character. The LED lights from the desk lamp and ceiling fixture shone but didn't really illuminate. The window gazed upon New Jersey but it was a misty day, making the Garden State look like a half-formed idea. The only serious furniture was a big oak desk that sat rather high and unevenly, reminding me of a bull intent on a tuft of tasty grass and at the same time wondering if it should gore someone.

D'Artagnan Aramois stood between the front door and the desk. He was short and sturdily built, wearing a blue-and-white-checkered suit that was probably made from cotton. Shod in brown leather shoes, he was white, clean-shaven, and wary.

"Can I help you?"

I smiled broadly and held out a hand.

"Philip Wrog," I said, "from East Saint Louis."

We shook with abandon.

"How do you spell that last name?"

"Double-u, are, oh, gee," I articulated. "It comes from the Polish. Means something not so good, I think."

"You think?" The man named after the fourth Musketeer had an engaging sneer.

"I'm originally from Pittsburgh. My parents died before I knew 'em and I was fostered by a Polish family for a while there. They were named Wrog. I like it that the name's unusual."

"Have a seat, Mr. Wrog," Mr. Aramois offered.

There were two chairs set out for visitors. They probably came from one of the big, cheap stores but I doubted if Aramois bought them. The office gave the impression that everything, except for the big brooding desk, had been leased.

The little man gave me a wary sneer and asked, "How can I help you, Mr. Wrog?"

"I'm sure you've read about the political unrest in Haiti," I said.

D'Artagnan nodded slowly.

"You're aware that there's a large community of Haitians in Brooklyn and down in Miami."

"Yes," he said.

"Well, then you may also know that there's a strong connection between these families and their relatives back home."

"Not, um, specifically but I can see where that might be the case."

We were performing a lawbreakers dance. Tentative and hopeful, maybe our gyrations would lead to a pot of gold.

"There's a lot of poverty back home. People who don't have and cannot afford the basic necessities."

"It's a shame how some people have to live," d'Artagnan said, his head swaying from side to side.

"Their families here are burdened with providing their people with the means of survival. They send appliances, money, and other necessities. They need everything down there, from straight razors to . . . to coffins."

"Don't I know it."

"Yes," I said with a smile. "That's what I've been told. I come here to you today because I represent a consortium of Haitian nationals that wish to purchase sturdy but affordable caskets for families that are sending their departed loved ones back home."

"That's why I went into this business," Aramois said devoutly.

"I'm told that while being inexpensive, your caskets are extremely durable. So much so that they resist even X-ray examination."

"That's true."

"Don't get me wrong," I said. "I'm not some smuggler or

terrorist, but it is a custom among these people to place memorabilia with their loved ones. My clients wouldn't want misguided authorities to disturb their dead."

Aramois studied me then. His aspect was less human and more coyote or rat; some creature that had the natural ability and inclination to gauge threat.

"Tell me something, Mr. Wrog."

"What's that?"

"How do you know to come to me? I mean, this is a business that doesn't advertise."

"An acquaintance gave me your name."

"What acquaintance?"

"A fellow named Thad Longerman."

That was the gambit. I knew a few names and came to a conclusion or two about their businesses and how they were run. Being a private detective was less about pinpoint accuracy and more about gambling. In poker I always lost a few hands before coming up with my opponent's tells.

D'Artagnan thought a moment and then nodded.

"My fee is twenty-five hundred dollars. You pay me that and I send you on to a contact I have in the Bronx. There you will be provided however many caskets you might require. Any additional items you wish to send to the grave with them can be added at the docks before they are sent on their way."

"And how much will this final transaction cost me?" Philip Wrog asked.

"Twenty-five thousand dollars for a twelve-count, shipping is extra."

I raised my eyebrows convincingly.

"The people I work with can almost guarantee that

the coffin will pass unmolested through customs in both countries," Aramois assured Wrog. "There will be a government seal on each unit that you will attach after your own inspection."

"I will be the last one to examine the unit?"

"Certainly so."

I looked closely at the little blue-checkered coffin salesman.

There are certain species of cuttlefish in the ocean that can change color as quickly and as effortlessly as a man might take steps on a path. But there was no order of beasts on Earth that could feign innocence like we could. *It's a gift,* I thought.

"The people I'm working with," I said, "have their own ways of sending their loved ones home."

"That's not the usual approach," the Frenchman said. "But I'm sure you can work something out."

"So how does it work from here?"

"I send you off to a man named Tex. You tell him what it is you want and come to some kind of payment arrangement. After that he will deliver the sarcophagi to the address you say."

"Along with the government seals?"

"Yes. Of course."

"And you guarantee that these sacred properties will not be molested?"

"Only God and the devil can make absolute guarantees, Mr. Wrog. All I can tell you is that we haven't had a dissatisfied client yet."

I froze up there for a few moments, a cuttlefish that had taken on such a complex range of hues and textures that he, I, needed a moment to reset.

"I get paid now," d'Artagnan said, filling in the moment of silence. "After that you can work out with Tex how to pay him."

"What if you're trying to cheat me?"

"You know my address. And, just to be clear, I can't promise that you will be able to finalize a deal up the line. My job is merely to make the connection."

I hemmed and hawed a little so as not to make the little man suspicious. But he had me at the word *Tex*.

Personalized Services was down the block from the old Grand Concourse Plaza Hotel. I parked my little Bianchina on the street about two blocks away and then ensconced myself on a bus bench across from the closed exporter.

PerSer (as I named it in my iPad notes) was bracketed by Tomas Jewelers and a dentist's office. The two side businesses were open when I got there, around 1:15, but Tex's concern remained shuttered.

Waiting wasn't a problem for me. Wearing dark blue cotton slacks, a tan T, and a many-pocketed army jacket, I perused my iPad with no feeling of urgency or expectation. Melquarth sent me a short missive about Cormody, the MoA, and other organizations mixed up with them. Mel had met many white supremacists at the various prisons he'd been sentenced to.

"It was a matter of survival, not philosophy," he said to me the first, and last, time we discussed the subject.

His information was nonconsequential to the case, but the fact that he took the time to compile the data told me that he thought I might need his help sooner rather than later.

At 2:00 I inserted earbuds and made a call.

"Art Tomey's line," a woman's voice answered.

"Hey, Amy, it's Joe."

"Well, hello. Art told me you might be calling."

Amethyst "Amy" Banks was the most overqualified *assistant* in all of New York. She'd been a high-powered defense attorney for a couple of decades when she fell for a client, Nina Morseton. Nina had been charged with killing a man she'd partnered with to defraud a Swedish insurance company. Amy had never before realized her affinity for women.

"I really don't think I'm a lesbian," Amy once said to me about Nina. "I just believe that she is my soulmate."

She, Amy, falsified a few documents and some evidence to prove her client's innocence, honestly believing she was. When it came out that Nina was definitely guilty, she turned on Amy, trying to get a better deal. It didn't work.

Both lawyer and client were convicted. Because of previous felony convictions Nina is doing life without possibility, and Amethyst did a very enlightening three years. Disbarred, disgraced, and displaced in her own heart, Amy went to prison, a mastermind of the law with a broken heart that no felon could challenge.

When she came out again Art Tomey hired her at 3K a week just to answer the phones and talk to him now and again about interpretation and approach.

Once a month Amethyst goes to Bedford Hills Correctional Facility for Women to visit Nina. You know love is true when it survives the devastation it causes.

"What can I do for you, Joe?" Amy asked.

"I was wondering how Art's doing with the Tesserat thing."

"I had a case like this one time," she said dreamily. "It was a suspected terrorist all bundled up and ready to be dropped into a black site. The evidence was circumstantial at best and the government refused even to let the judge in on their investigation. They demanded the full amount for bail in that case too. I know the right people and got them to countermand the issue. Come up with the ten percent and they'll have to let him go."

"Do I even need to talk to Art?"

"No, darling, it's all taken care of."

11.

WHILE WAITING ON the bus bench I got a call from Roger Ferris.

"How's it going, Joseph?" he asked me.

"The sun is out and the game's afoot," I said, feeling good about finally being able to use the latter phrase.

"Can I be of any help?"

"You can put your people on looking up the probable alias Thad Longerman."

He asked about the spelling but all I could give were phonics.

"And another thing," I said.

"What's that?"

"I'm going to need an interest-free short-term loan."

Buxom Tex Bradford showed up for work at 3:48 p.m. At 4:16 I pushed open his metal-reinforced glass door. There were waist-high glass showcases before me to my right. They were pristine and empty. Tex was standing behind a counter to my left. He was posing there like some kind of actor in a play just before the curtains were to rise.

"Can I help you?" he asked. There was no friendliness to the offer.

"D'Artagnan Aramois," I said.

"What about him?"

"He told me that you could supply me a dozen coffins and government seals for twenty-five thousand dollars."

"We usually oversee sending our own products abroad," the huge man muttered.

"My clients are sending their remains to Haiti."

I'm five-eleven weighing 199 pounds. When Tex moved around the useless counter I could tell he was near six foot four and his weight, twenty-one stone at least.

"How many did you say?" he asked.

"Aramois told me that I get an even dozen coffins for twenty-five."

"We call d'Artagnan's boxes *items*," he said, almost reluctantly. "It's twenty-five for twelve items when we send them, but that price doubles if we leave it in the client's hands."

"Oh," I said, feigning uncertainty. "Fifty thousand is an awful lot."

"There's no give on it either."

"I see."

I was making some headway with the bodybuilder. My apparent parsimony made him feel that I was a real contender rather than a ringer sent in to bring him down.

"It seems that if I did all the work it should cost me even less," I suggested.

"You'd think so," Tex agreed. "But in this business it's a liability to allow the items and their seals out of our hands."

"Huh," I fretted. My left eye, of its own accord, started to flutter. "I'm told I can move certain materials that are forbidden by the Patriot Act when protected by your units and seals."

"I don't know what you're talking about," Tex said in a flip tone. That's what warned me.

Putting my right arm akimbo, I said, "Then maybe I should talk to your partner."

"What partner?" Tex asked, looking from side to side.

"You know," I said, "Curt Holiday."

That's when Tex swiveled his head to regard me.

Speed and accuracy, stealth and strength, and an arsenal of specialized weapons are all keys to any physical contest between most animals—although it helps to also have the indomitable will of the honey badger. With humans, however, there's an extra added element—specific intent.

Tex was quite a bit faster than I had imagined. He grabbed me by the throat before I knew what he was doing.

There I was, three or four inches off the floor, choking. My eyes felt like they were about to pop out of my head and my thoughts were nearly useless. I believed that his intent was to incapacitate me because he needed to know why I was there before killing me.

I'd had my hand on my hip because there was a gun there, a .45 with no kind of muffler system. While my grip on consciousness was quickly fading, I held the side of the pistol next to Tex's left ear and fired—twice.

The big man yowled and fell to his knees. With my last clear thought I slammed the side of the pistol into Tex's temple. He toppled over and I, unwillingly, fell down next to him.

That was a serious situation. Whichever man regained his wits first would win the impromptu contest. If he won I would be tortured and probably killed. If I revived first he, Tex, might lose his business, his freedom, and possibly even his life.

Luckily the struggle for breath that I was experiencing brought me awake at a quicker pace. Within three minutes I was up on my knees. When four minutes had passed I hit Tex one more time to make sure that he'd stay down.

I secured the metal-reinforced front door and then made it to a back room, where, after a few minutes of scrounging around, I found a packet of files that was identified by the initials C.H. I would have liked to search further but the gunshot had been loud and I was quite sure the neighbors would have called the cops.

So, taking the foot-thick pack of files, I made it out a back door, crossed two blocks over, and located my car.

Driving across the line that divided the Bronx from Manhattan, I was fairly certain that I'd be out of trouble. Tex was a smuggler, a security threat, a defiler of the dead, and very likely guilty of even worse crimes. He'd tell the police a story that'd have them running in circles for weeks.

While taking the Verrazano Bridge to Staten Island I was trying to make sense of the bind that Quiller was in. I supposed that d'Artagnan Aramois, Tex, Thad Longerman, and, of course, poor deceased Curt Holiday might have been working for what Quiller called the Deep State. But the quartet of thugs and thieves, murderers and kidnappers, seemed more like simple criminals, their actions based on the motive for profit rather than false nationalism.

Once on the island that contained the fifth borough I headed for Pleasant Plains. There I went to a medium-size deconsecrated church that was surrounded by a high stone wall and protected by all kinds of advanced and old-time defenses. Recently Melquarth had added six Rottweilers to guard the grounds of the church.

I pressed the bell at the outer gate while the deeply suspicious canines paced on the other side. They knew me but I was not their master.

"Hey, Joe," Mel said as he strode toward the gate.

The dogs wandered off when they heard their master call to me. He opened the gate and I drove in.

The nave of the deconsecrated church still had twelve rows of pews that led up to the raised altar. Rather than a podium for the minister's sermon Mel had set up a table with a Go board built into it. The pieces were made from very high-quality jadeite gems, apple green and snow white. Before any salient conversation, we played a game that lasted around an hour and a half.

Forcing myself into the logic of strategy and the promise of theoretical victory calmed me down a bit.

When the moves began to take longer and longer, a conversation developed.

"I don't know which is worse," Melquarth said while considering his strategy or mine.

"The Russians or the alt-right?"

"You or me."

"Has to be you, Mr. Frost. I'm on the side of law and order."

"You are a Black man, are you not?" the white ultra-criminal asked.

"So?"

"Rather than *enforce* the law, more often than not the system jams itself down the throats of people of your ilk."

"Sometimes," I agreed.

Mel smiled, picked up a green jewel, and threatened a small cadre of my pieces.

"They got you outnumbered, Joe, and here you go trying to live by some rule."

"We all got rules, Mel."

The thief, killer, blackmailer, and all-around madman looked up into my eyes. He liked me. He'd murdered his father and burned away the body in the basement of a property he owned in Lower Manhattan, and yet I considered him a friend.

"I know it seems like that," he said. "I mean, yeah, sure, we all got rules, but that's not what makes the things we do so complex."

I knew the man, understood what he was going to say before he opened his mouth, but still I asked, "What's that?"

"It's the unexpected exceptions we have to our own commitments. You're not a killer, a murderer, but you might become one. You easily could. I'm not a sane man, a company man. I'm a lone wolf, but that don't mean I might not find myself in a domestic situation one day."

"What's goin' on with you, Mel?"

The now-and-then maniac smiled, placed another green

jewel in an unexpected square, and said, "I think I got the upper hand here."

He wasn't going to divulge the thought process behind secrets about himself; he rarely did.

"I concede," I said.

"I could go talk to Cormody for you," Mel offered.

"You could." I was in an agreeable mood. "But I think I want things to play out the way they are now. I mean, if you go in all gangbusters they might clam up. You know what I mean?"

"You wanna play another game?"

"No."

"Who cares about what happened to get Quiller where he is?"

"My employer does."

"Could get you killed."

"If that was the outcome, you'd protect Aja, wouldn't you?"

He gazed at me for a very long time.

"With my life," he said at last.

"That's all I can ask for."

There was another long pause. This time Mel was looking inward. At the end of this self-evaluation he nodded.

"You'll never make a good general, Joe, but you're one hell of a guerrilla."

Later on Mel went downstairs to work on refurbishing antique watches that he sold from a little shop in the West Village. I stayed at the Go table perusing the documents stolen from the cowboy, Tex.

It was the most eclectic set of documents I had ever examined. First there was very little English used where language was inserted. Much of the prose was in Spanish, German, and French, but there were also entire pages filled with symbols from Asia and the Middle East.

Mostly there were snapshots of people, mostly men, taken from clandestine angles. There were also maps showing locations both circled and underlined by red pencil markings. I was pretty sure that this was the diary of a hit man.

Outside of the covering initials I didn't see the name Curt Holiday scrawled or printed anywhere; that was business as usual. What surprised me was that Tex had kept these documents at all. What use could they have been to him or his masters?

When I got to the bottom of the stack I realized that that was where I should have started. This five-sheet file started off with a picture of Alfred Xavier Quiller with Mathilda Prim on his arm. He had on a dark suit, the kind that cowboys wore in the late nineteenth century when attending a wedding or funeral. She was dressed in a white lace gown that dimmed anything and anyone else in her vicinity.

The back side of that page was an architectural map that I was sure depicted the compound where Quiller lived in the West African nation of Togo.

I considered that last file for half an hour or more. When there was nothing else to glean, I took out a burner and entered a number.

"What's up?" answered Melquarth Frost.

"I'm headin' out, man. You mind if I leave my car in your garage?"

"Call me when you land."

12.

NOEMI TRISTEL LIVES on the top floor of a one-time tenement building on 145th a block east of Broadway. The new owners have transformed the working-class apartment house to upper-middle-class studios and one-bedroom condos. The tenants across the six floors are multiracial, middle-class, at least, and definitely transplants to a Harlem that is fast becoming something else. Maybe one day they'll be calling it Harlow Heights or possibly Haarlem, harking back to its Dutch roots.

The new tenants were all races but mostly white. There's nothing wrong with that. Things change in America, in the new world, the new Earth, things change all the time. And so it is especially nice when you come across something or someone that defies the relentless tide of transformation.

Carter Tristel was a pickpocket and general sleight-of-hand thief. He could have been a superior magician. He might have become a contender in whiff-whaff at the Olympics somewhere. But he used his skills to steal what he needed to take care of his daughter, Noemi, and her mother, Nimbal

Orestry Tristel. When I was still a cop I had a warrant for Carter not two days after Nimbal died of complications from diabetes. I came to the house and seventeen-year-old Noemi answered the door.

"Mom died and we just came back from the mortuary," she told me. "We got to bury her Sunday. He's in there on the couch if you want him."

Carter was a large man. His size made most people feel that he was slow, even lethargic. That's why no one expected his hands to be so fast. He lay on his left side on the broken-down couch, his big brown belly hanging off the edge. Staring at the far wall, his eyes dropped a tear now and then. I don't think he saw me.

"Daddy," Noemi called.

I put a hand on her shoulder to stop her from introducing me.

"What?" he asked pitifully.

"Um, you want some water?"

"No, baby," he said, choking back whatever sadness kindness caused.

Back at the front door I told Noemi about the antique silverware her father was supposed to have stolen.

"If the next officer with a search warrant doesn't find anything, I don't think they'll be able to arrest him," I told the girl.

She nodded and I left.

Two years later I was a detective third grade in an office I shared with three other officers. It was about 3:00 in the afternoon when Noemi walked in. She was wearing a lovely peacock-blue silk dress and had a pocketbook that probably cost three thousand dollars. She sat on my visitor's chair and smiled.

Noemi was not a beautiful woman. As a matter of fact, as she aged she became rather plain. But she had eyes that held the power of old-time royalty.

"Carter?" I said.

"He died."

"What happened?"

"He won the Lotto and then had a heart attack. The funeral is Wednesday next and he asked me to ask you to come."

That was then.

At 10:07 in the evening after I lost my ninety-second straight game of Go to Melquarth, I rang Noemi's bell. Through an electric eye she pressed the lock-release button and I walked through. As I headed toward the far end of the slender first-floor hall, someone hailed me.

"Excuse me," the woman's voice called.

I don't know why but I took another step.

"I said excuse me," the voice insisted.

I stopped and, after a little hesitation, turned.

The young white woman standing there was indeed very pretty. Her figure, her skin, her probably naturally blond hair that bunched on slender shoulders.

Everything about her was lovely except for the twisted expression on her lips. That was quite ugly.

"Do you belong here?" those lips asked.

"Right here?" I asked, pointing at the floor.

"I will call the police," she threatened.

"That is your prerogative, ma'am. The police are here to serve everyone—living and dead."

"Are you threatening me?"

"If I was threatening you, you would feel it." Rikers Island hadn't done me any favors.

At the end of the first-floor hall there was a two-person elevator on the right and a doorway to the stairs on the left.

I took the stairs to the sixth floor.

The day the new owners of the ex-tenement put the units up for sale, Noemi bought the entire floor with a million dollars taken from the $9,364,912 passed down from Carter's Lotto winnings.

I knocked on door number three and she answered.

"Come on in, Mr. Oliver," she said.

Crossing the threshold I asked, "When will you start calling me Joe?"

"My father called you that. He told me to call you Mr. Oliver."

"Noe?" a woman called from the room beyond the one we were in.

When she came in I got a good look at her. Light brown and maybe twenty-five, she wore an emerald bodysuit that was semi-opaque.

"Oh!" she said, covering herself and backing away to the room from whence she had come. "I didn't know anyone was here."

"It's okay, Stash," Noemi said. "This is an old friend. I told you about him—Joe Oliver."

"Hi," the now bodiless woman called from around a corner.

"Hey," I called back.

"We're going across the hall," Noemi said to the doorway. "I'll be back later."

"You want me to bring anything?"

Noemi looked at me and I shook my head.

"No, honey, we'll be okay."

Noemi and I hadn't gotten to sit down when there was a knock on the door. Surprised, my host called out, "Stash?"

"Police, ma'am."

"I forgot to tell you that a white lady downstairs thought I might not belong here," I said.

Noemi sighed and frowned.

"Just a minute," she told the door.

She took the full sixty seconds to suppress the anger, then opened the door on two NYPD uniforms. Both white. Both young.

"We've had a complaint about an intruder," the taller officer said to her while looking at me.

"Oh?" Noemi replied. "No intruder has been up here."

"What about him?" the other cop asked.

"Mr. Oliver is an old friend of the family. He rang the bell and I buzzed him in."

"And you know him?" Cop number 1 asked.

"I know all my good family friends."

"No need to sound off."

"No need for Miss La Fina downstairs to question every Black man that comes to visit this building."

"Are your neighbors at home?" the shorter cop wanted to know.

"I own the entire floor, Officer. Will that be enough for

you or do you need me to call Captain Brown? He's on duty tonight, I think."

The young officers knew when it was time to retreat.

"Sorry, ma'am," the taller cop said. "You two have a good night."

"It sounds like you should be taking a vacation," Noemi Tristel was saying an hour or two later. "I mean, I know what it's like to live under threat, when someone might break down the door any minute, but when they'd arrest Daddy back in the day I could always see him in jail, find someone to pay his bail. Your problem sounds like a fresh body dropped in the bay."

"Fish food for sure," I agreed. "But it hasn't gotten that bad yet."

"That man tried to choke you to death."

"That was a miscalculation. But I was ready for it."

We were sitting on a long couch in a living room only used for visitors like me, and I was pretty sure that I was the only one like me. Noemi, wearing a plush baby blue robe and no shoes, leaned back against the opposite side of the sofa, tucking her feet under her thighs.

"Daddy broke laws every day except Sunday his whole life," she said. "There was always some cop or angry mark after him. But I swear he was like a nun shacked up in some convent compared to you."

I'd brought a bottle of peach schnapps and it was almost gone by that time.

Once, when I was having trouble with my ex–brothers in blue I dropped by Miss Tristel's place.

"You think I could stay here a couple of hours until I work out some things?" I'd asked her.

"You could spend the night if you want," she said. "The couch turns into a bed and I can put a little food in the fridge."

I had a key to the front door of the building and that apartment, but I always rang out of deference.

On this evening I said, "Thanks for takin' me in, girl. You know you usually need to be family for somethin' like this here."

"I don't mind. It reminds me of when I was a kid and Daddy needed to hide. He was what he was and I loved him anyway."

"That Stash seems like a good catch," I said to take some of the shine off me.

"Oh no," Noemi said with maybe a hint of regret. "She's just a girl who needs a place to stay where they don't shove fentanyl in your pudding."

"So you're not lovers?"

"Oh yeah, we are. We're together until we aren't anymore."

It was pretty late when my host left for the company of her temporary girlfriend. I didn't unfold the bed or disrobe, just took off my shoes, lay back, and considered the options.

I wasn't going to walk out on Ferris or Monica. When I was a cop I always wanted to be a detective solving crimes and maybe making things a little bit better. I wasn't so much into enforcement and more about resolution.

Quiller and his Black wife intrigued me. How did they end up where they were, and how did that meeting impact the crazy, self-destructive racism of the Far Right? Ms. Prim was an enigma, but Monica was easy to figure. My ex would be rudderless without her fool of a man.

13.

I ARRIVED BY taxi at the front gates of Silbrig Haus at 7:17 the next morning. There was no one at the front, no button to push—but, like the world in general, there was always somebody watching.

"State your business," a discorporate woman's voice commanded.

"Joe Oliver," I said. "I'm here to see Ferris, but you can ask Forthright to let me in."

There's almost always a moment of silence when you mention a worker's boss. Most laborers want to avoid notice by their superiors. All of us do something wrong; that's the nature of the workaday world.

The gates began to part maybe four minutes after I mentioned the number two on the list.

Halfway to the gate I saw my grandmother coming around from the far side of the house.

"Hi, baby," she called, the grin all over her words.

We smiled and kissed, laced hands and walked toward the fanciful front doors of the manor.

"This mighty early for you, ain't it, Joe?"

"Make hay while the sun shines. Isn't that what they told your grandmother on the old-time plantation?"

"Not only that; they used to tell all us sharecroppers that hard work brought us closer to God," she added. "That's why so many of us went the other way."

The front doors opened before we got there.

"Two of my favorite people," Roger Ferris hailed.

"Hell with that," Grandma Naples growled. "Why you got my favorite grandson up in here when he should be safe in his bed?"

"Come on now, honey, I only have Joe gathering information. Isn't that right, Joe?"

"Yeah," I said, knowing that my grandmother could read even between the letters of a single word.

"Don't fuck with my blood, Roger," Brenda warned.

I think he heard her.

"So you're saying that he's sticking to the story that he was kidnapped?" Roger asked. We were in his stripped-down *serious business* office cube.

"And that the man he killed was trying to poison his buttermilk."

"Sounds just stupid enough to be true."

"I believe him. Here." I placed the multimillion-dollar coin down on the desk. "He also said that he has a gigantic blackmail file and that the Ferris name is on it."

"That may be," my temporary employer conceded, "but it's not about me."

He held my gaze for a moment or so.

"You have that hundred and fifty thousand I need?" I asked.

"You staying for breakfast?" was a reply of sorts. "Your ex-wife and daughter will probably want to talk to you."

Brenda and Roger didn't make the breakfast part of our meal. It was only Aja and her mom.

"How was he?" were the first words Monica said to me.

"Fine," I said as the breakfast platters were being deposited on the long table.

"Fine? How can he be fine when he's locked up with all kinds of criminals?"

"You don't have to shout, Mom," Aja said.

"I'm not talking to you," Monica replied.

"We're all gonna be civil at this table or breakfast is over," I said, the toothless tyrannical father of old.

"What did he say?" Monica asked.

"He's nervous. I mean, he has the feds threatening him with a long prison term, and then there's the people he's been working with, who might be even worse."

"What do you mean worse?"

"All that money he's been making?" I said. "I hope you don't think he's brought it in because he's such a genius."

Aja made a sound that would have been an *amen* in church.

"He's mixed up with a mob, probably Russian. They've been breaking federal tax laws and raking in millions, maybe even billions. The choice the feds have given him is to turn witness or spend twenty years in prison."

"No," Monica said. It was an absolute denial. These problems weren't happening and, even if they were, Coleman was not involved.

"Yes."

"How can I help him?" she begged.

"Help him?" Aja snarled. "Better let him go and get on with it."

"You're an awful child," mother told daughter.

"You're already doing the best you can, Monica. If you stay here Coleman's business partners can't get to you. And because you got me on it I found a lawyer that has lowered the amount he has to put up for bail. He'll represent Coleman."

"I want him here with me."

"No way."

"Why? Because I chose him over you?"

Monica was a good-looking woman and she knew it. She was a good person too but still saw herself as a kind of . . . prize.

"No, Mon, no. Your husband has two kinds of targets on his back and I will not bring that added danger on the house where my grandmother lives. If I manage to get him out of the hoosegow, you two will have to have a telephonic connection until the big problems are solved."

"You never liked Coleman," my ex charged.

"I hate him." It felt quite refreshing to say those words. Truth is so often deemed unsavory. "But I'm doing my best. And you staying here will make my job a lot easier."

"Why would I want to make things easier for you?" she sneered.

"That's simple," I said evenly. "If the Russians grab you and give me the choice of handing over your man, I will give him to them without a qualm and he will have died because of your love."

Monica had never looked at me like that before. It was as if I were a grand priest bathed in light who had just proven the existence of God. Not some beneficent old white man with a long beard but a pulsating eye that might wipe all humanity away without a second blink.

Monica turned her eyes to her plate and ate slowly, with small bites.

I knew I had gone too far because Aja reached out and laid a hand on her mother's shoulder.

"Hey, Joe," Roger Ferris said from the entryway.

He was wearing a black-and-cream-colored exercise suit made for fast walking. My grandmother was at his side. She'd changed into a gray calico dress that was printed with abstract red forms. I remembered back twenty years when she bought sixteen of the exact same dresses at a clearance sale in Brooklyn.

When he reached the dining table Roger said, "I transferred the money to Tomey and he's made you the executor."

"Thanks, Roger," I said. "I'll get it back to you as soon as I can."

Monica wasn't paying attention. That was probably for the best.

Brenda was giving my ex a scornful look. The great thing about old-time country relatives was that their love was fully armed and dangerous.

I stood up from the table, shook Roger's hand, kissed my grandmother, and said, "I got to be going."

"Can I come with you?" Aja asked.

"Not where I'm going right now, but I'll pick you up when things are a little less dicey."

"Okay."

* * *

Art Tomey was waiting for me at the entrance to the Metro-politan Correctional Center. The federal lawyer was short with a big belly showing in spite of his impeccably tailored dark blue suit. His skin had a gray pallor but did not seem unhealthy. His eyes were quartz blue, deeply faceted, and seemingly omniscient.

"Mr. Oliver," he hailed. "It's a great pleasure to see you."

"Art. How's the family?"

"Nita's a sophomore at the University of Texas and my wife left me."

"Sorry to hear that, about your wife, I mean."

"Don't be," he assured me. "She was unhappy and there's nothing worse for the marital bed than unhappiness. When she left, with her yoga instructor, I gave her twenty-five percent and the promise of friendship."

Tomey liked me because I saved his daughter's life and her future by leading the police to a dead body and not mentioning her name. That kind of intimacy makes honesty more free-flowing.

"What about Mr. Tesserat?" I asked.

"He's in a holding cell. All we have to do is go to the warden and set him free."

"Bail paid?"

"All ten percent."

"And what about Raoul Davies?"

"The FBI has backed off for the time being. I've promised them full cooperation after having a chance to debrief my client."

"How does one debrief a fool?" I asked no one in particular.

*   *   *

Teresa Valdon, a Black woman, probably not born in the U.S., was the acting warden of the MCC. I didn't know if that meant temporary or not but she had an impressive presence. She was six-two at least and maybe two hundred pounds, and her face would have been lovely if she wasn't so serious. Her hands wanted to curl into fists when we met and I found myself hoping they didn't have to.

"Hello, Mr. Tomey," she said to the man who had brought me. Then she turned her head in my direction. "Mr. Oliver, you have quite a presence in the files of the federal prison system. That's unusual for a man who was never an employee, an inmate, or a lawyer."

"My father once told me that if they're talking about you then you must be doing something right."

"I see," Warden Valdon said. "So the right thing is to take Tesserat out of here?"

"On bail," I added.

"Under my responsibility," Art Tomey put in.

"The FBI has asked us to take his passport," the warden said as a counter.

"That sounds about right," I said.

The warden didn't like me and for some reason I was tickled by the attention.

"I can't say that Coleman wouldn't hurt a fly," I went on, "but if he got into a fight with one, it's a toss-up who'd win."

Valdon's smile invigorated me. That was the old dog in my heart, maybe my soul. I wanted to get this woman who didn't like me to change her mind.

"From what I understand about this case he'd be better in a cell," she said.

"From what I understand about organized crime he's about as safe here as he would be in Afghanistan."

That made Valdon's shoulders rise. Her eyes changed shape to accent the anger.

"Are you saying—" she began.

"He didn't mean anything, Teresa," Art said, cutting her off. "Joe was once arrested on false charges. Prisons worry him."

"You were a con?" she asked on a smile.

"I was, and I am, an innocent man." I'd had no intention of using words with such gravitas. But no matter how much I don't want to believe it, the content of one's heart is not make-believe.

The warden's demeanor softened. She smiled ever so slightly and said, "Your man will be at the outer door by the time you get there."

He was waiting for us where people moved freely. Two uniformed guards stood close by, in case he had to be suddenly rearrested, I thought.

Art Tomey walked up to the guards, shook their hands, and greeted them by name, then turned to Coleman. Tesserat was wearing a nicely cut but rumpled gray suit, and, for some reason, he still had on paper shoes. He looked haggard and a little stunned.

"Mr. Tesserat," Art said.

"Yeah?"

"I'm Art Tomey. You already know Mr. Oliver, I believe."

Coleman looked at me warily.

"Yeah. I know him."

"We're going to go down the street to a coffee shop, have a

little something, and then lay down the plans for your safety and defense," Art told his client.

Coleman either nodded or shuddered, I couldn't tell which.

At Babylon Diner the three of us sat at a window table. I had coffee; Art only wanted water. Coleman ordered scrambled eggs with ham, bacon, sausage, a water bagel, a triple latte, and a tumbler full of orange juice.

"They have all your records," Art said after the food arrived. "Unassailable proof that you defrauded everyone from the oil company to the federal government, from the bank to the investors who you had buy stock in the made-up corporation. There's no way we can claim innocence or even ignorance. The only thing we can do is make a deal."

"I need some real shoes," Coleman said through a mouth-ful of bagel.

"To wear to your funeral?" These were the first words I'd said.

Coleman's eyes flashed fear.

"The only thing you can do is make a deal," Art said, then added, "Do you know who Tava Burkel is?"

"The first time I ever heard that name was when they arrested me."

"That's who the feds want."

"I never met the man; never heard of him." Whining comes easily when you're helpless.

"I've asked around," Art told the bailee. "People say that you'd need to get protection from the Kremlin to be safe from him."

"So you're telling me I can't turn against the people I've worked with?"

"It seems like that," Art agreed. I was surprised that he did so. "But the type of information the FBI wants doesn't have an expiration date. Burkel knows that you can turn state's evidence at any time. Do you think he'd let you live in prison?"

Either Coleman had never considered this potential outcome or it was so frightening to him that his mind couldn't home in on it. He pushed the rest of the food away, knocking over Art's water glass.

I was fast with my napkin while Art pushed his chair back from the table. As I sopped up the water Coleman just shook his head.

When the mishap was righted Coleman asked, "What can I do?"

"Joe?" Art said.

"We have to believe that this boogeyman of yours will know that you're out and the threat you pose. They'll be looking for you," I said to Coleman. "So we need to put you someplace where you will be protected and whoever's after you can be identified."

"You wanna use me like bait?"

"You heard what Mr. Tomey said, brother. You are bait whether I use it or not."

That was the standoff. Neither my ex nor Coleman wanted to look directly at the diagnosis. It's hard to accept that your power in a situation is nil, that your only chance is to put your life in the hands of someone you hate and who hates you back.

"What do you want from me?" he asked at last.

"There's a man in a blue Mustang parked across the street," Art said. "Get in that car with him and go where he takes you."

"Think about what you know," I added, "about how you want to play this. I'll be in touch to work out the angles."

The hardest jobs a PI has rarely have to do with law enforcement. It's settling beefs between criminals that's the trickiest thing.

"Can I trust you?" Coleman asked me.

"I'm gonna do my best."

"But you don't like me."

"True. But, luckily for you, that doesn't matter. I'm going to try and save you for Aja."

"She doesn't like me either."

"But she loves her mother, and keeping you in one piece is what Monica needs."

14.

I **RENTED A** Mini Cooper from a new place called Moment to Moment. It was painted periwinkle blue, a little too bright for my taste, but that was better than my own car. Too many parties were aware of my involvement; the FBI, alt-right, Russian mob, and who knew who else had my scent.

I purchased twelve burner phones at an electronics store on Twenty-Eighth Street. The work I'd taken on called for many levels of protection, anonymous communications being the top need. After that I went to visit my storage space a block from West Fourth Street. There, sitting in a comfortable chair under electric light, I called the people who needed to know how to reach me.

"Okay, Daddy," Aja said when I told her I was off the grid for a bit. "I guess I hope you do help out Coleman. Mom's crying all the time."

Melquarth only grunted when I gave him my numbers.

Roger Ferris had information about Thad Longerman.

*　　*　　*

Longerman, aka Benjamin Ingram, called himself an independent consultant working exclusively for a company called Zyron International. Zyron specialized in prison systems. They built and operated private pens around the world. Thad's position had him acquiring land while hiring architects, builders, and security forces. He also oversaw an international group of agents to man prisons, facilitate the transfer of international detainees, and investigate and also alleviate threats to the smooth running of ZI's interests around the globe. If Roger's sources were right Longerman had relationships with many world capitals and a shadow network of people brokers that ensured the interests of ZI.

ZI's headquarters were located in Atlanta, Georgia, and Longerman, as Ingram, lived there at the Bentley Hotel—room number 406.

The prison's consultant would be the hardest nut to crack. He was obviously dangerous and had backing of the highest order. The federal government might well have given him the go-ahead to grab Quiller, and his prison systems contacts would have made the crime unassailable.

Once again I had to consider whether or not to drop the case. I mean, what could I possibly learn about a crime committed in Belarus by some huge and shadowy corporation? And even if I did figure a way in, why would I put my life on the line for someone like Quiller?

I had every reason in the world to stop the investigation. If it wasn't for Longerman's profession I would have probably taken a vacation. But a company that specialized in prison systems, that had the power to pull anyone they wished out of one country and deposit them in another, a business whose product was the abrogation of human rights...well, as much as I wanted to, I couldn't turn my back on that.

My little storage space was exactly 500 square feet. In there I had everything I needed to survive, the most important of which was a bookcase containing the old hardback *Merriam-Webster's Dictionary.*

I took down the heavy tome and looked up *poverty.* There were many terms used to *define* the word: *penury, destitution, indigence, lacuna, privation...debt.* Mostly the definitions were more or less accurate synonyms; many of these used the words *extreme* and *absolute* to underscore meaning. But for me the absoluteness of the experience of poverty was a word not used—*prison.* And the only words that got close to defining that special brand of nothingness were *privation* and *wretchedness.*

Solitary confinement, aka isolation, was the certainty of having no rights whatsoever. My hunger and thirst, my loneliness and need for love, my freedom to pick up and go—all of these were gone. This was true poverty. This was the experience of being slowly murdered by a state of being, by uncaring humans, by systems that did not, could not, share my suffering.

I couldn't beat Longerman or Zyron International. But I'd be damned if I got down on my knees to them, damned if I ran from them even if there was no escape.

After that tumultuous inner-psychic examination I took out a DVD player from the wardrobe cabinet and played *The Hunter* starring Steve McQueen. It was his last movie, I think, and there was a kind of inescapable sadness to his performance that echoed my own feelings.

When the movie was over I called my electronic answering service. There were two messages.

The first was from Coleman.

"Okay," he said as if we were in the middle of a conversation. "I guess you and Tomey are right. I have to stand up and do something. Call me and we can figure out what's best."

Then there was a very short call. Even though we'd only spoken one time, I knew the voice.

"I'd like to speak to you," she said. "In person. Send me a text of when and where."

I sent a rather complex text that indicated the exact location in the large building and set a time. Looking back on that moment, bunged up in that storage room, I now realize the act of making that appointment marked the last time I'd consider abandoning my responsibilities.

"Hello?" Coleman said through the radio waves of modern-day telephones.

"How's the room?" I asked.

"You think it's some kinda joke to put me in this flop-house?"

"It might be a little funny," I admitted. "But you're there partly because no one you know would ever expect it."

Most of Brooklyn was gentrifying by then, but the SRO Art Tomey's man put Coleman in was not part of that transformation.

"I can't stay here, Joe. It's worse than the MCC."

"You can always go back there."

"This is no joke, man. A guy was shot across the street just an hour after I got here, and the woman next door got the shit kicked out of her by her pimp."

"That was my beat one time when I was in uniform. I walked those streets at night."

"You had a gun."

"Don't go outside and you won't have any problem."

"I need a place that at least has a shower."

"Then call Art and tell him to find you one."

"That's all I have to do?"

"Well, you also have to pay for it."

"You know my money's frozen."

"Ask Monica."

"Her money's tied up with mine."

"Borrow it, then."

Silence on the other end of the line.

"Oh," I said. "That's right, if your Russian business partner knew where you worked, who you talk to, they might tumble to your location. If you just ask an old friend a question, that might sign your death warrant."

"You're enjoying this, aren't you?"

"You left a message saying you wanted to talk," I replied. "So talk."

"Are you the only one on the line?"

"Just two burners with no names attached."

"This stays between us."

"I'm gonna do my job, Coleman. Information may be shared in some places, but I won't tell the so-called authorities."

After another silence he said, "I don't know his real name, but the one he had me use was Alain Freeman."

"That's not much help, Coleman. I mean, how do you expect me to get anywhere with just an alias?"

"I don't know, man. He was a little guy, had an accent like Eastern Europe but mild, you know?"

I understood fear. It was the bread and butter of the world I inhabited. So, finally I said, "Alain Freeman?"

"Yeah."

"Where can I find him?"

"Look, man. It'd be worth my life if he knew I even told you this much."

"The minute he finds out where you are he's got to kill you regardless of what you say."

After many seconds Coleman said, "He had an office across from Penn Station but he was gone from there after the first time the FBI came to my bank. I tried to call him but the number doesn't even ring."

"When was this?"

"About three weeks ago."

"Three weeks? And when did they arrest you?"

"Maybe an hour after I made the call."

"If Freeman's the connect, why are the feds talking about this Tava Burkel?"

"I don't know."

"Don't shit me, man. The name scared you when I mentioned it."

"Only because the FBI guys kept asking me about him. I thought, I don't know, I thought that you maybe were working for the Russians."

"That's good."

"What do you mean—good? Are you?"

"Naw, man. It's good you're worried. Worry will keep you on your toes."

"That's all you got to tell me?"

"Hey, you got two names and no way to get in touch with either one. They probably aren't even real names. No one knows where you are, but the minute I dip my toe in those waters people are gonna start to wonder—about me."

"I get all that," Coleman said. "I know you don't have to do this but I'm goin' crazy sittin' here."

"I know," I said. "I been there. But the only thing you can do is sit it out. Call Tomey's office. A woman named Amethyst Banks will answer. Tell her I said that I'd like it if she helped you out. She can do simple things for you. You know—foods, DVDs, books—stuff to help make the time pass."

"Okay." Lee capitulating to Grant. "All right."

Understanding how things work is the only way that we, humanity and I, can make it in this world. And making it is never a sure thing because nearly everything changes gears every thirty-six hours or so. All one can do is weigh the possibilities and move with great caution; hear the words being spoken and wonder what they could possibly mean.

Coleman was afraid for his life. But unless he got involved with the prostitute next door he'd probably survive being isolated. Probably. And if I could follow down the almost nothing he knew, I might not die this season.

After failing to come up with anything useful about Freeman and Burkel, I spruced up a bit and headed out for the Metropolitan Museum of Art. Once through security I turned right, going through a maze of various master- and minor pieces, past a series of ancient sarcophagi, and into a great sunlit room that contained very old Egyptian structures. There, sitting on a stone bench, was an elegant and lovely Black woman in a stark-white one-piece dress, appraising the huge edifices that America had somehow claimed as a gift from Africa.

The moment I laid eyes on her she turned, smiled, stood, and walked in my direction.

"Mr. King Oliver."

"Why don't we go back to your bench, Ms. Prim?"

"It's kinda public," she worried.

"Yeah, but no one will wonder what we're talking about. They'll know it's either art or love or both."

So we sauntered back to the bench and sat, both of us looking up at the Temple of Dendur with mild awe.

"I am always stunned by this exhibit," she said. "You'd expect something like this to be nestled away on some billionaire's estate, behind barbed wire and silent alarms."

"Where you from, Mattie?"

She smiled at my familiarity, even showing her teeth.

"A town called Peanut," she said.

"In Kentucky?"

"How'd you know that?"

"There's a chemical factory there, I think."

"You are a good detective," she said.

"How long ago did you leave there?"

"Long time."

"Your whole family?"

"No." There was a dark tone to that one word.

"Something happen?"

"You could say that. There were only two legal businesses in Peanut at the time—coal mining and the syngas factory."

"Syngas?"

"Synthetic natural gas. It comes from coal. Peanut was a big coal-mining town. Back then you either sold meth, hootch, ass, or your soul to coal."

"Back then but not anymore?"

"No. Not anymore."

"Do you mind if I ask you some questions about your husband?"

"No." But she wasn't happy about it either.

"Everything I've read paints him as racist and more. An enemy of Black people, of women, of any kind of thinking that didn't originate in Europe."

"I don't know him like that," she said simply.

"And exactly how is it that you know him?"

Mathilda Prim was exquisite: her face, her elocution, her gait . . . Her gaze told me to drop the line of inquiry, but I was stubborn.

"I got into trouble back home," she said. "As a consequence people looked down on me and my parents. That's why they wanted me in the gas factory. They were even happier to see me gone from town. For them it was like I never existed. Alfie has a similar life history, but his path was harder than mine. Much harder."

"But he saw a fellow soul in you."

"Among other things."

My heart grabbed right then. It wasn't love or lust or anything like that. It was a connection she'd made in her life that resonated with my own.

I took a deep breath and asked, "Was there something you wanted to tell me?"

"Have you heard the name George Laurel in your investigation?"

"No. Who is he?"

"That's what you need to find out."

15.

BESTIAL. **THAT'S THE** word that comes to mind when I remember walking through the vast entry hall of the museum with Mathilda Prim. I wasn't breathing any harder but was aware of every breath. I was walking normally but it felt as if I was hunching with each step, turning my head from side to side looking for threats—or rivals.

When we reached the crowded curb in front of the museum she took a cell phone from her sapphire clutch and entered a number.

"Can I ask you something, Ms. Prim?"

"What's that, Mr. King Oliver?" There was a smile in her voice.

"Those white men around your house."

"Yes, what about them?"

"Are they working for you?"

"No," she intoned. This time her mouth formed the shadow of a smile, but there was no humor behind it.

A black town car slid up to the curb, the door swinging

open. Minta Kraft was driving. My museum date lowered into the passenger's seat and closed the door, and Minta drove off, a dark samurai fish joining the school of brightly colored koi.

It's never a good idea for lawyers or detectives to have real feelings. It's okay to shout or frown. It's fine to channel old spirits into threats or even violence. But once you feel connected to any part of the job, you end up like Amethyst Banks—giving away everything for a roll in the hay.

These thoughts in mind, I turned in my Mini Cooper and took a train to Yonkers. There I went to a small hotel I sometimes use, the Nurya Inn on Second. I liked it because the slender Black man who always manned the front desk preferred cash and hardly ever made eye contact.

I was unarmed and feeling a fool, Mathilda Prim's fool. That woman got under my skin.

Nurya's rooms were like small dens off a main living room in a big house. The chamber I liked was 304. There was a roll-top desk, a sofa that folded out into a bed, and an old-time stand-up lamp that had three forty-watt bulbs that gave off soft but certain light. The one window looked out on a small side street that shone under the yellowy streetlamps. It had started to rain. Everything outside glistened and pedestrian traffic was nearly nil.

I stayed at the window for a long time, savoring the moments of anonymity, safety, and, most of all, quiet.

After a while I pulled away from the window and made

a few reservations via iPad. Then I called two men, asking them to help me. I got two yeses.

At 6:45 the next morning I was at Delta Gate 22 sitting very near the boarding gate. Across the way from my row of chairs sat Cousin Rags. He was leaning back in his chair studying a fishing magazine with great interest. I wondered if he really was a fisherman. We were blood but never really all that close.

Four seats down from me sat a thirty-something Black woman dressed for upper-echelon office work with good posture and a pink carry-on bag. I noticed her because now and then she would glance at my cousin.

I had a novel taken from my storage space library. It was *Joe Hill,* a biographical novel written by Wallace Stegner. Stegner was a good writer and a political activist of sorts. The man he wrote about, Joe Hill, was a martyr of the IWW back in the late nineteenth / early twentieth centuries. Ever since seeing Forthright and dealing again with Roger Ferris, I wanted to feel that I was about something meaningful. I mean, I realize that I was just another gumshoe working for a few dollars, prone to looking the other way if the client or the job was less than savory. But still it's good to read about flawed heroes attempting to do something good on a field of bad intent.

I'd gotten through the foreword when I looked up to see that the Black woman with the pink carry-on had moved next to Rags.

They were chatting away about something—fish or fishing, boarding flights, or maybe how crazy the news is getting.

I imagined that Rags had a whole story about why he was going to Atlanta. He was dressed like a day laborer, so he wouldn't pretend to be commuting for work. He didn't have a southern accent so probably wouldn't say he was going home. Maybe that's why he had the fishing journal. Maybe, in his mind, he was going fishing in some stream or lake.

And her? I imagined she was a little nervous about flying and he reminded her of some family member who calmed her down. Rags was a good listener and so she could put her worry into words about a job or boyfriend, sister or some specific task that she had to perform on one Peachtree Street or other.

I sat toward the front of the regular passenger section of the plane. Rags passed me at some point, but the woman with the pink carry-on did not. She sat in business class in the second row.

I was in the aisle seat. A white woman and her nine-year-old daughter sat next to me.

The woman's name was Ida Denton and her daughter was Florence. They were moving down to Savannah to live with her new husband, Clark Rowel.

"You think you'll like it down in Savannah?" I asked the child.

"Uncle Clark's got a swimming pool and a big tree where I can have a tree house."

Ida glanced at me. She seemed embarrassed that she'd allowed her daughter to be bribed with material promises.

"What are you doing in Atlanta?" the newlywed asked me.

"I'm working for a company that builds and operates private prisons."

"Oh," Ida uttered. "I see."

"You don't like the idea of private prisons?" I asked.

"I don't believe in prisons—period." There was back-bone there.

"Even for murderers and molesters?"

"Prisons criminalize," she said. It was a welcomed rebuke.

"My daddy went to prison," Florence offered. "They beat him up and then they killed him."

I took the passenger train to baggage and then looked around until I found carousel 3. The lady with the pink carry-on was there. She waited patiently, glancing around now and then. Looking for Rags, I'd bet. But my cousin hadn't checked a bag. He'd told me that anything *special* we'd need he'd send overnight.

My suitcase was the last one out of the chute. It was a gag bag that Aja gave me for a birthday one year—jet black with a big red eye painted on either side.

"Now everyone'll know you're a PI, Daddy."

"Won't that just be peachy," I said, and she laughed and laughed.

The Airbnb was in an apartment building on Marquee Street in the Bankhead neighborhood. It was a lively Black enclave with music pouring out of windows and from passing cars. Men and women talked and laughed on the streets.

The studio was on the sixth floor amid a crowd of trees that housed an aerie of birds that, I later learned, sang both day and night. It had a small terrace that looked down on Marquee. I pulled a padded chair out there and looked down upon my new environs. Working-class and down-market, it was a lively place. I saw two men get into a fistfight toward late afternoon. They hadn't been loud or boastful before engaging so I figured they must have had a deep disagreement. When one of the men got the upper hand, he kept on beating his opponent as the poor man lolled against a wire fence.

I saw that the loser was in danger of losing more than the fight, but I was too far away, and besides, I had a job to do and couldn't afford getting mixed up with the APD. I was considering going into the apartment so as to not be identified as a witness when...

"Back it up!" a woman's loud voice commanded.

The victor kept hitting his victim until the large Black woman advanced on him armed with a baseball bat. She went right into the sphere of the fight and hit the aggressor hard on the shoulder—to get his attention.

He looked up from the bloody loser and said, "I'm'a—"

What cut him off was the woman swinging the bat like a National League pro. It only missed because the man ducked. By the time he raised his head again she was ready for strike three.

Other older, and some younger, Black folk had come out to back the slugger up.

"You beat him," the woman said. "Now get the fuck outta heah."

Back in the studio I put on a pair of eight-year-old blue jeans and donned a white T-shirt. I wore a gold pinky ring festooned with an onyx square that had a tiny, glittering diamond at the center. Finishing the ensemble with a pair of Air Jordans, I made my way down to Big Bob's Barbecue on Arthur. There I ordered a slab of ribs with extra spicy sauce on the side.

Waiting for the meal to arrive, I happened to be looking at the front door when a young Black woman came in. Five-three or four, she weighed maybe 138 filled out just right. She had a lazy eye and one gold-capped upper canine. At first glance she looked like a young office worker, but then you noticed the coarseness of the cloth and the subtle dissonance of greens and blues that made up her outfit. One lime pump had a deeply scuffed toe.

She was beautiful.

I made no gesture toward her, however. I was in Atlanta working beyond hope to finish a job before it did me in. So it seemed almost mystical that as she looked around the room that wandering eye settled on me.

She waved as if she knew me and then walked up to my table.

"You mind if I sit here, mister?"

"I'd mind if you didn't."

"I don't wanna give you the wrong idea or nuthin'. There's a man out there lookin' for me and I don't wanna talk to him."

"Have a seat."

She smiled and pulled out the chair.

"This man mad at you?" I asked.

"Uh-uh. He think he in love."

"Thinks?"

"He likes a woman with my kinda figure and he broke

up with his girlfriend just last week. Now he got his eye on me."

"So? Just tell him no."

"Yeah, I know, but I like the way he look too. I know if we talk he gonna make me do something I'll be sorry for."

"Like what?"

The waiter came up with my ribs. He eyed my date with definite suspicion.

"You want something to eat?" I asked the woman wearing the lime-colored shoes.

"I like their brisket," she said.

"Bring it with everything," I told the server.

Her name was Lula McKenzie and she was born on the living room floor of an apartment not seven blocks from that restaurant. She was twenty-seven years old January last.

"What do you do for a living?" I asked for no reason in particular.

"Why?" she asked me, an edge to the tone.

"I just want to get to know you better."

"Why?" The hard tone was gone.

"Because I was sitting here alone when the prettiest girl I've seen down here walks through the door. Not only that, she walks up to me."

"I told you that I was tryin' to hide from Alfonso."

"That don't change a thing."

Lula took a sudden intake of breath and I told her that I was staying two blocks away.

We started kissing on the stairs. It took maybe twelve minutes to make the five flights. She told me that she liked it when her boyfriends kissed her *down there* and I moved to oblige. She returned the favor and then we got down to it.

When I awoke the next morning, just about sunrise, Lula was gone. She'd only taken two of the seven hundred-dollar bills from my wallet so I knew she liked me.

Atlanta is my kind of town.

16.

I SPENT THE next few days walking around the southern city. Atlanta's a good-looking town even when it's hot and sticky. It's very southern down there, so people talk to you and seem to really mean what they say. They look in your eyes with a greeting on their lips.

The other two things about ATL were that it is modern and also Black with a deep progressive culture. A town that awakened one morning with the realization of who and what it was with no regrets or antipathies.

I spent long nights in the Airbnb asking questions of the Internet. There were few solid answers. No connection between Zyron International and Rembert Cormody, the Men of Action, or any other alt-right or nationalist group—at least no connection that I could find. Alfie Quiller hadn't been public about prisons, private or otherwise, and the U.S. government hadn't said anything new about him for months.

Mathilda Prim graduated summa cum laude in information studies from Syracuse University in 2011 and was not heard from again until 2019, when she was granted a master's degree from Harvard in something called theoretical chemistry. It was just a name on a list of Ivy League accomplishments. There was no evidence that that name was *my* Mattie, but I thought it might be.

George Laurel was no more than three lines in an obituary published in a small newspaper from La Jolla, California. It seemed that his death was tragic but I could get no more about it. His father was already dead at the time of the publication and his mother, Nora Blandford Laurel, had died in 2000.

On the morning I woke up to find Lula gone I also received a text from Rags. He sent a locker number and its electronic combination. At the bus station we decided on before coming south, I used the code on locker 1011B. There to find a rather elegant pigskin briefcase.

When I got home I opened the attaché to find a newspaper wrapped around a nine-millimeter FN 509C semiautomatic. There were also six loaded clips.

The gun took my breath away. It was reliable, concealable, and expensive, but my inner gasp was because accepting that weapon meant that things had turned a corner. I was no longer *snooping*. Now I was at the precipice of war.

The underground newspaper wrapped around the pistol was called the *Rotten Peach*. A publication for the more adventurous Atlantan, it was composed of explicit personal ads, stories of police violence, veiled warnings about drugs on the street, sex offers, and other promises of ecstasy. On the second day in town I put a personal ad in the virtual version of the *Rotten Peach*.

At 5:39 p.m. on the third day I went to Wreckless Dancers

strip club. It was lesser known than some of the famous joints, but WD had space and really lovely women. The food and drink were good too. I was sipping Cordon Bleu from a generous snifter and munching on chicken wings. It was early and the night shift was just arriving. There weren't many customers then—the lunch crowd had gone and the nighthawks were still preening somewhere.

"Hi, mister," a lovely honey-colored woman said. She was wearing one big synthetic feather that covered everything but a generous nipple. "You want a dance?"

"What's your name?"

"Tantalea."

"That's a great name."

She smiled and said, "Thank you."

"I tell you what, Tantalea." I handed her a fold of three hundred-dollar bills. "I have a meeting and need to be left alone except for drinks and such."

As the lovely woman counted, her smile broadened.

"What's your name, honey?"

"Joe."

"Your wish is my command, Mr. Joe." From then on she was the only person I had to talk to.

I sipped my cognac and chatted with Tantalea from time to time. Mr. Joe was a contractor from Newark, in Georgia to build a small bridge for a rich man's estate down near Savannah.

I like strip clubs because they never tempt me. The naked dancing and money changing hands, drinking and loud talk, the smells both natural and artificial, and the constant beat of the bass were all just fine, normal, expected. What excited me was the unforeseen, the newly formed.

So sitting there, mostly unmolested, I floated in the sensory environment of red lights and Black faces, confident hilarity and relief from the hard edges of life.

An hour or so later a familiar voice called, "Hey, Joe."

"Rags."

"Why you got us meetin' here?"

"When in Atlanta..." I said.

Rags nodded and took a seat at my little table. He was wearing a tan suit with a one-button jacket and a black T. His shoes looked to be woven from straw and his socks were most definitely red.

"It's not a place I would have chosen," he said. "But nobody's gonna ask what we're talkin' 'bout."

"You get in touch with that woman with the pink bag?" I asked.

"Jesse Martin? Naw. She was just lonely and I had work to do."

"How's that goin'?"

And so we got into it.

Rags had taken a room in the Bentley Hotel to keep tabs on Ben Ingram. He'd been following the prison master for two days.

"He's mostly unpredictable," Rags reported. "But he does seem to go to the same little hole-in-the-wall café every day around one forty-five and then has his first meeting at two."

"What kinda meetings?"

"All kinds. Men and women, singles and pairs, now and

then there's even a trey. Sometimes a few sheets of paper change hands but not too much. It's all pretty dry.

"I followed one of the men who met with him."

"Oh?"

"Dark guy but not Black. I thought maybe Arab but he turned out to be from Brazil. He went to a hotel in the business district called the Antietam. I took a chance and followed him in. It was one of those old-time places where they hold your key behind the front desk. I had my briefcase camera running so later I could enlarge the picture enough to see that the guy was in room 204.

"When the dude went out that evening I jimmied my way in."

Rags handed me an envelope with pictures. The first was of an open passport issued to a Goncalo de Jesus. He was a good-looking man with a little too much mustache for my taste. There were a few papers printed in Portuguese and another sheet that had eighteen thumbnail photographic portraits with a name underneath each.

"I'll try and get the letter translated," I said.

"Don't bother. It says that the people in the pictures have been transferred from government custody to a site some-where in Austria, where they will be *debriefed*."

"How good is your Brazilian Portuguese?" I asked.

"Okay. Why?"

"I kind of doubt they'd let Zyron run their own prison in Austria."

"I was thinkin' that. Maybe Austria is a code for some-place else."

"Excuse me, Mr. Joe," Tantalea said.

"What is it, hon?"

"There's a white man here says he wants to join you two."

Standing maybe thirty feet away in semidarkness, Gladstone Palmer was as recognizable as a beacon in a storm. Lean and six foot one, the NYPD dispatcher smiled and raised a hand of recognition.

"He's ours," I told the feathered beauty.

Tantalea went to retrieve the third member of my unofficial covert mission.

He walked behind her like visiting royalty surveying a recently acquired colony.

"Hey, boyo," he said upon arrival.

Gladstone was always smiling, or at least getting ready to do so. He was almost a caricature of your classic Irishman. His hair couldn't decide whether to be red or brown. I would have called it cinnamon. His eyes were green, of course, and his skin as close to white as a Caucasian can get.

"I'm in love," he said before he sat, watching Tantalea walk away.

"Glad, I'd like you to meet Richard Naples."

Holding his hand across the table, my cousin said, "Call me Rags. I know you, don't I?"

"Maybe you saw me somewhere," Glad said on a grin. "So what do the great minds have to tell a poor Paddy from the Lower East Side?"

We filled him in on the important points.

"So you made it up the stairs and into his room?" Glad beamed at Rags. "Weren't you afraid of the vids?"

"I wasn't gonna kill him so I really didn't have all that much to hide."

Glad grunted pleasantly.

Looking at him brought to mind when he had sent me on a mission that was a frame. The plan at first was to kill me, but Sergeant Palmer put me in Rikers and then talked the powers that were, at that time, into letting me go. In the end all I lost was my profession, my family, and my faith in the world in general.

"You get here this morning, Glad?" I asked.

"No. I decided to come down a day or two early."

"Why?" I didn't like that.

"A few days ago I called down to talk to Craig Stork," he said.

"That's Sergeant Stork from Staten Island?"

"Now he's Assistant Warden Stork down around Galveston. Making six figures at a Zyron prison. I called him and said that I was thinking about changing jobs. He asked if I wanted national or international. After a little back-and-forth he told me to come down and talk to Ben Ingram. So I made an appointment."

"You actually talked to the man?" I asked.

"Talk?" Glad said. "I had a meeting with him."

"That's where I saw you," Rags remembered out loud.

"Why didn't you tell me?" I asked both men.

"I didn't know who he was," Rags told me.

Turning to Glad I said, "I just wanted you for backup."

"I can do that too."

That was the good and bad about my friend and traitor. He did things his own way, which sometimes was a boon and others a bust.

"What did he say?"

"He said that there was a position in the corporation called high marshal. A kind of enforcer who moves between countries trying to keep the peace and assess threats. Stork told him I was good at keeping balls in the air—in the air and the nutcracker too."

"Was he any more specific?"

"He said that there were times when a high marshal had to work outside of local law. Times when there might be a higher calling."

"And how much would you be paid for all this?" That was Rags.

"I'd get a base salary of two hundred seventy-five and then bonuses in cryptocurrency. That could go up to near a million. I tell ya, it was mighty tempting."

"Did you take him up on it?" I asked, my teeth feeling and tasting like iron nails.

My old dispatcher gauged me with shamrock eyes. He understood the question and knew the consequences harbored in my heart.

"No, brother," he said. "I wouldn't betray you and I wouldn't work for a company that big anyway. On the force we're all friends. You eat at people's houses and know their children's names. You would put down your life for a brother in blue. We're not a business, we're a church."

"Damn," Rags said. "You're good."

"Just a cop," Glad replied. "Honest or not."

We worked out a plan for the next day. What it lacked in brilliance it made up for with simplicity. That done, we ordered a round of drinks, ready to call it a night.

That was before sloe-eyed Lula came in with three girl-friends.

That kismet thing was still working. The moment I noticed

her she turned to see me. I smiled, instantly dispelling her
first instinct, which was to run. Instead Lula grinned and
said something to her girlfriends. They conferred for fifteen
seconds or so, casting glances in our direction, then forded
the now crowded room, headed for our table.

I got to my feet feeling a little giddy. Women have always
been my weakness.

Lula was the first to get to us. She kissed me on the lips.

"Hi, baby," she said.

"Lou." I guess I just like nicknames. "These are my friends
Glad and Rags."

"Glad rags," an astute white associate of Lula's said. "I'm
Roxanne and this is Nona and Chichi."

Roxanne was tall and blond, naturally so. Nona was very
dark-skinned, where Chichi was a deep amber Mexican lass.
These ladies spent at least three hours readying for Wreckless and now they bubbled over with cleavage, conversation,
and laughter. I ordered three bottles of champagne thinking
that this might well be my last night.

Gladstone left with the white girl, no surprise there, while
Rags went off with the other two. There were many things
I didn't know about my cousin. I made up my mind that
night to find out what they were.

17.

I'M GLAD YOU stayed the night this time," I said to Lula.

We were sitting on the little terrace eating buttered toast and jam off a paper plate set on a small cast-iron table. I'd made a pot of coffee and Lula was smoking a filterless Camel.

"I figured if I was lucky enough to meet you the second time that maybe we should get to know each other a little better," she said through a rising screen of exhaled smoke.

"Wasn't so much luck. I noticed you had a few matchboxes from Wreckless and so I hoped you might drop by."

"Sorry I'm on my period, then. You would'a been luckier with Nona or Chichi."

"Why not Roxanne?"

"You don't like white girls. Not like that."

"I'm happy with you, Lou. Anyway I was too dizzy to do much after all that champagne."

The 24/7 birds were chirping in the treetops and the streets were populated by people going to work and school.

"It's real nice up in here," Lula said. "I like spendin' time with you."

"As much as with Alfonso?"

"That man is just a hard dick and a hard time, like my grandmother used to say. He'd never make me toast and coffee. When Alfonso wake up in the mornin', the only thing he has to say is it's time to go."

We spent the early morning talking about life and how it seems to work, her charms and mine. After that I got dressed in my gray suit, surreptitiously pocketed my gun, and brought Lula down to my rented car. We drove to the affluent Buckhead area, where I bought her a silk dress and a citrine necklace.

"Where we gonna have dinner?" she asked as we exited the boutique.

"Where would you like?"

"Are you rich?"

"Not really. But I can afford a good dinner."

"Okay, then. I'll call you at five to tell you where."

I gave her money for a cab and she kissed me good-bye.

Watching her walk away, I was hoping I would be able to make that date.

My destination was the U-Turn Café, also in Buckhead. I decided to stretch my legs and walked the six blocks to the little espresso bar.

He was sitting at a small round table at the innermost end of the long room, reading a newspaper. The clock on the wall above his head registered 1:47. The news must have been engrossing. It wasn't until my shadow spread across his table that he became aware that someone was there.

When he looked up, his face at first darkened, but then he smiled broadly.

"Mr. Oliver," said Ben Ingram, also known as Thad Longerman. "It's a pleasure to meet you at last."

The familiarity threw me off a moment. I opened my mouth to speak, but he held up a finger with one hand and picked up a cell phone with the other.

Speaking into the phone he said, "Hold my next two," then disconnected the call. "Sit, sit."

I obeyed the offer and said, "Tex Bradford must've had a hidden camera."

The affable jailer nodded pleasantly. "Over the front door. Amazing what image software can do nowadays. It should be illegal."

"Lots of things should be."

"What can I get for you today, Mr. Ingram?" a young man asked.

He was of medium height with strawberry blonde hair that would have put Roxanne to shame.

"Café con leche for me, Mark. What'll you have, Mr. Oliver?"

"Sign over the bar says something about pastrami soup? What's that like?"

"Better than it sounds," the smiling heir of the Vikings allowed. "It's a cream soup with pieces of pastrami and bitter greens in it. Pretty good."

"I'll take it."

"You're the adventurous type," Ingram noted as Mark went off on his tasks.

"Only with food."

"If that were true you wouldn't be sitting at this table."

The words, the tone of his voice, made me want to reach for the gun in my pocket.

"I'm not here to get in anybody's way, Ben. I'm just gathering information for a client."

"What client?" His smile was infinitely patient.

Ben had a round head and close-cut brunette hair. His shoulders looked sturdy and I imagined he was close to six foot.

Mark returned with our orders. Ben thanked him and the boy went off to some distant table.

"I'm prohibited from revealing clients' names," I said, answering the prison professional.

"But you expect me to answer you?"

"*Expect* is a strong word," I said. "I expect the sun to rise in the east, the sky around it to be blue, the Democrats to believe in their impossible dreams, and the Republicans to revel in their own stink."

Ingram laughed out loud, turning a head or two in the sparsely populated establishment.

"Okay," he said. "All right. I'll tell you."

"Tell me what?"

"I was involved in the clandestine abduction of a certain gentleman named Alfred Xavier Quiller from an exurb of Belarus called Little Peach. Why, you ask? Because the man in question is an unredeemable idealist."

I was shocked, truly. In all my years as a cop and then a PI, I had never run across a seemingly sane criminal who would confess so easily.

"What do you mean—idealist?" I asked.

The prison master hunched his shoulders and gave a wan, apologetic smile. "Although he's a genius, Mr. Quiller doesn't understand the rough-and-tumble of politics, of power. Ideas in themselves are wonderful things, but the force of will behind these thoughts—that's what greatness is made of."

He believed that this answer was coherent. Maybe he wasn't quite sane.

"I don't understand you."

Again that maddening weak smile. It was like a limp-wrist handshake.

"Mr. Quiller thinks that merely saying something is enough to effect meaningful change. He thinks that most human beings are rational creatures that act solely upon logic. On top of that he believes that any and all systems of logic are open to argument, that any accepted truth might be overturned."

"So if he were to question himself," I postulated, "that might be disadvantageous to certain interested parties."

I was beginning to understand. Ingram's unexpected broad grin told me so.

"Exactly."

"Excuse me, Mr. Longerman, but you don't seem to be the kind of person who would be bothered by a man question-ing the innate racism of his theories."

"True." He didn't seem to notice me using his pseudonym. "Neither niggers, honkies, nor chinks make a difference to me. Cracker barrel or dark continent—who cares? It is, as I have said, power and politics that rule the day."

"And Mr. Quiller's scientific method has derailed him from your truth."

"It's a real pleasure talking to you, Joe. You have the ability to understand simple facts."

"So what's the problem?" I tried to get the tone of my voice to be that of an interested adviser.

"Not, as you have said—his innate idealism. But the half-assed nature of his approach to change."

"The file he has on the rich and powerful," I surmised.

"Got it in one." Mr. Ingram smiled and nodded.

"You want the file . . ."

"Out of his hands."

"Because?"

"You've met his wife, I hear." It was not a question.

"But she's his wife," I argued. "Wouldn't she be protective of him and his beliefs?"

"That doesn't matter. What does matter is what appears to be true."

"So because the Men of Action don't like his love life you kidnap and imprison a man you agree is important?"

"No. The people I'm working for are working with a larger organization that wants to control Quiller's database."

Of course they do, I thought. This made me consider Roger Ferris's reason for hiring me. My grandmother had told me not to trust him, that I was just a crumb on his table.

I needed time to work out my own situation.

"You have him already," I said. "Why not just get him to turn it over?"

"Well before Mr. Quiller met Ms. Prim, he put conditional access to the database in the hands of a man who also had the ability to move it further along without the originator knowing where. The only thing expected of Quiller is that he has to make a public appearance once a year in certain unpredictable places, along with his wife. If this prerequisite is not met, the information goes public."

"And there's a reason you can't go after the man who took control of the database?"

"So far he's been beyond our reach."

Ingram was staring deeply into my eyes.

"Don't look at me," I said defensively. "This is the first I've heard of the man."

A hint of disappointment informed Ingram's bearing. This frightened me.

"So how do you manage to place a wanted man in a public prison without the slightest ripple in the news or on social media?" I asked the question to delay an unknown inevitable.

"Business is business, Mr. Oliver. I know the agents that arrested Mr. Quiller in Paris. I'm on a first-name basis with wardens and their assistants across the nation. Quiller, as I am sure you noticed, is a guest at Rikers, not a convict."

"That's a hard place to be in for both you and him."

"And you," Ben added.

Exhalation had never given me a problem before that moment, but all of a sudden the air I breathed in seemingly sought refuge in my body. I wanted to deny Ingram's claim concerning my jeopardy, but that tack was useless. I knew hardly anything, but just that was way too much knowledge. With no other recourse I decided to taste my soup.

It was delicious. The greens were collard and the pastrami was not only salty but flavorful. I was a rat in a man-made maze, but still I'd gotten to the cheese.

Now the only problem was getting out again.

"Me?" I said. "I don't have anything to do with it. My job was to find out if Quiller was illegally removed from Belarus. The answer is—he was. The question of the murder of an

American citizen in Togo seems moot, and so there's nothing to say about that."

"Except for the identity of the person or persons that hired you."

Of course it was. And as much as I suspected my employer, I had no proof that he had me engaged in anything illegal. Roger Ferris was powerful, but even he might not be proof against the machine behind Ingram. It was my duty to protect him.

"I can't tell you that," I said with great reluctance.

Ben sipped his coffee.

"I like you, Joe," he said as the latte mug touched the table. "But you got your nose way up in the ass of some very important people. They need to know who put you in their business. You can understand that, can't you?"

"Of course I can," I said with nary a quaver. "But what you need to know is that I was a cop before I went private. There's something tribal about cops. We follow our creed and we never betray our brethren. I will reach out to my employer and ask if I might share his name with you. If he says yes, then I'll tell you."

Ingram sat back in his chair, laced his fingers, and looked at me.

"Tribes have gone the way of the nation-state, my friend. Religion, race, gender, age, even parentage no longer carry much weight in the world we inhabit. It is, as I have already said, politics and power—not in that order—that rule us. You have to tell me what I need to know right now, or I won't be able to trust."

I was that rat in a maze, a fly with one herky-jerky foot in a spider's web.

Ingram was not necessarily a bad guy. He was a man who had a job working for an evil so deep that it seemed virtuous. We sat in silence for a few minutes.

The soup was still good and breathing came back to me. I considered Ben Ingram—deeply. The experience of talking with him was astonishing to me. Usually when I met with someone over a case, or in life in general, I had to decipher their meaning. I took it for granted that people lied in order to reach their goals, to maintain their relationships, to survive, and, sometimes, simply to keep in practice.

But not Ben Ingram. I believed every word he said. There were things he wasn't telling me, but I couldn't even put the words together to ask about them.

In a way he was a paragon, a state of humanity to emulate.

In Ingram's sense of the world my fate had already been sealed. I was a dead man, a shadow burned into the concrete by a light a thousand times brighter than the sun.

"I'm sorry that we can't come to some kind of agreement, Mr. Longerman. You seem like the kind of man that one could trust. You're educated and confident."

"Thank you. I'm not very political and whatever powers I have are small. But be that as it may, you're right about me."

"How do you mean?"

"You and yours can bleed and die just as well as I and mine can."

18.

WALKING DOWN THE sweltering streets of Buckhead, I felt exposed to attack. This wasn't paranoia. Ingram could very well have called an assassin to follow me, to shoot me or run me down as I waited for red to turn to green. Maybe the message he left, *hold my next two,* was code for *get ready for a kill.*

My tongue was dry despite the humidity. My feet felt as if they might tangle up from the simple act of walking.

As disturbing as my situation was, it was not unfamiliar. I'd spent a good deal of my work life conniving against the machine. I could have, I should have, said no to Roger Ferris. When Monica came to me crying about Tesserat, I should have told her to call Art Tomey and mention my name—period.

There were other jobs, other ways to pay the rent. Aja was right about that.

So, turning on the residential block where I'd parked my rental car, I accepted that there was no one to blame but myself.

*　　*　　*

The forest-green Kia Rio was parked at the far end of the block, under, of all things, a peach tree. I was half the way there when I realized that there was a man seated behind the steering wheel. I couldn't make out his features but he was either Black or deeply tanned.

I stopped and considered running while feeling around for the pistol.

Neither response made sense, so I straightened my shoulders and forged on.

Eight steps along I saw that it was Rags sitting in the car.

"Hey, Joe," a man said from a step or two off to my right.

I flinched before recognizing Gladstone Palmer.

"You scared the shit out of me, man."

"We were waiting for you to come," he said, ignoring my flightiness. "It was a good idea your cousin had to put that tracker in your car."

"Why?"

"Right this way."

Glad walked up to my car and peeked through an open window into the cramped back seat. There was something there under a large black plastic tarp. Rags turned to wave at me and then pulled the edge of the cover up, revealing the face of a very dark-skinned Black man. The tops of the definitely dead man's cheekbones had equivalent horizontal scars on them. His left eye was open and sightless.

Rags covered the corpse over again.

"You should get in," Glad said to me.

A little stunned at the sudden bewildering spectacle of

death, I did as my old boss suggested. Glad closed the passenger's door behind me and then immediately walked away down the street.

"I got an Airbnb on the outskirts of Smyrna," Rags said as he ignited the engine and pulled from the curb. "A house with an attached garage kinda half in the country, you know."

"I thought you were staying at Ingram's hotel."

"I am," he said, giving a smirk. "It's just the kind of work I do often needs a pressure valve."

"Like when you suddenly find a dead man in the back seat?"

"Me and your friend set up a camera in his car and parked it across the street from this one. When I saw Fayez—"

"You know this guy?"

"Knew him back when I was a merc in Southeast Asia. He was the deadliest motherfucker I'd ever seen. One time I saw him kill four out of five men using stealth and a home-made machete. So, when I saw him climb into the back seat of your car I knew that Ingram was serious."

"He just climbed in?"

"Jacked the lock like a pro, slipped in the back, and disappeared. We came at him from both sides. I knocked on the window and when he rose up with a Glock in hand Glad shot him from the opposite side."

"That shattered the window?" I asked.

"Yeah."

"Why didn't anybody call it in?"

"Silencer."

"Whose?"

"Gladstone shot him but I gave him the gun."

"You run around with a silencer for reconnaissance and backup?"

"Zyron International," he said, as if those two words were the Eleventh Commandment.

Making it to the highway and then toward the suburb, I was on high alert. What if we got stopped? How do you explain a dead man with a bullet in the back of his head?

"What happened to the fifth man?" I asked the question as a distraction.

"Fayez knew how to put pain to work. He bled the soldier till he gave up the information we needed."

"Then he killed him?" Some distraction.

"I stopped doing that kind of work."

It took less than an hour to get to the house my cousin had rented. The garage was big enough for two cars the size of mine. Gladstone was already there. He'd made us lime rickeys in tall frosted glasses that were designed for that libation.

"How the fuck Rags get you to shoot a man in broad daylight in Georgia?" I asked Glad.

"Well," he said, grinning. "If I'm gonna do somethin' like that, it should be down south, don't ya think?"

"I think it's murder."

"He was hiding in the back seat and had a gun in his hand. I *am* a cop, you know."

"You need to get out of Georgia," Rags said to me. "And wherever you go, it should not be New York. You say Aja and Grandma B are with Ferris?"

"Yeah. Why?"

"I can go check out the security and either stay there with 'em or take 'em someplace else."

"Uh-huh. What about Fayez?"

"Who?" Gladstone asked.

"We'll stay here and dissolve his contract."

"Who's this Fayez?" Gladstone asked again.

While Rags explained, I wondered what I could do. I had to go back to New York, had to.

"Joe," Glad said.

"What?"

"What you gonna do?"

"Rags is right. I shouldn't go home, but I have business there. I'll make sure our family is safe and keep a very low profile."

The handsome Irishman looked at me, still grinning.

"What's funny?"

"Some people have heart attacks," he said. "They get cancer or too drunk and fall down the stairs. All kindsa ways a man could get killed. But you, Joe, you walk through a fucking minefield with blinders on and never even step on a pile of shit."

"I got a gig in Munich in three days," Rags said. "I'll leave you my number but that's still twenty-four hours away."

"I can't be doin' this shit in my own backyard," Glad added.

"That's okay. Both'a you boys have done enough."

In the taxi to the airport I made the reservation from yet another of my burners. After that I made another call.

"Who's this?" Melquarth said over the line. I was at the departure gate, drinking coffee.

"It's me, Mel."

"Wow."

"Wow what?"

"You sound like what the crime writers call hard-pressed."

"The guy I went to meet tried to have me killed. At least I think he did."

I explained the situation, naming names.

"Now I have to work both jobs without pissing people off so bad that they want me dead after."

"That's the trick," my murderous friend agreed. "Give me the flight number and I'll try to put something together."

"Hi," she said.

She had the aisle and I was next to the window. The seat between us was empty. The plane was taxiing for takeoff and I was looking out through a foot square of reinforced glass, feeling very much out of my depth.

"Hey," I replied, wondering if my tone revealed the pressure.

My row mate was a Black woman ten or fifteen years older than I. Her skin was oxidized gold and there were freckles—a whole field of them—across her cheeks. Gray and brown hairs curled together easily on her head and the clip-on earrings she wore were crystal and sterling silver.

"Do you mind if I move next to you?" She was already unbuckling the seat belt.

"They'll probably yell at you."

Smiling, the older woman heaved up and landed in the next seat.

"Please remain in your seats," a voice said over the speaker. "We can't take off until everyone is seated with their seat belts fastened."

My temporary friend was already buckling up.

"I know I shouldn't do this but..."

A flight attendant stalked down the aisle, stopping at our row. She had soft red hair and angry blue eyes.

"I'm so sorry, ma'am," said the woman who was now settled next to me. "I had to say something to my, my cousin here."

After looking to see that the seat belt was buckled, the flight attendant shook her head and smiled.

When she walked back toward the bulkhead my neighbor asked, "Would you mind holding my hand?"

For only a second I wondered if this seemingly kindly, late-middle-aged Negro woman doubled as an assassin in Zyron International's high marshal system.

But that was paranoia.

"Sure," I said, holding my left palm up.

Her hand was sweating, but that didn't bother me. It was my job to help clients. She was just another in a lifelong list.

"Joe Oliver," I said.

"Gillian Haft."

"You not used to flying, Gillian?"

The elder considered the question with gravitas. She seemed to be grilling herself with silent inquiries.

Finally she said, "Last week a young man named Tito called me from Atlanta. He said that my niece, Omolara, had a heart attack..."

"How old is your niece?"

"Only twenty-nine and she's always been so healthy. Anyway, I dawdled for a day before I bought my ticket, and by the time I got there she was already dead. Already dead."

Ms. Haft's hand clamped down on mine, allowing me to feel the pain she was going through.

"That's hard on the heart." It was a term my grandmother often used.

Gillian looked up at me, a sheet of tears covering the freckled cheeks under her eyes.

"I don't know what I'm going to do," she said. "My sister died and I'm the only one Omo had."

"That's what hurts so much. There's nothing you can do, nothing you could have done. You're no doctor. And I bet you she was unconscious from the time of the attack until the moment she passed."

"You think so?"

"And she had that young man…"

"Tito. He was there for her. She wasn't alone."

When the plane lifted up in the air Gillian's grip lightened. For the next hour or so we talked about her younger sibling and niece, how the sisters were raised in Ohio but came to New York to be models. That didn't work out but they had good lives.

I picked up my baggage at the carousel and walked toward the outer doors.

Melquarth was standing there wearing a black suit and a limo driver's cap. He was holding up an iPad with the name Redbird emblazoned on it. He stepped forward adroitly, grabbed my bag, and said, "Right this way, sir."

He had a black stretch limo in the parking area and even tried to get me to sit in back.

"Naw, man," I told him and then went around to the passenger's door of the front seat.

After we'd cleared the parking area I asked, "What's with all the dress-up, Mel?"

"Doin' what the situation calls for."

"I just said wow. How much can you read into that?"

"I got a call from a man named Ingram yesterday."

"Oh."

"Yeah. Oh."

"What did Mr. Ingram have to say?"

"He told me he had a call from a cat named Rembert Cormody."

"What did the high marshal want?"

"What's a high marshal?"

"I'll explain later."

"He asked me if I vouched for you."

"And?"

"I told him to keep his fuckin' nose outta my business."

"Maybe not the most friendly reply," I speculated.

"Maybe not. But right after you and I spoke I called a cracker I know down in Florida. Asked him to go up and take a look at your boy. By the time he got there word was Ingram was gone."

"What you mean, gone?"

"Either buried in Georgia clay or sipping mimosas on foreign soil."

"Huh," I grunted with maybe a little too much emphasis.

"You don't need to get all flustered, man. If your beef was with Ingram and Ingram has been removed, then there might be some wiggle room to deal in."

"Like in playin' poker with the devil?"

"No," Melquarth said optimistically. "He called the killer on you without thinking it through. You proved too much for him and they sent Ingram away."

"I can't count on that," I said. "I need to find a place I can work from and to set up a meeting with Roger Ferris."

"You also need a bodyguard."

"Hey, man, I'm not no Whitney Houston here."

"Maybe not, but I got one for you anyway."

19.

MEL DROVE US to a sushi place in the Bronx. I didn't ask why the restaurant or the borough. A schemer, a planner extraordinaire, he knew my troubles. I assumed he'd brought us out there to offer me assistance, and also, maybe a place I could stay.

I worked on a spicy tuna roll, an eel roll, and a few pieces of uni while Mel munched on a seaweed salad.

"Eatin' light, huh?" I said. "You're the one that's worried."

He smiled, quoting, "Never eat heavy before a battle. You can feast on the enemy's liver when he is dead at your feet."

"Who said that?"

"Masashige. A great samurai."

"What are we doing here, Shogun?"

"Waiting."

"For what?"

"There's something I want to show you in the park."

"Pot of gold?"

"Somethin' like that."

"Come on man. What are we doin' here?"

"It's better to see after dark."

Van Cortlandt Park. Big enough to be a wildlife preserve. It has its own zoo.

Mel brought us to a pretty desolate parking lot with fewer than a dozen cars. There he drove through a pretty much camouflaged space bracketed by two trees. This led to a dirt road. Ten minutes later we came to an empty dirt clearing.

We climbed out and Mel led me into a stand of pine. We walked no more than seven minutes through the trees, finally coming to a large hill made mostly of stone. That knoll was likely older, and definitely larger, than any dinosaur.

It was night by then, but Mel had an electric torch to light the way. He led me to a crevice the size of a doorway. We passed maybe fifteen feet and then came to a blank wall of stone. Mel produced a flat panel that fit easily in his hand, pressed a button, and the stone wall rose, revealing a room of some size.

"What the fuck?"

A light came on, defining the room as an entrance area for an even larger space.

"Jacobus Van Cortlandt bought the park, along with this stone hill, from John Barret at the end of the seventeenth century," Mel explained as we walked into the most secret place in New York City. "Barret wanted to keep the use of his gunpowder and alcohol storage area. He was a paranoid motherfucker and planned to hole up here if his enemies ever decided to do him injury.

"They hid weaponry here during the Revolution. It was

such a highly guarded secret that after a while there was no one around that knew it."

I was what they call gobsmacked. For the first time in days I wasn't thinking about Quiller or Ingram, the Russians or even prison. The entry hall opened into a neat little two-story apartment.

"If nobody knew, how'd you find it?" I asked Madman Frost.

Mel winced. That's an unusual response for a man who's shouldered evil for every minute of his life.

"It's a long story, Joe. Maybe some other time."

"Okay. Then tell me where you get the electricity."

My friend smiled brightly at this reprieve.

"Off the city grid," he said. "Connection is way underground so nobody's likely to find it, but there's a gasoline generator in the storage room just in case. Even if they cut the cord I could keep this place running for months."

It was the First Wonder of New York. Mel showed me how to work the stone barrier entrance and all the little tools he had put in place over the years. There was even a well that provided water.

"I looked into that bodyguard thing," Mel told me when he was about to leave.

"I don't want a bodyguard."

"You need somebody anonymous to watch your back. The guys you're going up against know my face."

It was a standoff. I shook his hand and he left me to figure out next steps.

*　　*　　*

The Bronx hiding place was a marvel of architecture and technology. There were six monitors that looked out on the park from every possible vantage. Nine rooms, a kitchen, and a bathroom with a walk-in vestibule like they sell on TV for elderly individuals who have trouble climbing in and out of a tub. The cupboards were filled with canned meats, soups, vegetables, and fruits. There was even canned brown bread on the shelf with butter and half-and-half in the refrigerator. The television was connected to some satellite that offered shows in a dozen languages.

After I felt comfortable with the ins and outs of the hole in the ground, I called Aja.

"Hi, Daddy."

"How's it going at Silver House?"

"Mr. Ferris has this great library. And, and, and he has a full-size theater with digital and film projectors."

"A real Joe Stalin."

"Stop it, Dad. He's been very nice to me and Mom."

"Yeah. You better let me talk to her."

"Joe?" Monica asked a minute or so later.

"How you doin', Mon?"

"I talked to Coleman. He says he's out and that you're going to help him."

"All he has to do is be truthful and do what I say."

"He hates the place you put him in. Can't you do anything about that?"

"He's lucky to be out of stir."

"Can't you let him come here?"

"No."

"But—"

"Monica, I'm doin' what I can. He's safe and we're working to get him out of trouble. Leave it at that, okay?"

"I guess. I'll talk to you later."

After that I said a few more words to Aja before returning to my solitude.

I was asleep in the blue bedroom on the second floor when the phone rang. I answered immediately because only the most important people had that number.

"Hello?"

"I'm at the stone door," a woman's voice said.

My consciousness poked through the veil of sleep only enough to hear the words but not really to comprehend, at least not immediately. At first I thought that it must be a wrong number. But who could this wrong number be calling who also had a stone door? A stone door.

"Who is this?"

"My name is Oliya Ruez," she said, "and you are Joe. I've been sent here by the Int-Op Agency to assist you."

"You're gonna have to give me a little more than that. I never even heard of the word *Int-Op*."

"Redbird."

She was Ali Baba and I the forty thieves.

I pressed a button on the universal remote that ran the joint. This lifted the stone door, revealing my late-night caller.

Oliya Ruez was five-five and 150 pounds without an extra ounce of fat. It was hard to be certain about her age because of the severity of her expression, but I placed her at about thirty. Short-haired, she had fingers like pilings and forearms with writhing muscles reminiscent of the steel bands that formed the inner workings of some nineteenth-century perpetual-motion machine. Scarred upper lip, discolored left forearm; she wore black knee-length tights under a short black skirt and a loose-fitting black T-shirt. She could have been white or brown, a Pacific Islander or Spaniard from the south of that nation. Her haircut was too short to reveal texture.

There was a pretty big rucksack on her back and a duffel bag at her side. Both black, of course.

"Ms. Ruez?" I said, blocking her entrée with my body.

She looked up into my eyes in a stance that could allow her to take a step across the threshold or throw a round-house kick at my head.

When she didn't reply I asked, "What are you doing here?"

"I already told you, Joe."

"I didn't send for no assistant."

"I'm here to assist you, but not as an ordinary girl Friday. My duties are more . . . specialized."

"Melquarth sent you?"

"I don't know anyone by that name. Who is he?"

A chill breeze was coming through the doorway, but I wasn't satisfied yet.

"Where'd you get the word *redbird*?"

"It's what I was supposed to say if you questioned my being here." Her expression added, *Of course.*

"Okay," I said after a gusty pause. "Come on in."

As she strode past I lowered the drawbridge door.

"Have a seat," I said when we entered the living room.

Oliya put her bags down and sat in a plush blue sofa seat set at a perpendicular angle to the emerald-green sofa. I watched her a moment and then lowered onto the couch.

"You want a drink?" I asked.

"Not right now, thank you."

"So let me get this right—you're here to provide specialized assistance."

"Yes."

"But you don't know Melquarth."

"He may have contracted for the services of Int-Op but I take my orders directly from Luxembourg."

"What is this Int-Op you're talking about?"

"The term stands for International Operatives Agency. My designation is Int-Op 17."

"And your special services?"

"Bodyguarding, hostage retrieval, some specialized mercenary work, and intelligence reclamation are all in my job description."

"And which of those services are you here for?"

"As I understand it's bodyguarding mainly, but I am to provide help in any way I can."

I was wearing a white T and gray exercise pants that I'd found in a drawer upstairs. I didn't feel embarrassed and doubted that my guest would have turned red in the Saharan sun.

"You wanna drink?" I asked again.

"Not right now, thank you," she said once more.

I popped up and opened a cabinet door set in the shelves of little sculptures and books in every language from Latin to Esperanto. The liquor cabinet had a twenty-eight-year-old Delord Armagnac. I poured myself a double shot.

"Sure I can't tempt you?" I said to the woman who was reminding me more and more of the king's black rook.

"Not yet."

Sitting down again, I asked Oliya, "Do you know the players in the game I'm playing?"

"No. When I asked I was told that you would have most of that information."

"Do you know Zyron International?"

"Yes."

"Have you ever worked for them?"

"I can't give information about Int-Op or anyone that we have or have not provided with our services."

"Okay. That's good. But what if I'm having a problem with a company like that and part of your job would be putting you at odds with them?"

"If that were the case, Joe, I wouldn't be here."

Our eyes met.

"You look pretty tough," I noted.

"Sometimes you have to fight." Her manner was nonchalant. "But no matter how tough anyone is, there's always somebody stronger, luckier, or smarter. I try to avoid confrontation. That makes it better for me and my clients."

I sipped my brandy.

"So," I said, my talking tongue more than satisfied by the alcohol. "What if I were to tell you that I didn't want or need your services?"

Suddenly the stony-eyed young woman's face was vulnerable. Even the suggestion that I might dismiss her was completely unexpected.

"I wouldn't be here if you didn't need me, Joe."

"Why you keep usin' my first name like we're friends? Don't you usually refer to your clients as mister and miss?"

She had a smile that was something to behold. It felt as if I had been walking on a paved road that gave way to pounded earth that then became a less-trodden path through a wood. There I come upon a peasant woman tilling the soil with a huge hoe made from the horn of some beast of burden. That path could have been anywhere in the world. And that woman was the reason there's life anywhere. She was both a fortress wall and the only home anyone would ever need.

All of that in a smile.

"Part of my instruction was to call you by your first name, Mr. Oliver."

I took in a deep breath right then. Melquarth was a good friend in spite of his close relationship with evil. His understanding of the world led him to hire this woman of violence and defense. As much as I wanted to deny it, there was something about her that was right.

"To answer your question," she said, her tone now lighter, "I've been assigned to protect you. If you ask me to leave, then of course I will, but I'd have to call Int-Op. If they tell me to break off I'd move on. But if they say to stay and protect you I'd try my best."

I looked at her, thinking about that universal woman wielding her great horn.

"Okay, then," I said. "You stayin' here?"

"That would be best."

"The blue bedroom upstairs is mine. You can have either of the other two."

She stood, grabbed her bags, and headed up.

"We can talk about my troubles and your services in the morning," I told her back.

I waited a quarter hour, savoring the drink. While there I looked at my phone and saw there was a text from Mel.

Her name is Oliya and she's the best Int-Op has to offer.

After that I went upstairs and tumbled into a sleep that was better than I'd had in days, maybe even years.

20.

IT WAS ONE of the few times in my life that I overslept. The stone house was quiet as a tomb and the idea of being concealed by the earth itself dispelled all fear.

I showered, shaved, and dressed in a dark suit I'd brought along to Atlanta. That done, I was ready to go downstairs.

There Oliya was seated in the blue chair—knitting. She had on a bright yellow, loose-fitting jumpsuit, her feet tucked up under her.

"Good morning."

"Good morning, Mr. Oliver."

"You can call me Joe," I allowed. "I just wondered why you were so familiar."

She smiled, gave a quick nod, and went back to her knitwork.

I ventured out to the kitchen, where I made coffee and canned toast.

Twenty minutes later, back in the living room, the stocky fingers of my bodyguard were still furiously at work.

I sat and watched her for a while.

"Today," I announced. Int-Op 17 put down her needles and cloth. "I won't be needing you because I'm not doing anything that has to do with the situation you've been hired for."

"I could come along anyway," she offered.

"I'm gonna go see a couple of old friends. You being there just wouldn't work."

Looking at me, she nodded and kept on looking.

"Maybe I could do something else for you."

"Not really. You got that special skill set. I wouldn't wanna dull it down with grocery shopping and laundry duty."

Oliya smiled using her teeth and then went back to her woolly task.

Before leaving, Mel had shown me around his underground domain. Off the kitchen there was a small armory stacked with hunting rifles, shotguns, semiautomatics, fully automatics, and one or two specialized firearms designed for assassination. The arsenal had everything from Teflon to poison bullets. In an upstairs closet there was a chest of Morgan silver dollars, all of them shiny and dated from the late nineteenth to the early twentieth century.

A few hours after Mel had left me he sent a text that said, *E-key in mag-case under back front wheel.* There was a photograph of a six-year-old nut-brown Kia Soul attached to the text. The car was pictured in the area where Mel had parked his limo.

So, I counted out 250 silver dollars, bid good day to my bodyguard, and headed out to a very special place.

*   *   *

Sometimes, when one finds oneself cheek by jowl with a brick wall of indeterminate height and thickness, it might behoove that clandestine traveler to turn away to seek access less daunting. So I ventured out from the Bronx to Manhattan's Upper West Side.

The address was not far from Roger Ferris, though the neighborhood was not nearly as posh.

That's one of the things I like about New York—rich and poor are never that far apart. Walking down the street, living one block over, or descending the subway stairs—New Yorkers of every class are continually rubbing shoulders.

The six-story walk-up apartment building was on Seventy-Seventh Street. I walked up the dozen or so stairs of the stoop and looked for her name among the buzzers.

"Yes?"

"Hi, Loretta. It's Joe Oliver."

"Oh. What do you want?"

"To come upstairs and talk to him."

"Is he expecting you?"

For some reason I never was bothered by Loretta Gorman's rudeness. She was a liberal New Yorker and therefore, despite her whiteness, she had little tolerance for cops or ex-cops. And since she had moved in with her boyfriend, her patience had worn even thinner.

"No, he's not," I said, "but I'm sure he'd like to see me."

Silence. I was sure she had gone to her boyfriend trying to talk him out of letting me upstairs.

Maybe three minutes later she said, "Okay, then. Come on up, I guess."

The buzzer screamed and I pushed the door open.

*   *   *

The one-lane staircase snaked all the way to floor six, apartment 27.

I had to knock. She kept me waiting a few minutes more before opening up.

Ms. Gorman stood five and a half feet with a sleek figure and blond hair cut short. She wore skinny black jeans and a pink T-shirt. Her eyes were an impossibly light blue. It would be hard to make eyes that lovely challenging, but Loretta managed it.

She blocked the doorway the way I had with Oliya.

"Hi," I said.

"He's been tired lately," she replied. "Don't take too long."

"Okay."

That should have been enough but she was stuck like glue to the doorjamb.

"The case is over, right?" she asked. "I mean A Free Man is gone, isn't he?"

I'd met Mr. Lamont Charles when investigating a murder a few years before. He was in a nursing home at the time. Loretta had worked as a volunteer there.

"All over," I assured her. "This is just a friendly visit. You know that man of yours is like a great Greek philosopher. He's got answers to any question you could imagine and many more that you don't have words for yet."

Defeated by kindness, Loretta moved back from the door and I eased into the apartment.

"Come on out here, Officer," came a musical tenor from the veranda.

"Here I come."

"Honey," the man's voice added, "can you bring out some bourbon, a glass, and some ice?"

"You shouldn't be drinking," she said to the air.

"That's why I only asked for one damn glass. You know the detective likes his whiskey."

"Okay."

The veranda was nine or ten feet wide and six deep. There were flowering plants along the lattice metal wall and an ornate table inlaid with blue and red Moroccan tiles.

Maybe sixty, he was leaning against the wrought-iron railing, wearing a deep red housecoat with a royal blue T-shirt underneath. The pose was pure 1930s. William Powell considering his next quip. Humphrey Bogart's wry but comfortable stance in the face of insurmountable odds. Only, for Lamont Charles this was not an act. With skin black and lustrous as tar, his smile was a starry palate. He'd lived the lives of the characters that populated Depression-era films. Born in Acres, Mississippi, he'd chopped cotton until his father left and his mother died. Then he wandered down to New Orleans and played blackjack, stud poker, banco, and even the slot machines in back rooms, gin joints, and whorehouses, first in Louisiana and then around the world. He was banned from the main floor of every casino in Vegas, not for cheating, not even for counting cards, but because he was the luckiest man on earth—so dubbed by almost every gambler who had the bad luck of sitting across a gaming table from him.

He turned from the view of the Hudson to regard me. Letting one hand loose from the railing, he almost fell but then righted himself.

Grabbing hold of the back of a nearby cast-iron chair, Lamont worked his way around until he could fall back on the cushions.

When I'd met him, the professional gambler was triplegic, with only his right arm functional. He lived fairly comfortably in that convalescent home. Loretta was a nursing student doing an internship there. That's where she got to know Lamont. Even after she took a paying job, Loretta dropped by every week or so. She'd fallen in something beyond love with him. She took him out of that nest of senility and got him so that he could stand upright and even take a step or two. His left arm was weak but he could use it to steady an object while his right hand did the work.

In the beginning Loretta took extra shifts as a nurse at New York Presbyterian to pay for Lamont's doctor bills and their rent. But for the last year, on the first day of every month, Lamont and Loretta have gone down to Atlantic City for a game literally run by kings.

"How you doin', Detective Oliver?" he greeted. "Have a seat."

"You know I haven't been a cop for nearly fifteen years," I said as I settled.

"Once a cop..." he insinuated on an airy smile. Then: "What you got in the satchel?"

It was a slender blue briefcase I'd found in the blue bedroom. I laid the case on Moroccan tile, then opened it to reveal 250 shiny silver disks.

"Oh my God," Lamont said, his eyes alight with the promise of treasure.

"You got the cards?" I asked him.

"Blackjack?"

"Just what I had in mind."

"Loretta," the luckster called out.

"Yeah, baby?"

"Bring me out a hundred ones."

"Okay."

"There's more than twice that here," I said.

"I see," he assured me.

From somewhere in the folds of the housecoat, my friend brought out a blue deck of Bicycle Standard playing cards. Mr. Charles's face glistened with the fever of gambling. Somehow he managed to shuffle the deck using the good hand and the infirm one.

Blackjack. It was the first word of an ancient incantation that sometimes allowed a poor man or woman to dream about deliverance. Lamont grinned at those cards.

We played for nearly three hours. I do believe that he could have beggared me in forty-five minutes, but Lamont was having a good time, wanting to savor the feeling of victory.

After letting me take a pot or two, the hustler asked, "You want another drink, Officer?"

"No, thanks." I looked up to see him smiling.

"That's right, son," he said. "Alcohol is poison for the serious gambler."

After that exchange he won fourteen out of the next sixteen hands.

Loretta had come to the sliding glass door of their terrace. She stayed inside, watching intently from shadow. Now and then Lamont would look up at her, his eyes expressionless.

I could feel the potency of their connection. There was a hunger between them. Somehow this want was satisfied by him playing and her looking on.

I didn't know exactly why I was there. Lamont didn't know anything about petroleum bootleggers or alt-right warriors. He didn't have any contacts that would have helped me. But he was a prodigy of calculated risk and had spent his life in the hazard lane of a race to the death.

"You ever play two hands at once?" I asked when I'd lost half of Melquarth's dollars.

"Sure," Lamont said to his hand. "Sometimes I'll buy two places at the table. It's a good way to understand who you playin' against by competing with yourself."

That was an interesting idea, but I was after something else.

"I mean have you ever played at two different tables at the same time—against different opponents?"

"I don't use the word *opponent* in cards. It's not straightforward like chess is. What makes gambling fun is the element of luck. You could be your own worst enemy or the cards might just fall your way."

"I get what you mean."

"Hit me."

I did.

He glanced at the card and then at me.

"You pat?"

I nodded.

"Twenty-one," he murmured.

Showing me the cards, he then raked in a thirty-six-dollar pot.

It was his turn to shuffle.

"But what if you were playing at two different tables at once and you had to win at both to take the antes?"

"Whoa," he crooned as he cut the deck with one hand. "That would be a great game. I don't know how you'd do it. I mean, three people sitting at the same table is like that in a way, but...that extra hand would hurt you."

He offered me the cut.

I waved it off.

He dealt.

I lost.

"That's what I was thinking," I said. "If I lose either hand, then I lose it all."

"If you were in some crazy situation like that, you could go at it like most gamblers, I guess. I mean, you could just go for broke and hope for the best. Problem is if you go for broke that's usually where you end up." Lamont was looking into Loretta's eyes as he spoke.

"That's what I'm afraid of," I said. "Is there another way?"

"The wild card."

"What if this game doesn't have a wild card?"

"Every game got a wild card."

"How does that work?"

"I was playin' this guy down in the Keys one time. I was too much with the rum and he was just good enough to take advantage. Almost all my money was on the table and my cards tallied seventeen. It was a strong number but I knew he probably had a face card behind his nine."

"So what did you do?"

"I smiled."

"Smiled?"

"Smirked, really. Usually when I play, nuthin' shows on

my face. It's not no act. I concentrate so hard on the cards or dice or that little ball that I ain't got no energy to mug. And that there was my wild card. He knew he could beat me. He knew he probably would. But when I gave that brief grin he started to worry. He said, *hit me,* and that was it—the wild card had won."

"How did you know that just a grin would push him?" I asked.

"You never know, Detective. You never know. If you wanna know you shouldn't be at the table. If you wanna know, really you shouldn't even be alive."

I glanced at Loretta as he said those words. The thrill went through her like an icy breeze.

"I think the game's over, Officer," Lamont said.

"I still got seventeen dollars here."

"I see, but a good risker knows not to leave a man totally broke. It's mean and it's bad karma too. 'Cause, you know, gamblin's a game, not a war."

"Are you tired, baby?" Loretta crossed the threshold into the light.

"I am."

"Well, I guess it's time to go." I stood up feeling a little stiff after so many hours' play.

"I hope I was helpful," Lamont said. "I'm'a put these dollars up on my trophy shelf and hand 'em out to little kids at Halloween."

Loretta walked me out. On the way she looped her arm with mine.

When we got to the door she leaned into me, saying, "You should come by more often, Joe."

"Really? I got the feeling you didn't approve of me."

"I'm sorry. I just get into protective mode. But...you make him feel alive."

"He's a good man."

"I know. I'm having his child."

21.

THE NEXT ADDRESS on my list was on Fifth Avenue but not so far that I needed a taxi, or a trip in the dreaded subway that reminded me so much of Rikers. I walked to Central Park, crossed over to Fifth Avenue, and then to a slender, modern-looking building on Sixty-Sixth and Fifth.

I hadn't been there in a couple of years, and, on top of that, when last there I had been in disguise. Back then the doorwoman was a man.

She had straightened blond hair the texture of dry straw but was still rather fetching. Her eyes were light brown and, at half the blackness of Lamont Charles, she was still dark-skinned—around my color.

"Excuse me."

"Yes?" she asked through a leery half grin.

"Nigel Beard for Augustine Antrobus."

Her auburn eyes tightened around that questioning sneer. She waited a moment, maybe giving me a chance to change my mind.

Maybe I considered leaving.

"A Nigel Beard for Mr. Antrobus," she said into the micro-phone attached to her right ear.

Then the blond Black woman pursed her lips and nodded to some inner melody that took up the space of waiting. I remember wondering if she was a dancer or musician.

"You can go on up," she said, shifting her gaze to me.

The three women office workers were all different but still young, beautiful, and of various so-called races. Lyle was the only actual remnant from my last visit. Pixie-like and thin, smelling of rose water and deadly as Cleopatra's asp, he wore a lime-colored suit and leaned against the doorjamb that led to his master's domain.

"May I help you?" the apparently Native American woman receptionist asked. All eyes were on me.

"You can show me in to see Augustine."

"And you are?"

"Nigel Beard."

"I'm sorry, but I've never heard of you and there is no meeting set on the schedule."

If somebody asked me I would have said she'd been educated somewhere in the Ivy League.

"I don't have an appointment, true, but he does know me."

"Maybe it's time for you to leave," slight Lyle suggested.

He was armed, I was sure, and he probably had other tricks.

At a corner desk sat a very tall, very thin, very black-skinned woman. She had an earphone anchored to her left lobe. Her head and shoulders jerked up suddenly and she said, "He wants to see him."

The nervous energy in the room evaporated.

"I know the way," I said.

Pushing himself up and away from his post, Lyle countered, "I'll take you."

He led me down the slender outer hall with its window slits that looked down on Central Park.

It took nineteen steps to get to Augustine Antrobus's office / man cave with its autumnal colors and dark wood furnishings.

That day the big, big man wore a three-piece maroon suit with a pale blue dress shirt and a tie that seemed to be derived from the colors of the dark rainbow that adorns a shallow oil slick.

"Mr. Beard," Antrobus allowed. Even his voice was muscular.

"It's good to see you again, Augustine."

Lyle stiffened.

Antrobus smiled and then said to his death-dealing Passepartout, "You may leave us."

Lyle sneered at me and moved from the room, a wraith being exorcised but at the same time infusing the atmosphere with his spite.

"Sit down, Mr. Beard," Antrobus bellowed.

There were two wide-bottomed walnut chairs set at the outer orbit of a three-foot-wide globe of the moon. I took the closest seat while Antrobus moved his bulk from around his grand piano–size desk. When he sat it was with a satisfied sigh.

"Most people have globes of the Earth," I observed.

"That's like having a picture of yourself doing the job you've done your entire life. I'd rather think about the future."

"Luna in your future?"

"I'm an investor in an international conglomerate that means to start colonization within the next ten years."

"Then why not have a map of Mars on the wall?"

"I have that in my son's room in Southampton."

The demon master's dark eyes were on me. His words were some kind of test, though I couldn't discern the subject.

"The last time you were here you were bald with a beard and an extra forty pounds," he said.

"There were a few people after me at that time—including you."

"You cost me a very good agent."

"If he was that good you two would have never parted company."

Antrobus laughed. It was a loud sound—cannon-like. But it was also, in its own way, forgiving.

When the crashing mirth ended he said, "Tell me your name."

"Joe Oliver."

"What can I do for you, Joe Oliver?"

"Talk to me about illegal oil trafficking in the U.S. and elsewhere."

"I don't understand." The words felt intimate, like a good friend trying to give advice.

"What I'm asking?" I wondered aloud.

"No. It's just that you don't seem to be a strike-it-rich kind of fellow."

"I'm not. I just represent people like that—sometimes."

Again that punishing and yet merciful laugh.

"Diesel fuel is modern-day hooch and the criminals that sell it are today's bootleggers," he said, still smiling. "They buy the heating oil for homes at a government discount and then sell it for vehicular fuel. The markup makes billions of illegal dollars every year, in every part of the globe."

"Yeah," I said. "I know that much."

"Did you know that some of the smaller international oil cartels are up to their elbows in this trade?"

"I suspected it. But that's as far as it goes."

"So, Joe Oliver, what you need from me is the only thing in the world more valuable than illegal petroleum. Information."

"Yes."

Antrobus's eyes might have been long-range heat-seeking missiles and I was the test target, far out at sea. Seeing this revelation in my eyes—he smiled.

"You really planning to populate the moon?" I asked.

He nodded, Sydney Greenstreet on steroids.

"What if," I speculated, "I could maybe get the plans, at least some of them, based on Alfred Xavier Quiller's space-exploration cannons?"

The puppet master's brows went up so far that his whole fat face smoothed out, making him look like a baby would to a gnat.

"How would you do that?" he asked.

"I got a way to get to him."

"If you were to provide me with that way, then I would be happy to help you with the problems your client is having."

"Come on, Augustine. Be for real, man. What I'm asking you for might be worth a gold coin, but it ain't all the way to the goose that laid it."

"You can't blame me for trying."

"So, will you help me?"

"Yes. But you will owe me the information."

"Okay."

"I will also need some kind of down payment."

Another test.

What to get for the man who has, literally, everything?

Gift giving is one of the most challenging conundrums of the modern age. Most people don't know how to ask for what they want; most don't even know what it is. They spend entire lifetimes looking for, finding, and then leaving behind what they've been told they wanted by everything from sacred texts to television. Some want children but realize, too late, that kids often don't want them. Men and women search for love, find it, and then wake up one morning to the harsh reality that the cap was left off and the precious passion has dried up. Monks meditate on consecrated mantras, hoping for enlightenment, then realize that awareness doesn't change a thing.

On the other hand, in ancient, and modern, tribal cultures, everything given is already known by everyone you know. Manhood, womanhood, your first trinket, your last rite. Back then, and over there, they expected happiness and therefore achieved that state.

The trick to gift giving in the modern world is either real need or surprise. If you can't pay the rent and someone covers it with no strings, you are going to smile and feel edified. Warm socks during a subzero season, food in an empty stomach...a snifter of cognac when your heart is broken; these are real and perceived needs for us when we are most vulnerable.

But Augustine Antrobus was not the vulnerable kind. He was apex. His hungers would always be satisfied, and even if he were captured and caged, his nature would always be dominant, even supreme.

So what AA needed was wonderment, something to make him smile.

Me having access to the secrets behind Quiller's Cannon was such a thing, but I had yet to deliver on that front.

"Do you play Go?" I asked.

And there it was. Something I couldn't have, or at least shouldn't have, known.

"Yes," he ventured. "Why?"

"I just wondered if you wanted to sharpen your skills on a novice."

When he pulled out the Go board from a bottom drawer, I knew I'd hit the right note. Made from oak, it was old and battered, with pitted stone disks that had rattled around in their lambskin sack for at least half a century.

He could see in my eyes the appreciation for a history in an object and for one of his few weaknesses.

"I'll tell you what," he said. "I'll discuss your problem between moves. You have until I defeat you to get what you need."

We played.

I lost.

"Another game?" He was having a good time.

By 11:07 p.m. I had all I needed to at least try to help Coleman.

"Another?" I asked the grizzly bear dressed up like a man.

"I think you've learned enough for one day."

"You talkin' 'bout Go or oil?"

He stood, extended a hand, and said, "I hope we remain friends, Mr. Oliver."

The sirens of the front office were gone but Lyle was still there. He was sitting in the tall Black woman's chair with his feet up on the blotter, staring into the void of dead men he'd left behind—at least that's what I imagined he saw in solitude.

His eyes flicked upward the instant after I entered the room.

"Still here?" I asked.

Sitting up and then standing he said, "You should show more respect."

"Never yielded much profit in my experience."

22.

AS I WALKED down the street at a few minutes shy of 11:30, the world was feeling pretty good. I had a few names and quirks of some players in the international fuel bootlegging business. I had a personal reason to talk to Quiller again and a bodyguard.

I crossed over to the park side of Fifth. There I took out a phone.

"Hello, Joe," Oliya Ruez said, answering her phone after the third ring.

"You sound like you're outside."

"I went out for dinner."

"A little late for that, isn't it?"

"I live by a European schedule. Where are you?"

"Midtown Manhattan."

"Do you need anything?"

"No. I'll be home in under an hour."

"See you there."

It was just before I disengaged the line that he grabbed me from behind and pulled me into the park. At first I thought it was Lyle making good on his warning, but my attacker was too big. Then I thought maybe the fay assassin had enlisted help. I reached out with both hands to grab the man's neck and hair. Then I yanked hard.

"Uh," he grunted, loosening his grip.

Pushing him off-balance, I followed up with the heel of my palm against his cheekbone.

As he fell I saw his two friends closing in from the A and C sides of the right angle we formed. I thought about running but did not. I wondered if I'd die there because I didn't have a gun. Then I just waited.

In a street fight I prefer close quarters, especially when facing multiple opponents. They tend to trip over each other when rushing at a solitary target.

The attackers wore business suits. I noticed this just before throwing a body blow at the skinny guy to the left. He grunted but didn't go down, and the man on the right hit me above the ear. This caused ringing but no immediate pain or dizziness. I jumped on that man, bringing him to the lawn with my weight. I felt another man's heft on my back and twisted to avoid whatever he was trying to do while bringing my left elbow down on the man under me. In a perfect world that strike would have landed on his throat, but it felt more like shoulder.

Then, using all my adrenaline-enhanced strength, I pushed up hard enough to dislodge the man on my back and make it half the way to standing. It was a good maneuver, but two of my adversaries were already up while the guy on the concrete was almost there. I hit the latter with a comic book haymaker. He went down again and I turned using the speed of fear to attack the closest one.

That was my waterloo.

I had the man by his arms but he had me too. I tried to kick him. Missed. He managed to kick me but only got shins. In the meanwhile the third man, wearing the darkest suit, pulled out a handgun. He rushed up at us. I was sure that he intended to put a bullet in my body before I fell, when he could put another in my brain.

He was right on me. I could feel his breath. Then a warm spray hit my face.

The man dropped the handgun, bringing both hands to his throat as he fell. The gesture was useless. Oliya had severed his jugular and no amount of pressure would stem the flow of blood.

The man I was dancing with let go. Oliya was on him immediately, her silent knife buried all the way to the hilt in his chest.

The luckiest of the attackers was the one I laid low. Darwin at work again.

"We should get out of here," Oliya suggested.

Her car was illegally parked two blocks away. Well, not actually illegally because she had some official-looking city placard on the dash of her maroon Dodge telling the world that whoever drove that car had the right to wait.

Ms. Ruez took a few packets of alcohol wipes from her black duffel bag. She used these to wash the blood off my wrist, jaw, and neck.

"Lucky you wore dark clothes," she said while wiping my face the way a patient mother scrubs a baby's butt. "Blood don't show there."

"Wasn't luck, Olo," I said, coining the nickname as I spoke. "Darkness is a Black man's best friend."

Oliya smiled at me. That simple expression filled me with pride.

"You took some chances but you were good in that fight. Real good. Just with a knife and you would have won by yourself."

"Speaking of knives, we should get out of here."

Oliya turned the key and we were on our way toward the Bronx.

I was still breathing hard, unable to keep thoughts in any kind of sequential order. Two dead men, blood everywhere. Aja. Yes, Aja was safe. They tried to kill me. Who did? Why? On Fifth Avenue, in Central Park.

"How're you doing?" Oliya asked. It was a simple question but also an intellectual lifeline.

"We got a problem."

"How do you mean, Joe?"

The question brought a hiccup-like chortle from my diaphragm.

"I didn't tell anybody where I was going. And if anybody knew my movements they would have stopped me at the stone cave."

"Maybe they were following you and got the go-ahead to attack when you left the office building."

"Those motherfuckers tried to kill me."

"Yes, they did."

"Did you watch me leave on the monitors?" I asked.

"Yes."

"Was anybody else watching?"

"Not that I could see."

"And how long were you on me?"

"I followed you the entire day, put a tracker in your wallet when you were asleep."

"I don't like that." I turned a stony stare at her.

"Maybe not. But it saved your life."

I took a deep breath into an angry cauldron of lungs.

"What about your cell phone?" she asked.

"I got a dozen burners to choose from. I mean, they might have a line on me in some way, but let's look at you too."

"Me?"

"Have you told anyone about the job?"

"Only . . ." she said and then stopped talking.

I was quiet too. The panting had stopped. The car engine wheezed on a steady flow of gasoline. Five minutes passed. Something about my bodyguard seemed a little less certain.

"I know you can't tell me about other clients and their business. But do you think—"

"I don't know," she replied to the darkness outside the windshield.

"Two days ago ZI sent out a man to kill me," I prompted. "He died before he could accomplish that end."

"It's possible," she said. "They know my codes. They could have located you."

"You want to go to a motel?" I offered. "I know a really disreputable one in Jersey."

We stopped along the way in Manhattan. I climbed down into the number 1 subway station and left the tracker on a southbound car.

Dingo's Retreat Motel was a horseshoe-shaped single-story

structure on the outskirts of Hoboken. The night manager had no problem taking cash. I bought a fifth of Jack Daniel's and a small box of Dixie Cups from the twenty-four-hour liquor store across the street.

Sitting up, facing each other on the pair of single beds, Oliya and I had three drinks apiece before we began the debrief.

The TV was tuned to a late-night talk show, up loud.

"Did you see them following me?" I asked.

She shook her head. "They were good. I only saw the one that grabbed you when he did."

"It's not all that easy to follow a cell phone, even if you got the number," I said, moving on.

"No, it isn't." Those three words comprised what would be, if official, a forty-page Pentagon document.

"You should probably reach out to your controller and tell 'em what you did."

I wondered if I could take the girl guard one-on-one. She was ruthless in a fight. I could see that in the way she eliminated the professional killers.

"No," Oliya said, studying my eyes.

"No what?"

"I will not turn against you and I won't leave."

"So you'll call 'em?"

"In the morning. Before we go."

After that we turned off the lights and TV, then stretched out on our bunks, fully dressed.

I was on my back in the semidarkness of the room. Light came in from the parking lot through battered shades. My nerves were still jangled from the surprise attack on one of the most well-known streets in the world. I felt very alone in the gloom until . . .

"You were on me the whole day?" I asked behind closed eyes in the dark.

"Yes," she stated. "I mean, it wasn't so much following as more waiting. First outside Loretta Gorman and La-mont Charles's place and then around Augustine Antrobus's office."

"You got all that information from the outside?"

"I did have that tracker on you," she said. "It's pretty accurate. Int-Op is aware of Antrobus because he is a key figure in much of the criminal activity in your country. And Mr. Charles keeps company with some of the most powerful and influential players in the world."

"Huh," I said.

"I saw you come upon an old lady on your way to Antrobus. Her shopping cart was too heavy and you helped her lift it. I could see that you weren't using her to test the waters, to see if someone followed.

"Helping for no reason, that is life at its best. Most people in your cities don't know it. Almost everyone in our business thinks that they cannot afford kindness. They don't have a reason for living and so go through life like the dead."

I slept well after that. I was alive. I had an ally. I'd probably live to see morning.

We stopped at a restaurant called Pic's on the way north. I had two soft-boiled eggs and she, avocado toast. After breakfast, in the parking lot, Oliya made a call with the speakerphone on.

"Seventeen," a man's voice answered.

"One seven," she replied.

"You were supposed to report last night."

"The client was approached by hostiles. I helped him but he was hurt and I had to move fast and silently."

"We lost his tracker."

"I didn't know you were following it."

"What happened?"

"He took off his pants . . . the blood."

"How is he?"

"Immobile but he'll make it."

"Where are you?"

She gave her contact the name, address, and room number at Dingo's.

"How long will you be there?" the controller asked.

"An hour or so. Mr. Oliver's friend is coming to take us for medical care."

"What friend?"

"Someone named Carlson."

"First name?"

"I don't know. Just Carlson."

"Where are you now?"

"In the car."

"And the client?"

"In the room, sleeping."

"Carry on."

And the call was ended.

We sat in the front seat with an iPad set between us. The image on the screen was the motel room we'd vacated. Neither of us talked. We just waited.

Fifty-six minutes later three men burst into the room with

guns out. They were well dressed like the assassins the night before. They spent no more than a minute checking to see if their targets were there.

Then they were gone.

"Your people?" I asked Oliya.

"I don't think so."

"Why not?"

"To begin with we don't have a hit squad. I would know about that."

"So—Zyron?"

Oliya hesitated a moment before saying, "Maybe. They're a big client."

"You think the top people at Int-Op would play this dirty?"

"I don't know if I'm the right person to ask that question."

"Yeah," I agreed.

Oliya turned to me, a blank expression on her hard face.

"I'm sorry," she said.

I gauged this apology.

"I should cut you loose," I said at the end of the assay.

She nodded.

"I mean, you put killers on my ass."

She gave another assent but with a wordless caveat at the end.

"What?" I asked.

"You need help with this, Joe."

"I got friends."

"You have me too . . . if you want."

Being a cop is a tough job. You have to make split-second decisions a dozen times every day. Is someone a threat? Do they see you as a threat? What's waiting behind that door? What would your mother think?

Since I was bounced out of the NYPD, without retirement, life just got harder. I had all those decisions to make without backup, without respect.

These thoughts in mind I asked, "You wanna take a ride out to Brownsville?"

23.

BROWNSVILLE. IT IS a place that creates heroes and villains, where people cling to their dreams because they know for a fact that that's all they'll ever have. It's poor and it's angry, intoxicated and hopelessly in love. It is a place where children learn lessons that they spend the rest of their lives trying to forget. Sharper than a razor, it is the cut you never see coming.

The place we were looking for was on Rockaway Avenue. An unofficial SRO where poor people go when they need a place to lick their wounds.

The broken granite stairs led up to an oak door that, I knew, was braced by corroded, but still strong, iron bars. I pressed the doorbell button and waited a full minute. Then I bumped it again, twice.

"Who the fuck is it?" a grizzled voice inquired. If you didn't know the speaker you wouldn't have been able to put a gender on them.

"King Oliver."

"King? In Brownsville? Tell me it ain't so." Now there was humor and maybe a woman smiling back there.

"Yeah, baby, it's me. You can tell Loopy to put down his shotgun."

"Loop!" the woman on the other end of the PA system called. "Let that bastard in."

A moment passed, then another. I turned toward Oliya and saw in her eyes that she had been in places like this before—maybe she'd honed her talents on a thoroughfare like Rockaway.

Something was happening behind the oak door. After a few beats it swung inward.

The man standing there was tall and wide, high yellow in color and bald, mostly. The whites of his eyes were a deeper yellow and his face was the general shape of a butternut squash—the big side down.

"King," he uttered. It could have been a greeting or a warning.

"Loop," I said. "This here is Oliya."

"Ma'am."

"Hello," my partner replied in the friendliest voice I'd heard her use yet.

"What you doin' here, King?" Loopy Wright asked.

"I had a lawyer man put up a guy with you, name of Tesserat. We need to see him."

"Coleman? He a mothahfuckah and a half. Lucky he don't get his ass kicked in. Man runnin' up and down the halls tellin' folks to be quiet. Quiet? Shit. Come on in, brother."

Loopy, the huge impediment to aggression, took two steps backward, making space for Oliya and me to enter the ghetto hotel.

*   *   *

Going down a hallway no more than a yard wide, we could hear Loopy's shoulders rubbing against the walls behind. Maybe forty steps into the journey we came upon a closed door that had a strong light coming from underneath.

I knocked.

"Come on in," she called.

I turned the knob and entered a room that hadn't changed much since before the old woman that lived there was born. Once-thick burgundy carpeting lined the floor and an orange felt sofa sat against the far wall. To the right was a doorless doorway leading to a kitchen. To the left was a desk supporting a large lattice of cubicles from which all kinds of papers, keys, and other, less recognizable detritus sat and hung. The swivel chair at the desk was brand-new, made from some kind of space-age material. Mookie, the woman who ran and maybe owned the seven-story guest-house, always said that *you need a good chair for comfort and concentration.*

She was sitting in the middle of the orange divan. Mookie was the only one allowed that perch.

"Loop."

"Yeah, Mook."

"Bring in some chairs for our guests."

The big man blundered out into the kitchen. I knew from past visits that there was a toilet beyond that room and a storage closet after that.

"Who's your friend?" the diminutive old Black woman asked me.

Mookie Hill was more than seventy but not yet ninety.

She was taller than my grandmother and yet less than sixty inches in height. Her expression was daring you to contradict deep-set convictions. She could quote from the Bible, chapter and verse, and curse like a sailor from centuries past.

"Oliya," I said, answering her question.

"Ma'am," my bodyguard added.

"Look like she could scrap."

Loopy came out with two metal folding chairs under his left arm. These he shook out for us.

"Wanna drink?" the hotelier offered.

"Not me, Mook."

"No thank you, ma'am."

"Well then, what else can I do you for?"

"I'm just here to talk to Coleman Tesserat."

Mookie's eyes were squarish and there looked to be a film over them. That aside, she saw everything.

"Why you gonna help a niggah like that, King? He look down on Black folk like he was a white man just off the plantation."

"He's married to my ex."

"What you care 'bout her?"

"She's the mother of our daughter."

That put an end to the interrogation. Mookie needed to hear truth in her parlor.

"He's on floor seven. Number five."

Mookie's place was lively. On the way up the carpeted stairs you could hear music and laughter, voices both threatening and with heart. Halfway past the third floor there was a young woman in a tiny red dress lounging comfortably and smoking weed. She took a hefty toke when we were ten steps down and released it when we reached her.

Dark brown skin with painted lips and impossible lashes; she reveled in the beauty of youth. The tips of her processed dark brown hair were frosted with gold.

"You guys wanna party?" she asked when I nodded hello.

"Gotta meetin' upstairs," I answered.

"Oh. Okay. You need anything else?"

I stopped and asked, "What's your name?"

"Toni with a *i*."

"What is it that *you* need, Toni?"

Toni gazed at me, speculating. I imagined that she could float a butterfly with those long lashes.

"You know Fat Cat Tom?" she asked.

"No." But by the name I knew his kind.

"He was my protection on the street."

"Was?"

"Then he fount out I had a bank account."

"I see."

"You don't know him?"

"If I did what difference would it make?"

"I thought maybe you could talk to him...for me, you know?"

"He live around here?"

"Uh-huh."

"You know the best thing you could do is not be where he's at."

"I'ont know no place else."

"You do anything stronger'n weed?"

"Nuh-uh. No."

I took a disposable mechanical pencil from one pocket and my business card from another. On the back of the card I wrote *Mimi Lord* and a phone number I knew by heart.

"Call this woman and tell her that Joe O suggested you. She does business in Manhattan mainly. You get out there to her and she'll set you up with something."

"Tom got people all ovah round here. I wouldn't even make it to the train."

"I'll ask Loopy to give you a ride."

"He scary," Toni said on a sneer.

"I know for a fact that he don't bite."

That got Toni to grin. She stole a look at Oliya and then asked me, "What I do for you?"

"Nothin' right yet."

With that my minder and I continued our journey upward.

No one answered the first or second knock on the seventh floor, number five.

"Not here?" Oliya suggested.

"Naw, he there."

I knocked again, a little harder, and shouted, "Open up, Tesserat. It's Joe."

It took him maybe thirty seconds to screw up the courage to let us in.

He was a darker shadow of the investment banker he'd been a week before.

There was the beginning of a beard along the jawline and his hair was disheveled. He wore a strapped T-shirt and a pair of dark suit slacks. His feet were bare.

A small revolver was nestled in his left hand, finger on the trigger.

213

After Oliya and I had hustled in, I tugged the piece out of Coleman's hand.

"Where'd you get this?" I asked.

"A guy down the hall."

"How much?"

"I gave him my watch."

"Your Rolex for this piece'a shit?"

"I got to protect myself."

I had to hold back from slapping that little pistol across Coleman's face. Instead I turned a chair he had for looking out the window and sat, heavily.

"You wanna sit?" I asked Oliya.

She looked around, saw the ruffled bed and a short dresser, then went to the stack of drawers and leaned back against it.

Coleman sat on the bed.

"Tema Popov, Yuri Fleganoff, or Yevgeny Gobulev?" I said to Coleman, repeating names Augustine Antrobus had given me.

His eyes registered a whole new kind of concern.

"What?"

"Come on, man," I said. "You know what I'm talkin' 'bout."

Coleman's hands clenched into fists, released, and then clenched again.

"The second one," he said.

"Fleganoff. So that's the one you called Alain Freeman?"

"How you find out his name?"

"It's my job to know the players in the games I'm playin'. Monica asked me to look into it and that's what I'm doin'. Was Fleganoff the only dude you worked with?"

"Pretty much. I mean sometimes, back when we started out, he'd bring some muscle, but they didn't talk. Why?"

"They were keeping their vulnerability down to you and him," I said.

"So the fuck what? Only thing I need is for Tomey to get the government off my ass."

"Yeah. Right. How'd it work with Fleganoff?"

It was a rare event in Coleman's life to have his ideas summarily dismissed. He wanted to curse me out, but thinking better of it he said, "I set up companies for him and worked them myself. I distributed cash and took care of taxes at year-end."

"How much you make?"

"What business that of yours?"

I just stared.

"Hundred fifty thousand a month. It's gone, though. Feds sittin' on it like a hatching hen."

"How long?"

"Two and a half years."

I stood up and turned to Olo.

"Let's get outta here."

"Look, man," Coleman said. "Look. He really used the name Freeman. I thought if you found him under that name then he couldn't blame me for it."

"This ain't sixth grade, brother. This is serious."

There were tears in the cheater's eyes. I couldn't blame him but, then again, I had nothing else to say.

When I turned toward the door he blurted, "What about my gun?"

"Loopy bringing you food and drink, right?"

"Yeah."

"Good. Stay in here. Look out the window. If you need muscle, just ring downstairs. Loopy or one'a his people be here in a short sixty."

Mookie owned a garage two blocks away. She hadn't been there in decades but Loopy spent every night there — working on his cars. When I asked if we could borrow one of his fleet he walked us over.

"I been workin' on this beauty for six years now." Loop was talking about a dark blue 1987 Mark VII Lincoln Continental. It was showcased at the middle of the garage. "This is my baby."

"We don't wanna take your best car, man," I said. "Any old clunker'll do."

"I don't have no beaters here, King. When I work on cars they all get a shine."

Loop turned to Oliya, held out the car keys, and said, "You take it."

Somehow my temporary partner was able to effect humility with a regal bearing. She took the keys saying, "Thank you, my friend."

Since she had the keys Oliya drove us out of that double-gated garage.

"Where to?" she asked me.

"Upper West Side," I said while entering a phone number.

After I finished the call Oliya asked, "How do you know all these people?"

"It's my city."

"No," she said. "Most New Yorkers are completely lost twenty blocks from home."

"I was a cop."

"Cops have beats and precincts."

"They bounced me and I had to make contacts if I wanted to make a living at this trade."

"You're alone?"

"Lone, maybe, but I have people like Loopy and Mookie all over."

My words seemed to have a big impact on the cold-blooded killer.

We made it all the way to the Museum of Natural History. Somewhere deep in the bowels of that place is a fiberglass replica of a blue whale—scaled to actual size. It hovered dozens of feet above the floor, arched like the real thing, master of the ocean.

"It's amazing," Oliya said.

"You never seen it before?"

"In my job there's rarely time for sightseeing."

"The guy we need to help us could meet anywhere," I said. "Why not here?"

The question seemed novel in her furrowed brow. Yeah. Why not?

"Joe," came a familiar voice.

"Mel."

He emerged from the throng of museumgoers. His ocean-blue suit was loose-fitting on a lithe frame.

"Hey, brother," he said, extending a hand.

We shook and I said, "I'd like to intro—"

"Oliya Ruez," Melquarth said with a big smile on his face.

"Have we met?" she asked him.

"I hired you four times in the last six years. The Int-Op Agency is the best there is."

"Maybe was," Olo speculated.

A disturbed shadow passed across my friend's face. Then he smiled and asked me, "Where to?"

"We take a jaunt out to Queens."

24.

OLIYA AND I sat in the front of the Lincoln while Mel lounged in back.

"You hired me for the Lanyard job?" Oliya asked our passenger.

"Yeah."

"That's strange."

"Strange how?"

"Paul Lanyard worked for exBank. It was presented to me like his employers wanted to protect him."

"Just the opposite. There was this high-up dude there that was worried about something Pauly knew; probably that this guy was stealing."

"And Lanyard was a friend of yours?"

"Never met the man."

"But you paid fifty thousand dollars for round-the-clock protection?"

"There's no price tag on right."

Olo was definitely puzzled by Mel. For some reason that tickled me.

"What about *maybe was*?" Mel asked her.

She explained about the six assassins sicced on me, probably by her bosses.

"Huh," Mel said when she was through.

Belle Harbor, Queens, is set out on the Rockaway Peninsula. It was the site of the crash of American Airlines Flight 587 on November 12, 2001. Everybody on board died. Five bystanders were also killed.

That tragedy aside, Belle Harbor is one of the poshest neighborhoods in the sleepy borough. Has its own beach. The house we were looking for was on Bay Circle, number forty-five.

Augustine Antrobus had provided me with three Russian names that had been known to move illegal oil. I'd looked them up on my phone at Dingo's. I was pretty sure that the guy I was looking for was Yuri; he was the only one who lived in New York.

It was a two-story home wrought from yellow stone, with a deck on top that probably looked out over the bay. Lots of windows. It was a rich man's residence.

Mel jumped out and attached a barely noticeable microtransmitter wadded up in something that looked like gum to the post of a mailbox across the street. Pretending to be checking addresses, he inspected the old-fashioned box, then turned toward the car and said aloud, "No, Joe, I told you it was on the other block."

From there we drove over to the local shopping area and parked on the third level of a three-floor parking structure. Mel brought out a computer and plugged it into the cigarette lighter socket. We watched the front of the rich man's house for the better part of four hours.

There wasn't much talk during that time. The few words we did say were of no consequence. We simply watched. I'm sure that between the three of us we had eyes on that home longer than the sum total of all other people looking at it since the day it was built.

Right at sunset the garage door lifted and a cherry-red Tesla slipped out and down the driveway. The driver got out at the curb and picked up a discarded beer can from the gutter. He climbed back in and drove off.

Still, we didn't talk. I started the car and drove down to the street. Within four blocks we were two cars behind the red Tesla.

Yuri Fleganoff drove to a yellow-and-green building in Brighton Beach. It was a Polish restaurant with a large bar area. A guy who looked to be loitering around the front jumped to attention when the electric car pulled up. Yuri climbed out and handed the lingerer something. The man hustled into the car and drove off.

Parking around the corner, the three of us walked to a pizza joint down the block and across the street from A Taste of Warsaw, the place Yuri went.

We ordered a large meat-eaters pie with black olives and three beers.

While waiting for the feast, Mel offered to check out the bar and the guy out front.

"Might as well wait for the food," I suggested.

"Naw, man. He could come out any minute."

So Mel split, leaving Oliya and me to watch the front door of the restaurant across the street.

"What is it with your friend?" Oliya asked after a few minutes of silence.

I sipped my beer and considered. I didn't want to lie but, then again, there were many things that only I knew about the sociopath.

"Back when I was a cop," I began. "More than a decade ago, I arrested Mel."

"What for?"

"He was climbing out of a manhole three blocks from where a heist had just been stopped by the FBI."

The pizza came. It took up most of the table.

Oliya and I chowed down on a couple of slices and then picked up two more.

"So what happened after you arrested him?"

"They put him on trial."

"For the heist?"

"Yeah. He was definitely a part of it. But there was nothing to prove that. Nobody in the crew would testify against him, so the prosecutor asked me to um...embellish."

"And you refused." It wasn't a question.

"I figure that if we want citizens to obey the rules, then we have to too."

"So you and Melquarth became friends."

"Sometime later, having nothing to do with Mel or the heist, I got into trouble with the force. They framed me, tried to kill me, and then fired me instead. I went through a hard time and then Mel showed up. He wanted to play chess."

"He wanted a friend."

"Yeah. He had decided to go straight and liked that I had rules."

"He's a very dangerous man."

"It's a dangerous world."

Mel returned almost forty-five minutes later. He told us that he preferred cold pizza and ate for maybe a quarter hour.

After the last bite he leaned back, letting out a very satisfied sigh.

"They keep the cars in an open lot just down from where we parked," he said.

"Can we get in?" Oliya asked.

"There's a fence in back. The guard got somethin' goin' on his cell phone."

"What about the restaurant?" I asked.

"Lotta young Eastern Euros looking for a good time. Wherever Yuri went I couldn't see. Probably up these stairs they have toward the back."

"Did you make it to his car?" I asked, meaning something more.

"I did."

"So all we have to do is wait."

"Yeah."

With that, Mel went into a story about a guy he knew whose dream in life was to escape from a supermax prison. He was an adviser to active participants in heists around the world. He had vast knowledge of electronics, locks, and explosives and knew about a thousand ways to confound pursuit from dogs to helicopters to angry mobs.

"He's the one who trained me in interrogation methods," Mel said.

I knew Mel's ways of interrogation. If I ever doubted that

he was crazy, just his way of getting information disabused me of that notion.

"He never got caught," Mel said. "Because he only talked to people, never selling paraphernalia or scouting. And, like I said, his big dream in life was to escape from a maximum-security prison."

"Did he ever do it?" Oliya asked. She was really interested.

Mel nodded and said, "Pelican Bay."

"That's the worst there is," she exclaimed. "How'd he end up there if he was so careful?"

"His wife was having an affair. He knew it. She was younger and needed more than he could give. But one day he came home early. Somehow she had broken their agreement and was feeding the boyfriend lunch. Brisket, I think. Anyway, Peter—his name isn't Peter—Peter walked in, saw them chatting, and for some reason he lost his cool. He got a gun from the den and shot the guy in the shoulder. Then, when his wife couldn't stop screaming, he called nine-one-one and reported the shooting.

"He pled guilty and was sentenced to Lompoc or something."

"I thought he was at—"

"Pelican Bay," Mel finished. "Yeah. He attacked a guard and so they sent him there. Spent four years cultivating a medical condition that had him seeing a doctor maybe three times a year. The doctor passed letters from Peter, not his name, and various people in the outside world."

"So he escaped from a hospital visit?" I asked, the sneer smeared all over my words.

"No. That would be cheating. The doctor had to visit Pete in stir. There was a special clinic. Well, one day there was a substitute for the doctor who smuggled in a small arsenal and various other tools. They subdued six guards and made it to the escape car without killing anyone. That was one of Pete's prerequisites—no one could get murdered in the operation. He's a little like you, Joe."

"Where is he now?" Olo asked.

"On an island in an ocean with his young wife and two kids."

"He took her back?" That was me.

"Here he comes," Oliya said.

Looking in the direction of the Polish restaurant, I saw Yuri talking to the semiofficial attendant who parked his car. The guy ran off, leaving the Russian doddering by the front door.

"I'll go get the car," Oliya said.

She left hurriedly.

"That's an extraordinary woman," Mel commented as she went out the front door.

"I think she thinks the same of you."

"Really?"

"Do I have to worry about it?"

"What you mean?"

"Come on, man. You know what I mean. Are you stalking Olo by secretly hiring her?"

"Never even seen her in person before today. I only hired her because I was told she was the best Int-Op had."

He seemed to mean what he was saying.

"There's Yuri's car," I said.

Yuri was already two blocks down when Oliya pulled up to the curb, but that didn't matter.

"What's the plan?" she asked as we trailed behind.

"If he takes the same way back, he'll go past that cemetery near his house."

"You want to ram him?"

"No."

"It was something about the way he shot the guy," Mel mused from the back.

We were approaching the border of Queens from the Brooklyn side.

"What guy?" That was me.

"Peter-not-Peter's wife's boyfriend."

"He shot him in some special way?" Oliya asked.

"Not really, but old Pete had never shown such passion. That's why the wife needed outside stimulus. Pete was as dependable as the old Ford your grandfather drove. When he shot the boyfriend her heart opened wide."

"Wow," I said. "Damn."

"Drop back a little," Mel said to Oliya. "We don't wanna spook the guy."

"We don't wanna lose him either."

"I put a transmitter under his bumper and a little surprise under the dash."

"What kind of surprise?"

"The kind that makes everybody's life easier."

It was fully dark by the time Yuri led us back to the peninsula.

We were cruising past the Memorial Homes Cemetery as we came to a red light. Yuri's red Tesla was in the lead, with a light blue Hyundai behind him and Loopy's Mark VII taking up the rear.

226

"This is as good as anywhere," I said.

There came a faint click from the back seat.

The light turned green but the Tesla didn't move. The light blue Hyundai honked and then veered around the red car angrily riding the horn.

"Killed a man one time for honking at me like that," Madman Mel observed.

I cracked the door and told Oliya, "Pull up on the cemetery road."

I got out and she pulled off.

The driver was unconscious behind the wheel. That was because of the gas bomb Mel had laid. I let down the back-rest and rolled the little Russian into the back seat.

Behind the graveyard chapel we moved Yuri to the trunk of the Lincoln and then drove for four hours to a good-size stone farmhouse just outside Brattleboro, Vermont.

25.

I WOKE UP with the morning sun on my face. The huge bedroom had a chilly stone floor and its own fireplace. The faint scents of burnt wood, plaster mold, and bacon sat me up in the big bed. I'd kicked off the down comforter in the night.

There were the faraway sounds of the labors of morning coming from downstairs. Probably Mel making breakfast.

My clothes were hung on a high-backed dark walnut throne. I thought about getting dressed but didn't have the heart for it yet. Instead I went to the twelve-foot windows. They gave a panoramic view of the pine forests and grassy fields that surrounded the hill where Melquarth Frost's northern New England home sat.

No barn, farmhouse, or even paved road could be seen. It was idyllic. Beautiful. Primordial. And there I stood, naked as Adam—or a youthful Cain.

In spite of appearances, the majesty of nature is just a fancy blanket draped over the malevolence of the creatures of earth.

The forest floor was populated by beasts that spent entire

lifetimes fighting and killing for food, for survival, for fun. And there I stood, a member of the most depraved species.

Every once in a while, naked and alone in the morning, I make up my mind to be better than my race, my human race. It's a vow that can't be kept for long. The call of nature will, sooner or later, drag you back down into the struggle that nothing and no one can long escape.

But now and then, if I concentrate, I have the chance of doing something right.

"Mornin', Mel, Olo," I said half an hour after my soul-searching.

"Good morning, Joe," Oliya said.

"Hotcakes or cheese omelet?" Mel offered.

"Both."

Over breakfast Mel talked about one day retiring to his woodland retreat.

"I could raise sheep, make maple syrup, and grow a garden that could feed a family," he told us.

"Are you married?" Oliya asked.

"Never."

"Then what family would you be feeding?"

The man named after the devil's grandfather hunched his shoulders and smiled.

"Yuri in the basement?" I asked him.

"Yep. You want me to milk him this morning?"

"I was thinking that I'd like to take a run at it first."

"That don't sound like you, Joe. What's up?"

"I don't know. I was just looking out on the countryside and thought that I'd like to try my hand at forced honesty."

Both of the specialists were looking at me, wondering. A sane man would have gone running from that room.

"Where's the door to the cellar?" I asked.

"You don't know?" Oliya put in before Mel could answer.

"He's never been here before," Mel replied. "I never had an uncoerced guest out here. Usually when we do this kind of work it's out on Staten Island."

I wondered if I should warn my bodyguard against learning too much but then realized that Mel was only flirting.

"At the other end of the sitting room you'll find a yellow door," he said to me. "It opens on a staircase that ends at blue and red doors. Red goes into the main room. Blue takes you to the prep chamber."

Through the blue door was a closet that contained long black robes and porcelain-like masks of either red or white; these were used to interrogate the penitent without revealing your identity.

I eschewed disguise.

Yuri was chained to a stainless steel chair that was bolted to the granite floor. He wore headphones and a thick pair of blinders. Mel usually played opera for his prisoners. He said that you had to have dramatic music for serious situations.

I removed the headphones and then lifted his blindfold.

The international mobster was short and wiry, his hairless face lean and olive-colored.

"What do you want?" he said with conviction.

"I want you to give me a name."

"Fuck you."

His accent was so mild that I thought he must have learned English at an early age, at some kind of American school. Forty or so, maybe one of his parents was some kind of diplomat who lived in D.C. during Yuri's formative years.

"You're going to tell me, Yuri. There's no question about that. I have a friend upstairs who gets pleasure out of breaking down resistance." I paused for a few moments and then said, "I was looking out the window this morning. It's really beautiful outside. So much so that I thought I'd come down here and offer you your freedom for some discreet information. I won't tell anyone that I got this information from you. And you will leave here with all your appendages in working order."

This was why I didn't wear a mask. I was hoping that the Russian was a pragmatist. But in order to achieve this end he had to look into my naked eyes, hear my unmuffled words clearly—honestly.

I could see the inner workings of the oil bootlegger's mind trying to encompass the situation.

"How would you know if I lied?" he asked.

"I'll test the answer. If you've told me the truth I'll call my friend and he will deposit you, safe and sound, in a red Tesla in any place of your choosing."

"What will stop me from finding and killing you and your family?" he said, trying his best to sound threatening.

"You won't find me. And if you did it would cost you dearly."

I was Adam's surviving son, free and unrepentant. If Yuri wanted to live, to go back home without fear, he'd have to get my approval.

We sat for a long while in silence.

He hated me and needed me.

I didn't care if he lived or died.

"What do you need to know?"

"There's a guy who identifies himself as Tava Burkel. I need to speak to him."

Sometime after our conversation I went back upstairs. Mel and Oliya were sitting across from each other in block-shaped padded sofa chairs that were covered in bearskins. Mel was opining about some schism in his character and she was studying him like a postdoc grad student majoring in evil.

They brought to mind a dog and cat of equal size living in the same house. They got along well but weren't the same. The call of nature outside the walls was always summoning and they couldn't help but listen.

"Hey, Joe," Melquarth hailed. "That was a goddamned masterpiece."

"You watched?"

"I got a vid up here. Oliya didn't want to, but it's my house."

"You liked it?" I asked my bodyguard.

"He knows your face."

"That's not gonna be a problem."

"You want me to take care of it?" Mel offered.

"I want you to sit on him until I call. Then gas him and bring him wherever he wants to go."

"But like your friend says, he knows your face."

"By that time it won't matter."

26.

A LITTLE LATER in the morning Oliya and I headed back to New York. The pace felt leisurely compared to the night before. The beauty of the day was still contrasting with the darkness of the tasks I would have to perform.

"Where does your friend come from?"

"From bad parents with a strong church background."

"He seems very capable."

"Strong words from a woman who can kill two assassins without breathing hard."

"I . . . am capable too."

Crossing the border of New York State, I called in to my electronic answering service.

"This is Winston Halbreadth," an officious voice said on the third message, "speaking on behalf of Roger Ferris. There's been a breach at Silbrig Haus."

"Daddy," Aja said on the next call, "Grandma B's been shot."

I disconnected the service.

"What's wrong?" Oliya asked.

She was looking at me, wondering, offering.

When I didn't answer, she turned away.

"My grandmother's been shot."

"Dead?"

"I don't know."

The next call I made was answered on the seventh ring.

"Forthright."

"It's me, man."

"She's okay," Forthright Jorgensen said.

"She's shot."

"One ball of a shotgun in the left buttocks. Didn't even hit bone."

"What happened?"

"Hit squad. I tried to call you but the phone was offline."

"How many?"

"Six. Four dead and two in police custody. I lost one. Two others were wounded."

"My grandmother in the hospital?"

"Ferris brought in a team of specialists."

"They good?"

"What do you think?"

Finishing the call, I felt, once again, at sea.

"How is she?" Oliya asked.

"They say okay."

"That's good."

"I guess. I mean, how does a ninety-three-year-old woman get shot in the safest place in New York?"

"Is this the job I was hired for?"

"It is now."

"Okay then. Let's get on with it."

*   *   *

We arrived at the mansion in the early afternoon. There were two uniformed guards at the glittering steel gate this time. They each carried a sidearm and compact assault rifle. They checked us out and passed us in.

Two more guards stood by the front door. One of them led us through the entryway into a large sitting room where nurses and doctors tended to the two wounded security guards and frightened domestics.

"Daddy!"

Aja ran up and hugged me tightly. She put her head against my shoulder and pressed as hard as she could.

"Where's Grandma?"

"In her bedroom."

After maybe a minute I pulled away, turning to Oliya.

"This is my daughter. I want you to stick to her."

"Yes, Joe."

"Honey."

"Uh-huh?"

"This here's Oliya Ruez. You stay with her. She'll protect you."

Aja looked at the compact bodyguard, a dozen questions in her eyes. But all she said was "Okay."

The curtains were drawn in my grandmother's bedroom. Extra-powerful lighting stalks had been brought in. A male nurse and Dr. Lucille Leon were in attendance. In the corner of the room sat Roger on a wicker chair that my grandmother had owned since before my father was born.

Roger was staring at Brenda, bereft but brave—for her.

She looked even smaller than usual in the big bed, receiving blood from an IV. There was some kind of electronic medical device, the size of a small dresser. This machine displayed her bodily functions on a broad screen. She looked distressed but not as bad as Roger.

"Grandma?"

She turned and smiled.

"Baby."

Dr. Leon turned in my direction. She'd been my grandmother's primary physician for two years. Her skin was mahogany brown under straightened, and shocking, white-gray hair. The mature woman was about to say something when my grandmother interceded.

"Leave me and my grandson for a minute, Lucy."

"I'm not finished with the examination."

"It'll only be a few minutes."

Roger got up and approached us. The nurse was already leaving.

"I'll be back in five minutes," Lucille Leon told us.

"Ten," Brenda corrected.

Roger moved close to me and said, "I'm sorry, son. I never thought they'd pull an all-out assault."

"She's alive," I said. "That's the best either of us could ask for."

I pulled the rattan chair up next to the bed. She smiled and gave me her dry hand.

"Ain't we sumpin'," she said.

"What happened?"

"Dropped from a helicopter! Six of 'em. A goddamned

helicopter! Could you imagine that? Forthright and his people were movin' as soon as the whirlybird come over the river. Me and Roger was havin' afternoon tea and two of 'em bust through the windah. One fired this shotgun, then they was both cut down. Roger wasn't hit at all and I was shot in the butt."

She started laughing. It wasn't hysteria, just the dark humor at the trials of being a Black woman in an inhospitable world.

"You look scared like you'd get when you was a boy, King."

"What you expect? They told me you were shot."

"In the butt."

"Butts bleed."

"That they do."

For maybe two minutes we sat quietly holding hands.

"Is this the mess Roger got you into?" she asked.

"I don't think so. I'm on a case got nothing to do with his kids."

"What kinda case? Is it safe?"

I told her about Alfred Xavier Quiller and the work Roger wanted me to do.

"Is that safe?" I asked after finishing.

"I know, baby. It's your job. And people die in pillow factories. Ain't nuthin' assured."

"But you're alive and that's all that matters right now," I told the woman I had known longer than anyone else.

"I'm gonna buy me a shotgun as soon as I can get outta this bed. Livin' with this rich white man have done made me soft."

I smiled and kissed her.

*　　*　　*

Aja and Oliya were standing just outside the door to the bedroom.

"How is she?" Aja asked.

"She'll be better after talking to you."

"It was so scary. They jumped out of a helicopter."

"I'm sorry, baby. I thought you'd be safe here."

"It's okay," she said, squashing down the fear. "I mean how am I ever going to work with you if I don't see what it's like?"

Over my daughter's shoulder I could see a smile flitting across Oliya's lips.

"Where's your mother?" I asked Aja.

"In the kitchen."

"Cooking?"

"You know how she is."

"I better go talk to her."

"Glad's here too, Daddy."

"He is? Where?"

"I dunno. Somewhere," she said with a shrug.

Monica was down in the kitchen making some kind of vegetable medley. Green and red peppers, broccoli, and onions mixed with garlic and mascarpone, hot peppers, and soy.

"Hey, Monica," I said from behind her.

"They shot at your grandmother," she said, not turning.

She splashed a little water into the sauté and clapped a domed lid on the pot.

Then she turned.

"Is this the kind of situation you put us in?"

"You're welcome to leave."

There had always been a choreography to the way we spoke to each other.

"You're a bastard," she twirled at me.

"Then why do you keep asking me for shit?" was my boogaloo reply.

"Coleman says that you came to his place and took his gun," she dipped and twisted.

"I did," I said, dropping her to the floor.

"How's he supposed to protect himself in that terrible place?"

"Terrible, yes. But maybe the safest building in New York City. Nobody gets past L and M."

"I want him here with me."

"You can move into his room in Brownsville if you want. I'm not adding one more target on this house."

Monica turned back to her comfort cooking. After a minute or so I left.

"Hey, boyo," Gladstone Palmer greeted. He'd been waiting outside the kitchen door.

"NYPD send ya?"

"Your grandmother's boyfriend wants to keep this all quiet. Don't ask me why. Seems like publicity would be a good shield."

"They're his kids," I explained.

"You sure it's them did this?"

"Zyron wouldn't get much from attacking a man like Ferris. And they think they have better ways to get at him."

"Maybe you're right. But you know there's no profit in bein' too smart."

"You got bodies on this?"

"Twenty-five officers, twenty-four hours a day."

"That's a whole lotta taxes."

Glad laughed.

"You're the best cop I've ever known," he said.

"And I'm not even on the force."

"I'll be around. Call me if you need anything in the city."

My last stop was Roger Ferris's pared-down business room.

He ushered me in and closed the door. I sat but he had too much nervous energy to stay that still.

"You need to calm down, Rog. All that worry is hard on the heart."

"How are you going to worry about me when I got your grandmother shot?"

"You didn't shoot her. And she knew what was happening. She could have gone somewhere else."

"I'm going to send her away to someplace safe."

"You must know by now that nobody sends Brenda Naples anywhere. Best thing you could do is buy her a twelve-gauge shotgun with a six-round clip."

The old man took in a deep breath and then went to the folding chair behind the pressboard desk.

"Your grandmother is amazing to me," he said. "I realized after she got shot that I've never seen her shed a tear."

"You ever been hungry, Roger?"

"Sure. Everybody knows hunger."

"I don't mean *it's time to eat* hunger. What I'm talkin' about is when you need to eat but there ain't nuthin' in the cabinet; when all you got is three stale crackers and four hungry kids looking up at you."

Roger empathized with my words. He shook his head slowly and then said, "No. I have not."

"Where Brenda come from, a smoked turkey leg would

be cause for celebration. Could you imagine what would happen to the poor fool tried to take that leg from her?"

Roger chuckled.

"Okay," I said. "We had the soft talk, now it's come to Buddha time."

Roger sat back and I leaned forward, putting an elbow on either knee.

"Who is George Laurel?" I asked.

Betraying barely a falter he asked, "Where'd you hear that name?"

"I heard it looking around for information on Quiller."

"From who?"

"Who is he?" I insisted.

Roger stood up from the chair and sat on the desk. He turned his head away, looking at the blank wall as if it were a vast field of dying crops.

"A long time ago, almost fifty years, he was a student at Yale."

There was power behind these memories. So much so that the recent events in both our lives receded into the background.

"What he die of?" I asked after a spate of seconds.

"Slaughtered." Roger's tone was almost matter-of-fact.

"By whom?" I get correct when talking about death.

"Some student at school. A scholarship kid, I think."

"What's that got to do with you?"

"I'm an alumnus of the school. I give them money. The death was a big deal."

"Did you know Laurel?"

"No, never met him."

Like silver in the ground, there was more to be mined. But

I knew the old white man well enough to see that there'd be no more answers that day.

"Quiller was kidnapped," I said. "I'm pretty sure of that. Maybe the rest of his story is true too."

Roger's eyes and heart were concentrated on that dry field.

"What do you want me to do next?" I asked.

Roger was quite limber for a nonagenarian. Grandma B said it was because he did a regimen of yoga exercises every morning. He crossed the left leg over the right and looked at me.

"I love your grandmother, Joe."

"I know."

"It's the first time I've ever felt like that about someone that wasn't blood. And even with relatives it's more a sense of duty than what I feel about Brenda."

There was really nothing to say about this admission.

"Look," he said. "You've done what I asked. Maybe you should take Aja and your grandmother someplace safe while I deal with what's happened here."

"Now you got the cops and all these extra hands, I can't think of anywhere safer than this house."

"Okay. You have enough on your plate with your ex-wife's problems. Leave dealing with Quiller to me."

"If that's the way you want it."

Roger stood up before saying, "It is."

27.

LOOPY'S MARK VII was still parked in front of the manor. My daughter walked us out. When Oliya climbed into the passenger's seat, Aja put a hand on my wrist.

"Can I come with, Daddy?" she asked, already knowing the answer.

"Not quite yet, honey. Oliya and me got some serious chop to get through first."

"What's the thing with her?"

"What do you mean?"

"She's...I don't know...different."

"That she is. She's kind of like the detective you keep on saying you want to be."

"And she's your girlfriend?"

"No. She owes me a debt and I'm in so deep I'm letting her pay it."

"Okay," she said warily. "Be careful."

"Nice office," Oliya said after I'd shown her around my rooms.

"Thanks. Me and Aja got a good rhythm in here."

"Her space is so much bigger than yours."

"She keeps the files and the office tools. The only thing I do is think."

"Why all the paper files? You some kinda throwback or something?"

"Something."

"Well, if you want to go think, I can do some work out here."

My first call was to Henri Tourneau. Henri's father was a friend of mine and I looked after the young man's progress in the police department. He'd risen to the rank of detective first grade in good time. He called for advice now and then, and on rare occasions, I'd reach out to him for help.

"Tourneau," he said, answering the call on the first ring.

"Hey, Henri."

"Mr. Oliver."

"Come on, man. When you gonna start calling me Joe?"

"When I bust my first international smuggling ring."

"You close to that?"

"Hold up. Let me get outside."

While the call was on mute I looked up the website for the Regency Oil Syndicate, based in Tulsa, Oklahoma.

I'd just found the name I was looking for when Henri said, "I'm back."

"How's your dad?" I asked, warming up to a request.

"He had what they call a ministroke two months back. Mom wants him to retire but he says that he likes being a pipefitter."

"What's a ministroke?"

"What it sounds like. A stroke that doesn't do as much damage."

"So he's okay?"

"Only thing you can see is that the baby finger of his left hand doesn't bend. He says he never used it all that much anyway."

"Is he home?"

"No. He's at work down on the Brooklyn docks."

"Give him my best."

"Will do."

"Um, I wanted to ask you to do me a favor."

"Name it."

"Half a century ago a student named George Laurel was murdered while going to Yale. I've been trying to get information about what happened, but it's too long ago. Does the force still have ties to the New Haven PD?"

"Organized crime has the most."

"Can you dig up some information on the case?"

"Try my best."

"Thanks, Henri. Give my love to your mother."

My next call was an 800 number so there was no way even to guess at its geographic location.

"Regency Oil," a pleasant woman's voice said.

"Hi. My name is Lon Preston and I was hoping that you could help me."

"Certainly. What can I do for you, Mr. Preston?"

"I'm looking to speak to John Sledge."

"Oh." There was a hint of hesitation in the young woman's voice. "I don't have a connection to Mr. Sledge's line."

"Might your supervisor know how to get in touch with him?"

"What is your business with Mr. Sledge?"

"A friend of his has had an accident and he wanted me to reach out."

"Does this have to do with Regency?"

"If your mother broke her leg, would that have to do with Regency? I mean, could somebody call you at work to tell you that?"

My words sounded like a threat. They were and, then again, they were not.

"What is this friend's name?"

"Yuri Fleganoff."

"Hold on."

It took five minutes for the second voice to come on the line.

"Regency Oil," a very masculine-sounding man said.

"Hi. I'm looking for John Sledge."

"And you are?"

"Lon Preston."

"And what is your business with Mr. Sledge, Mr. Preston?"

"Private."

"You said something about a friend of his," the voice coaxed.

"Can you put me through?"

"I need more information before that can happen."

"So, you can put me through, you're just refusing to."

"I need to know why you want him."

"What's your name?" I asked.

"Connor."

"Well, Mr. Connor, believe me when I tell you that

Mr. Sledge does not want this message out on the street."

"I'm the manager in charge of communications," Connor asserted.

"If your salary is below eight figures you really don't want to know what I have to say to your boss's boss's boss."

"Hold on."

This time there was music on the suspended line. Tina Turner singing "What's Love Got to Do with It." I like the song, love the songstress. I was moving my upper body to the rhythm when a knocking came on the door.

"Come on in."

When Oliya walked into the room I had the familiar feeling one gets when seeing an old friend.

"Oh," she said. "You're on the phone."

"On hold. What do you need?"

"I wanted to talk to you about something. It can wait."

"This is Aaron McCaffrey," Billy Goat Gruff snarled in my ear.

I pointed at the offended ear and my new/old friend backed out—closing the door.

"Hello, Mr. McCaffrey."

"Who is this?"

"You can call me Lon."

"Lon what?"

"Look, man, you're the third person I've had to talk to and I'm getting a little fed up. My name is Lon and I'm calling John Sledge to pass on a message from Yuri Fleganoff."

"I don't like your tone, Lon."

"Go home and kiss your kids. You'll forget all about the sound of my voice."

I could feel the upper-mid-management mandibles quivering on the other end of the line.

"Hold on!"

Most of human life is defined by waiting. Neanderthal hunters would wait in shadows to ambush prey. Foot soldiers wait for the signal to attack. Hopeful young men wait downstairs while their dates wonder which shoes to wear.

Yuri Fleganoff was waiting in a forest den, hoping against hope that he'd have future delays on foreign soil.

"Hello?" a mature woman said. "Mr. Preston?"

"Yes."

"How can I help you?"

"What's your name?"

"Delphine. Delphine du Champs."

"Whoa. Now, that's a name."

"How can I help you, Mr. Preston?"

"I need to speak with Johnny Sledge."

"John Sledge?"

I didn't see any reason to answer.

"What is your business with Mr. Sledge?" du Champs asked.

"Private. It's private business that he wouldn't want you hearing about."

"I know about all of Mr. Sledge's affairs."

I wondered if she intended the double entendre.

"Not this one," I assured her.

"Give me your number. I'll ask him to call you back."

"Now or never, Delphine."

"Hold on."

While waiting, I did a little math, coming up with a

number that was maybe the last digit of the combination to Roger's secret. I was about to test that calculation when a silken-toned tenor got on the line.

"Lon Preston?"

"Mr. Sledge?"

"How can I help you?"

"I have a problem that coincides with an issue you're having."

"I seriously doubt that."

"Oh? You mean the FBI, heating oil, and Tava Burkel's real name aren't things that make your dick soft?"

Blessed silence.

"Who is this?"

"Just a guy who wants parity. We meet, exchange a few words, and then all our problems will be solved."

"How much do you want?"

"Not a dime."

"So why are we talking?"

"Meet me and you'll find out."

"There's nothing you've said that would make me want to meet with you." He sounded very certain.

"No, Mr. Burkel? Really?"

More silence.

"Where?" Sledge asked.

"Dead center of the pedestrian passway on the Brooklyn Bridge. Tonight. Midnight."

"You think I'm a fool?"

"Only if you don't show."

I hung up. I wasn't worried about repercussions over using my office phone because I had the best protection software that blackmail could buy.

Feeling undeservedly good about myself, I went to the outer office.

Oliya was sitting in my daughter's chair reading a Spanish novel titled *She Opened the Box.*

"So what did you want to talk about?" I asked, taking the visitor's seat.

Oliya put down the myth made modern. "I called a friend at Int-Op. My mentor. The woman that brought me in."

"Somebody you can trust?"

"Nothing's for sure, but—I think so."

"And what did she say?"

"Int-Op is a very old company. More than a hundred years. They started in the United States and then moved the base of operations to Europe in the 1950s. My division works mostly for big corporations dealing with everything from kidnapping to corporate espionage, but the majority of the staff now consists of hackers researching and protecting sensitive data.

"Still, the company has deep roots in the kind of work I do. That's why I wouldn't tell you about our relationship with Zyron. In a perfect world any association we have with them should not compromise what we're doing for you."

"Uh-huh," I said.

"But it seems that Zyron and maybe others have bought off certain key representatives. That's what my friend says."

"Do they know who these people are?"

"No."

"But they know you."

"Yes."

"They trust you."

"As far as I know."

"You need to go take care of business?"

"Right now my job is to protect you." ·

An hour later I was sitting in my office again looking out on Montague Street. There was nothing to do until late night. Oliya would cover the Manhattan entrance while Mel would guard the Brooklyn side. In the meantime I could watch the pedestrians making their way down a street they could no longer afford.

I was so into the sights that when the phone rang I was startled.

"Hello."

"Joe?"

"Henri, my man."

"I don't know what you could be looking for here, but I got some of the story if you want it."

"Hit me."

"It happened nearly fifty years ago. A very popular junior at Yale, George Laurel, was killed in his New Haven apartment by another student named Sola Prendergast. Sola came from Argentina. He was poor but that year they were looking for bilingual students with fair grades."

"Did he give any reason for the killing?"

"No. He just pled guilty and took a life sentence."

"What prison he in?"

"He *was* in Bridgeport Correctional but got released in '92. Upon release he was deported back to Argentina."

I tried, in my mind, to connect this half-a-century-old seemingly senseless murder to Quiller. All I got was a mental cramp.

"You need anything else, Joe?" Henri asked.

"Yeah. A factory job putting cheap shoes in cardboard boxes."

I looked up Alexander and Cassandra Ferris and their college educations. He went to Harvard and she to Princeton. He was a fuckup at school; his sister, on the other hand, attained the distinction of summa cum laude. Neither one had anything to do with Yale. Their father didn't seem to spend much time there either.

George Laurel would have to wait.

I leaned back in the swivel chair and put both feet up on the desk.

I was at a country fair in the late day. It was different from most fairs in that they had a zoo but all the animals, from elephants to lions, were walking among the people come to gawk at them. There was a river with seals and sea lions lolling on the banks. The hot dog vendor didn't charge and the lions yawned lazily. There was a tall, very tall and lanky man who wore a stovepipe top hat the crown of which must have stood a good yard above his brow. His green dress jacket had big yellow stars sewn on it. This ringmaster, this circus boss, had a perpetual grin plastered on his face. He was looking around the crowd, for something.

When he turned that gaze on me I experienced a thrill of fear.

He took a step in my direction.

I set off at a run. I was hoofing it but for some reason made little headway. The man in the top hat was walking and still catching up. His tooth-filled grin was feral. I ran harder but he was closing the gap. Then I slammed into an extinct cave bear. Falling to the ground I saw that the circus boss had caught up with me. He held out a helping hand but I knew that he wanted to capture me, to make me a part of his carnival.

I cringed, closing my eyes and praying for escape.

"Joe."

28.

OLIYA WAS STANDING next to the chair, jostling my shoulder.

"It's ten thirty," she said.

I sat up, shaking my head.

"Joe," my newfound friend said again.

"I'm up."

"We have to go."

I pressed the heels of my palms against both orbital bones.

"Sure," I said. "Of course. You go get the car and I'll make it there on my own."

Looking down at my forearms and desk, I felt her considering my words. Then she was gone.

I was approaching the Washington Street pedestrian entrance to the bridge about forty-five minutes later. Melquarth was standing at the top of the concrete stairs.

"Joe."

"Hey."

We shook hands.

"Wanna grab some chili up in Harlem after we're through?"

"Okay."

I walked on.

There wasn't anything to go over with Mel. He'd attached microcameras overlooking the spot where the meeting was to take place so that he and Olo could watch without being seen. If any suspicious characters got on during the meeting, they'd follow—and respond accordingly.

I reached a spot where Mel had painted a small white X on the outer wall. If I stood there, the hidden, high-resolution camera lens would capture me—and anyone I was with. I also had a voice-activated digital recorder inside an empty pack of Kool cigarettes in my shirt pocket.

It's better to be early than on time. You can compose your thoughts, imagine the flaws in any plan. With fifteen minutes to spare I considered how an entire lifetime had brought me to that bridge, attempting to save the life and freedom of a man I detested. It felt right to be inside a life based on principle and not selfishness. Standards are all that the descendants of Cain have to keep them upright and respectable.

Over the next eleven minutes a few pedestrians sauntered by. Lovers, loners, late-night joggers, and a tourist or two. A couple of strollers wondered about me, looked back to make sure I wasn't following. None of them seemed to be on the job.

"He's on the way, Joe," Oliya said into my ear. "Alone."

We'd dug up a photo of Sledge online. He had a round head with a receding hairline and razor-thin mustache. You couldn't tell his height from the portrait but I wasn't there for a fight.

A few minutes later I saw him coming from the Manhattan side.

Surprisingly tall, over six feet, he was thin and fit, like a tennis pro. His loose trousers were light-colored cotton, and when he reached me, I could see that his short-sleeved shirt was dark green.

"Mr. Sledge," I said when he was two and a half steps away.

Stopping on my first word, he looked around—a soldier attuned to any threat.

"Mr. Preston."

"Nice night."

"Let's get down to business, shall we?"

"Okay—" I was about to go into my spiel but Sledge cut me off.

"Before you tell me what you want, I want to know who gave you my name."

"A man who, even just knowing his name is often fatal."

"I'm not worried."

"I am."

John Sledge measured me. His left eye got very small before he said, "I can be dangerous too."

"I'm sure you can. You and I both know that life is a losing bet at best. But right here, right now, we have a chance to avoid that fate for a few weeks, or years."

"Okay. Tell me what you want."

"The government is pressing very hard to find a way to stop the sale of heating oil for diesel fuel. Neither of us wants them to succeed."

"What horse you got in that race?"

"The dark horse is Yuri Fleganoff."

"Who?"

"Come on, man, you know who that is. The guy runnin' millions of barrels of oil from foreign tankers into a few of your distribution centers. The man who the FBI knows as Alain Freeman."

"If that's true, then why don't they arrest him?"

"Because they're looking for another name."

When Sledge licked his upper lip, I knew I had him.

"What name?"

"The one they have is Tava Burkel. The one they want is John Sledge."

"I don't know who you think you're dealing with, brother man."

I pulled a .38 out of my pocket and aimed it at his left eye.

"I am not your brother," I said in a civil tone.

The captain of industry kept quiet.

"Fleganoff needs to be out of the picture," I said, now holding the gun down at my side.

"Why?" The one-word question had all the passion of a Neanderthal fledgling philosopher looking up at the night sky.

"It doesn't matter why. You put Yuri out to pasture, place somebody else in his harness, and I will fade into the background, never to be heard from again. That's really all you need to know."

The lithe corporateer stared at me. After some seconds he began to nod.

"I do this and we're done?" he asked.

"Absolutely."

"You won't mention my name?"

"I only want one thing."

He pretended to think a moment or so and then said, "You got a deal."

"You can go now, Mr. Sledge."

"What's your name?"

"You don't want to know."

Charles's Chili was a basement joint above 150th Street. Oliya, Mel, and I were chowing down on bowls from different batches. Mel preferred beef while I liked pork. Oliya ordered something I never heard of before—shrimp chili.

"Why'd you pull that gun on Johnny?" Mel asked when we were halfway through the meal.

"I just needed him to know that I was as serious as it gets."

"I would'a shot him."

"I need him alive."

"Why?"

"I'm pretty sure that he's not the top man. Better to have him alive and afraid than to have his betters lookin' for me."

"All right," Mel said leerily.

"I'm sending you a recording I have of the talk with Sledge. I want you to go back to Vermont and play it for Yuri. I'm pretty sure he'll make tracks after that."

"Pretty sure? That good enough for you?"

"It's the best play I got."

"So you want me to let him go?"

"Ask him if he needs any help. It'd be great to have Sledge and his people chasing their tails."

Oliya didn't utter a word, just kept shoveling in those spicy red-stained prawns.

In the morning I did a little research. When rush hour was over I donned my best suit and headed for New Haven.

Once at Yale I went to the main office and introduced myself as Joe Oliver, the new representative of the Ferris Fund.

"How can we help you?" Trish Geiger asked without demanding documentation.

"Roger is interested in how the school managed its scholarships at the very beginning. He wanted me to talk to people that were here then."

"That was way back in the seventies," Underdean Geiger proclaimed. "Anybody who worked here is either retired or dead."

"Or both," I allowed. "But there are several staff members today that were students at the time. Mr. Ferris would like to hear their impressions."

"I guess," Ms. Geiger said. "If you give me their names I'd be happy to set up an office where you can interview them."

"I'd prefer seeing them in the environments they work in. If you just point them out on the campus map . . ."

Lionel Millman was a botanist who worked and sometimes taught in the campus greenhouse. He didn't remember anything about the murder except that it happened. He didn't even remember George Laurel's name.

Charlaine Fogle was giving a lecture to 150-something students about the Peloponnesian War, a memoir by a Greek doctor/philosopher/general's experience during that monumental conflict. I listened for nearly the full seventy-five-minute lecture and learned quite a bit. This made me hopeful about talking to the aged professor.

"The Ferris Fund, you say?" she asked when I buttonholed her on the bottom rung of the lecture hall.

"Yes."

"I was told by the last person claiming to represent the fund that there was no interest in the subject of history among the board members. You aren't interested in me and so I'm not interested in you."

With that she walked away.

Couldn't say that I blamed her.

Bexleigh Terrell was the ace I needed to stay in the game. The head librarian was tall, with proper posture and coarse hair dyed copper. She wore a maroon pants suit and sensible shoes. I imagined that she carried a knife and only worried about the health of her cat.

The imposing white woman's eyes were somehow and mostly colorless.

"How may we help you, Mr. Oliver?"

We.

Approximating a humble demeanor I said, "The board has asked me for information about the crime of a long-ago scholarship student—Sola Prendergast. He killed George Laurel in the dormitory back in—"

"Nineteen seventy-seven," the librarian said. "In March, as I remember. What on earth would the board need to know about him?"

"I really don't know. They asked me for information and I couldn't find a thing. So I thought I'd come here looking for people who were on campus at the time."

Ms. Terrell's judging eyes studied me like the proverbial book. I could only hope that my untrustworthy narrator was convincing.

"It was a terrible day," she said. "George was well liked.

I remember crying when I heard he was dead. Now I look back on that time and wonder about it."

"About what?"

"Nothing. The crying. I mean, I didn't even know him. I guess I was blubbering over the violence of the murder."

"Do you know why Prendergast killed him?"

"They said it was jealousy."

"Over a girl?"

"A woman," Bexleigh corrected. "The prettiest, smartest, strongest—she competed in the Olympics—and most sophisticated creature on campus. Everyone was in love with her—male and female."

"A professor?"

"No. A student. Valeria Ursini. Her friends called her Pixie."

"Was Sola going out with Valeria?"

"Valeria didn't go out. She would grace you with her company now and then but you just followed after."

"Did George Laurel follow?"

"Maybe." There was contempt in the word.

"So was she seeing Sola too?"

"I don't think so."

"Then why would he kill George?"

"I'm surprised you don't already know. Valeria and Sola got together sometimes because they were both Ferris scholarship students."

"I didn't know that." Even the untrustworthy could tell the truth sometimes. "So you think that maybe Sola killed George out of jealousy?"

"I wouldn't know." Bexleigh glanced to the right, giving me the sign that she needed to get back to work.

"Thank you for your time, Ms. Terrell."

"You're welcome, Mr. Oliver."

My iPhone told me that Valeria Ursini worked as a film archivist at Mandrake College in Yonkers. The urban university was easy to infiltrate. A Black man in a sharp gray suit was accepted easily. I asked around about the film archive and found that it was located on the sixth floor, through the library.

At just about seventy, Valeria would have still given Sophia Loren a run for her money.

She wore a coral-colored one-piece dress that came down to the middle of her calves and revealed a stunning figure — tastefully. She was flipping through film cans on a cart in the middle of a large room where students worked on various machines that examined and restored celluloid.

"Miss Ursini?" I asked the Yale bombshell.

"Yes?"

She raised her head, bringing a hand to her only slightly creped throat.

"Hi. My name is Joe Oliver. I'm the new director of the Ferris Fund."

Her expression turned from mild interest to definite distaste.

"Oh. How can I help you, Mr. Oliver?"

"The fund is about to celebrate a big anniversary. We'll be showcasing scholars all along the way. To some of these we'll be awarding a one-hundred-thousand-dollar prize."

"And?"

"We were wondering if you'd like to be one of the scholars we celebrate."

"I haven't done anything to be recognized for."

"You've restored hundreds of films that would have been lost. And you discovered hitherto unknown works by Alice Guy." Thank goodness for the internet.

"No one is concerned about her work."

"But the history of any field of study must include everything if it is to be considered complete."

Something I said, some emphasis, turned the lady completely against me. Her face hardened and my words drained away.

"Go back to your master and tell him that I will keep my word."

"You mean Roger Ferris?"

"Leave."

29.

JUST WHEN I got situated behind the wheel of the car my cell phone rang.

Answering the call I asked, "Are you following me again, Olo?"

"No." I could hear the subdued smile behind the word. "Just wanted to know where you were."

"I'm in Yonkers on the way to Rikers Island."

"What's there?"

"Alfred Xavier Quiller."

"What's that do for you?"

"Among other things, he's the reason Int-Op turned against us."

"Yeah, about that, my mentor has maybe found the one who sold us out."

"You going back to settle up with them?"

"After I finish this job."

"The way things look, I'm happy to hear it. I'll see you this evening."

*   *   *

Possibly the best thing about the Quiller Case was what I learned going to New York City's prison for the second visit. If I'd had a weak heart, the first time I went to see Quiller would have caused an infarction. But on the second trip I was only mildly nervous. For more than a dozen years I'd been so afraid of Rikers that it colored my dreams, made me wake up in a thousand cold sweats. But the simple act of facing the object of my fears dispelled the bugaboo from my mind. That was a lesson that would last me the rest of my years.

Two different guards met me and showed the way down to the undocumented cell. When the door slammed behind me, I detected an odor. It was bodily but more than that. Not exactly offensive, it was more like a warning.

There was also a mild buzzing sound in the air. Looking up on a shelf he had for a few books, I saw that Quiller had set up a small electric fan, maybe to make it seem that a free breeze was coming from the outer world.

Quiller rose from his chair when I entered the cell. The whites of his eyes had darkened. His hair was tangled and there were streaks of gray throughout that I would have sworn had not been there before. And for some reason, the prisoner couldn't stand fully erect. It was as if he'd aged a decade or more in a few days.

"Mr. Quiller."

"Mr. Oliver." It was the first time he'd used my name.

"May I sit down?"

He nodded at the stool in front of his desk. I sat. Rather than lowering into his chair, he let himself fall backward.

"What's happened?" I asked.

He laced his fingers before his face, a penitent in desperate prayer.

"They've judged me. I'm lost."

I glanced at the wall and saw that the cockroach I'd seen on the last visit had died only a few inches farther on.

"A federal prosecutor was here," Quiller said. "I am now officially under arrest. I will be charged with murder and espionage. If I'm lucky, she said, I'll be sentenced to ADX Florence for life—as long as it lasts. My so-called friends have abandoned me. I have been condemned for my adherence to the truth." Somehow he managed to keep melodrama out of his tone.

"What about Roger Ferris?"

Quiller smiled. "Even the richest man in the world cannot defy this pack of hyenas."

I couldn't argue with the man. This was his domain, his own private tragedy.

"You can't fight them in open court?" I asked anyway.

"The court won't be open. I'm a threat to national security. My fate will be sealed in secret."

We sat in that fearful silence for a very long three or four minutes: the dead cockroach, the condemned convict, and me.

"You met Mathilda?" the doomed philosopher asked at last. His tone was almost hopeful.

"Yeah."

"She's an amazing woman, is she not?"

I nodded and said, "What's confusing is you and her together."

Alfie could have taken that comment to a very dark place. But all he did was wince and nod.

"I spent an entire lifetime being alone," he explained. "Then I met Mattie. She never tried to convince me that I was wrong. She just told me that she wouldn't dignify my arguments with reply. Dignify, with reply. That was what she said. I knew right then I'd been wrongheaded—about everything."

"Why?" I had to know if he felt the same way I did. There was no reason for the question beyond that.

"She was right," he said. "I had no dignity."

"What can I do for you, Mr. Quiller?"

"Are you an intelligent man, Mr. Oliver?"

"Compared to what?"

He smiled and then nodded.

I was escorted out by only one guard. His name tag read SILAS. I wondered if that was a first or last name. At the entrance to the visitor center I was about to walk off when Silas touched my forearm.

"This is the last time you'll be able to see him," the guard told me.

"Why is that?"

"The tit's run dry."

They were waiting at my car. Two men. Both white and of normal build, wearing suits and standing at ease.

"Mr. Oliver," the one in the lighter-colored cloth said.

"Yeah?"

"What did Quiller say to you?"

"Don't you have a microphone on him?"

"He put an electric fan in front of it," said the man in the darker clothes. "He's smart."

"He's my client," I said lightly. "I wouldn't want to betray that trust."

"You'll never get your money," the first man said.

"Some things are more important than money."

"Not if you're smart," said the second man.

"Who are you guys?" I asked.

"What did he say?" asked Second.

I took a moment, pretending to consider the request. But there was no choice.

"He asked me to put an ad in the online magazine *People-for-People,* from an interested aardvark."

"What was it supposed to say?" asked First.

"T-F-I-A-B-O-A-three-two-one-N."

"Did he tell you what that meant?" asked Second.

"No," I lied.

The men stared at me, maybe expecting a mental breakdown under the pressure. I had no doubt that my life was on the line.

"Be careful, Mr. Oliver, these are dangerous times," Second said.

"You want me to put the ad in?"

"No. We'll take it from here."

I drove home happy to be alive and outraged at the kind of world I had to live in.

30.

OLIYA WAS WAITING for me. We squandered three or four sentences and then I showed her the blowup mattress Aja stored in the closet of her office space. She thanked me and was about the process of making her bed when I went into the office. There I logged onto a bogus activity board and entered the real code Quiller gave me for his wife. The website was TINNY-TINY-AND-WRONG-614. I included my name and a temporary phone number. Then I lowered the rope ladder that led from the trapdoor to my upstairs apartment.

Before I could start the climb the cell phone dinged. The entire text consisted of one symbol—∞.

I camped out in the bedroom upstairs, not sleeping all that much. Those intermittent naps were dominated by the dream of having to split a thousand-pound boulder more or less evenly. There were no tools, and even if there had been I didn't have the skill or experience to accomplish such a task.

When I finally got up I sat at the end-edge of the bed so tired that standing seemed impossible.

One of my many burner phones was in a pants pocket on the floor at my feet. I snagged the slacks with a toe, lifted the phone, and texted the word *RED* to a number I knew by heart.

Six minutes later the little radio-phone chirped.

"Hey, Mel, what took you?"

"I just dropped Yuri off in Montreal. Drove the sucker up in the trunk. Gave him a little cash and a few addresses."

"How much cash?"

"Fifty thousand."

"I can cover it but it'll take a few weeks."

"Don't worry about it, brother. I like having you in my debt."

"You coming back down?"

"Thought I'd spend the night and cruise back in the morning."

"I'll call you."

Oliya and I got to Silbrig Haus by 8:30 a.m. The front gate knew us and our car. My grandmother met us at the front door. She was using a hollow silver walking stick, but that was the only concession she made to the wound.

"Who's this?" Grandma B asked, her wide eyes taking my bodyguard in.

"Oliya Ruez," she replied. "I'm here helping your grandson."

"He could sure use the help of a good woman," GB agreed.

"Daddy." Aja was coming through a middle foyer door.

There was lots of kissing and hugging, relief that everybody was still alive.

After a while the little crowd made it to the breakfast

room. I wasn't surprised that the exploded window had already been replaced.

"Roger joining us?" I asked.

"No. He had to go out of town," Brenda said.

"Where to?"

"He didn't say."

We were halfway through the celebratory meal when Monica showed up. She'd lost at least five pounds. Her hair was wild and there was a button missing on her blouse. She moved woodenly and her eyes were glazed. Looking almost as bad as Quiller had in the bowels of Rikers, she lurched to a chair and sat down on it, somehow askew.

"He's dying out there," were her first words to me.

Looking at her, I understood that what we had was never love. Pure love, like distilled nicotine, was as deadly as a bullet through the brain.

"He's fine," I said.

"No, he's not!" she yelled, knocking her heavy chair over as she leapt to her feet.

"Monica!" Grandma B commanded.

"It's okay, Grandma. She's worried about her man."

"It's not a joke, Joe," Monica said, trying to keep her words in order.

"I solved the problem," I said. "Oliya here is gonna take you out to Brownsville, pick up Coleman, and then go to Art Tomey's office. There your husband can tell them everything he's done. He'll lose the money and he'll probably get fired, but at least he'll be free and nobody will come after him. You might have to get a job."

Monica righted the chair and sat back down. Her fists

271

were clenched. Her eyes, like fish eyes, were perpetually stunned and unblinking.

"What did you do?" she asked.

"More than I should have, that's for sure."

"Don't fuck with me, Joe. I need to know what to tell him."

"Oliya knows how to get there. Art has already made the deal with the feds."

"And what about the people after him?"

"They're not gonna be a problem anymore. You're just gonna have to take my word on that."

Her startled look turned to hatred. If she had a loaded gun I am sure she would have used it.

"I need to go to him now. Now," Monica insisted. "Now."

"Mom, we haven't finished breakfast yet."

Standing up again, Monica said, "Now."

I turned to Oliya and nodded, saying, "You can take the Lincoln."

The lethal jack-of-all-trades stood too. She motioned to my ex and the two left without another word.

"What's wrong with her?" Aja asked the universe.

"She's in love."

I found Forthright's observation center on the third floor of the mansion. There were a dozen monitors watched by a single sentry who moved her head back and forth across the screens like a barn cat on the hunt for her next kill.

Forthright was smoking a cigar, seated in a big blocky chair pressed up against the far corner of the large room. The outsize piece of furniture most resembled an old-time electric chair.

"I was just getting ready to come down and find you," he announced.

"Where's Roger?" I said. "I need to speak to him."

"I doubt that."

"You know something I don't?"

"Quiller's dead."

"How?"

"Cyanide, they say."

"Who says?"

"The news, Rikers Island, federal prosecutors, probably every conspiracy theorist in America."

"They said he was under arrest?"

"It wasn't so clear. They're saying that he'd been taken into custody for selling state secrets some time ago but only yesterday was when they charged him."

Of course he killed himself. Of course he did. They'd boxed him in, probably threatened Mathilda . . .

"You got a car I can borrow, Forth?"

I parked the mirror-bright chrome-colored Jaguar under the building I lived and worked in. Making my way upstairs I swore never to drive that four-wheeled looking glass any-where else.

The key dragged a little in the lock, but I had too much on my mind to worry about office repairs.

"Mr. Oliver," a woman's voice said somewhat graciously as I crossed the threshold. "It's so good to meet you at last."

Other than myself, there were three people in the room. The older woman who greeted me and two suited men, one big and the other slight. They were all on the lighter side of the skin spectrum.

Upon hearing the woman's voice, my mind cleared from its muddle. The first decision I had to make was—fight, flight, or wait and see. There was a longish hallway behind me and I had to believe the men were armed. My own gun was in a pocket. Getting to it would have taken too many seconds. I could have tried a physical assault, but I was outnumbered and the guys had a street sense of professionalism about them.

So, I affected a smile and said, "Hello."

The woman was standing next to Aja's desk with an expression on her lips that she probably thought was a smile. Not all that much past seventy, she was around five-nine, with a rose-colored serape draped over a darker maroon dress, or maybe just a skirt that was ankle-length.

"We were hoping you'd come back sooner than later."

"Who are you?" I asked pleasantly.

The smaller henchman approached me holding out both hands and reaching toward my chest. When he got close enough I jutted my palm into his sternum, making him stumble back a step or two.

"I don't get patted down in my own office."

The larger guy and his partner were moving toward me. There was just enough time to draw out and fire the pistol. I would have done so if the lady hadn't spoken up.

"Billings, Ray, Mr. Oliver is correct. This is his property."

Billings and Ray moved back to their previous positions.

"My name is Cassandra Ferris-Brathwaite," the woman said. "You've heard of me?"

"My grandmother might be your stepmother someday soon. So I guess we'll be step-siblings or cousins or something."

She lost the false smile completely.

I thought, goody.

"Would you like to take a seat?" Cassie offered.

"You don't tell me what to do in my office."

"No reason to be stubborn," she said.

"What do you want?"

"I need your help with a problem I'm having."

"I already have a job, two actually."

Nodding, she said, "Working for my father."

"What do you want?" I asked again.

"My father is old. He's been making bad decisions. That's not going to work because thousands of people depend on our company for their daily bread. MDLT needs new blood at the helm."

"As I understand it, that's for the courts to decide."

Shrugging, she said, "Maybe you can help."

"I don't see how."

"You have my father's trust. You can speak to him for me and my brother."

"And what would you have me say?"

"That it's time for him to step down."

"Look, I don't have anything to do with your business squabbles. Your father hired me to find out if Alfred Xavier Quiller was guilty of the crimes he was charged for."

"And was he?"

"I don't think so."

"And were you able to exonerate him, to keep Zyron International from bunging him in an underground cell?"

Hm.

"The old man's time is running out," she said into my bemused silence.

"He is old," I agreed. "Why not just wait?"

"Don't fuck with me. I could have you back in Rikers," she said, snapping her fingers, "like that."

275

I was thinking that this was probably the one responsible for my grandmother getting shot.

"I know what my father is afraid of, Mr. Oliver."

"And what is that, Mrs. Ferris-Brathwaite?"

"The truth."

"You mean if I told him that zero is neither a positive nor a negative integer he'd scream and jump out the window?"

The little guy had a large nose. Under that schnozzle his rubbery lips formed into an understanding smile. You never know when someone will appreciate a good joke.

"I think we should sit down," Cassandra said. "Won't you join me?"

The boss, of course, sat in the swivel chair behind the desk. The henchmen took their natural positions, standing more or less at attention behind her.

I pulled one of three visitors' chairs up as close as I could to the desk. That way the pistol pocket was hidden.

"What do you know about A. X. Quiller?" I asked the lady in charge.

She took her time with the question, relishing it.

"It's time for my father to step down," she said as if it were an answer.

"He thinks that passing the company over to its employees is a better move."

"Corporations are capitalist entities," the lady said, quoting something. "You know where I learned that?"

"No."

"My father." She delivered the line like a bad actor on a country stage.

Sitting back, pretending that the words had the intended effect, I let my right hand fall to its knee.

"Um," I articulated, "maybe he learned something along the way since then."

"My father," she said with true spite. "Did you know that he competed in fencing at the '58 Olympics?"

"That was Rome, wasn't it?"

"He didn't achieve a medal, but our family gave so much money that they made him an assistant coach to the American team for many years after that."

My client's daughter liked to parse out information like treats to a slavering lapdog.

"He worked with the team in '76, in Montreal." Her eyes took on a demonic cast. "That's where he met eighteen-year-old Valeria Ursini. Have you ever heard of George Laurel?"

"No." My expectant heart was pounding so hard that if I were hooked up to a lie detector it would have been shooting off fireworks.

"He was murdered at Yale in '77."

"How did you get my name, Mrs. Ferris-Brathwaite?"

"Aren't you interested in George Laurel?"

"No, ma'am."

"Why not?"

"Answer my question first."

The heiress did not like to be spoken to like that. It took her a moment to compose herself. As she suppressed rage I leaned over to rest my left elbow on the edge of Aja's desk. With that torque to my torso, my right hand now rested on the pistol pocket.

"Move it back," Billings, the larger bodyguard, said.

I did so, leaving the right hand where it lay.

"A confidential agent at Zyron International passed your

name along. They had done some work for me recently and you were involved in the same, um, arena."

"A. X. Quiller."

"Mr. Quiller keeps in-depth files on the rich and powerful. My father has an entry in that record. Did you know that?"

"Quiller's dead."

"Yes. But the records still exist."

"Okay. And that's why you're here?"

"My father had an affair with the Ursini girl. When she finished with the competition he gave her a scholarship to Yale. She met another, age-appropriate man, George Laurel. When my father found out he had Laurel killed."

"You're sure of that?"

"Oh yes. Quite sure."

"He told you all this?"

"I need you to deliver a message to my father," she said. "I need you to explain to him that it would be in his best interest to step down."

"Really? You *have* talked to the man, haven't you?"

"If . . . he does not accept this request, I would like you to help us in other ways."

Whoa. Detective work is often dubious, but this was the first time I'd ever been asked to take a life. I think that maybe that truth was writ large across my face.

"You could be a rich man," the lady offered.

I moved my hand away from the gun because if I pulled it out there'd be three, or four, dead bodies to clean up and cart off.

"How much?" I asked with complete insincerity.

She spoke a number.

"I'd like to be rich," I said, this time truthfully. "Really I would. Your father's never mentioned this George guy you're talking about, and when I asked him if Quiller had anything on him, he said no."

"Of course he did," the lady said, balling the words up in a sneer. "He's a murderer."

"Patricide is also murder," I pointed out.

The lady looked directly into my eyes. The effect was chilling. I looked up at the gunsels behind her.

"Don't worry about them," she said. "They're loyal to me."

"Will you be telling anyone else about this?"

"You think I'm a fool?"

"I think you have a brother."

"No, Mr. Oliver, my brother is a follower. I don't bother him with the details of what must be done."

I believed her. I wanted to shoot her. Instead I took in a deep breath.

On the exhalation I said, "I'm going to need half up front."

"So you can take it and run?"

"In a way," I agreed. "I mean, once he's dead, people are definitely going to look at me, look for me."

Cassandra Ferris-Brathwaite went to some deep inner place reserved for psychotics and the infinitely wealthy. I silently swore that I'd never again take a case like this. Grandma B was right about her boyfriend and his world.

"Ten percent," she said, and I knew that I was reprieved.

"In cash. Here. Tomorrow at six."

Giving me a curt nod, she ascended from the swivel chair without needing the aid of her arms. Aged Aphrodite.

"My men will be here then," she said.

I followed the entourage to the door and then watched them head down the hall.

I had twenty-four hours.

31.

I LITERALLY STAGGERED back to Aja's chair and sat down hard. The springs were still juddering when there came a knock on the door.

Pistol in hand I went to an awkward corner, pointed the gun at the midpoint of the door, and said aloud, "Who is it?"

"Olo."

It took a moment for the name I'd coined to break through the fear.

"Olo?"

"Yes, Joe, it's me."

When I opened the door and saw my Mel-provided body-guard I wanted to hug her, I really did. She saw the embrace in my posture and I think she would have allowed it. But I held back.

"Did you see them?" I asked.

"I heard you talking in here," she said. "I waited by the door in case of trouble. And then, when they came out, I went down around the corner until they were gone. That was Cassandra Brathwaite, wasn't it?"

"You know her?"

"Int-Op has done work for her before."

"I thought I was dead."

"Feels kinda good when you come out the other side, doesn't it?"

"I can see why Melquarth likes you so much."

I kept a fifth of sixteen-year-old hundred-proof single-malt Laphroaig Scotch in my office. Oliya joined me in a shot.

"How did it go with Monica and her man?" I asked while pouring the second hit.

"She was nervous all the way until we got to Mookie's. But the minute they saw each other they were fine. Better than that. They started taking off each other's clothes in the back seat on the way to the lawyer's."

"Makes you wanna think twice before falling in love."

"What's next, Joe?"

"I need to go out of town again."

"I'll come along."

"No. I want you to watch over Aja and her great-grandmother."

She took me in with her eyes and then nodded.

In the morning I called Minta Kraft.

"Hello?"

"Hey, Minta, Joe Oliver here."

"Mr. Oliver."

"I need to talk to Mathilda."

"Have you heard from her?"

"No. I'm calling because of what they're saying about her husband."

"She's gone."

"Gone where?"

"I don't know."

"How can that be? You're the one that drives her around."

"When she didn't come down for breakfast, I went to her room and she was just gone."

The story sounded true enough—as far as it went.

"If she calls will you tell me?" I asked.

"Yes. And if you hear from her please let me know."

Three hours later I was on a flight to Blue Grass Airport in Lexington, Kentucky, birthplace of the incomparable Muhammad Ali.

There I encountered a smiling redheaded young woman standing behind a counter. Her name tag read SHAWNEE. Shawnee managed the local car rental concession at the far end of the small airport.

"I need a car," I told her.

"What kind you want?" she replied, a big smile on her face.

"As small as you got."

"We have a six-year-old Volkswagen. That's the smallest. It's in good shape 'cause nobody hardly ever wants it."

It took about four hours to get to the tiny town of Peanut in southeastern Kentucky. The Wikipedia entry still described it as a coal miners' town with a mostly Black population. Main Street was paved and quite lovely, but many of the roads that led away from the downtown were still dirt lanes.

Across the street from city hall was a big glittery cube that encompassed an entire country block. It was, and is, the most anomalous piece of architecture I've ever seen.

It could have been a beached spacecraft as far as anyone might know.

I went into the city hall, finding what once might have been called an effeminate Black man sitting behind a small oak desk in a large atrium, alone.

"May I help you?" the pecan-colored dandy asked. His suit was very yellow and his shirt a cobalt blue. The slant of his satin white necktie reminded me of a smile made vertical. It brought the grin out in me.

"Yes, I'm looking for a young woman named Mathilda Prim."

"Oh," he said exhibiting some surprise. "Mattie. I haven't thought about her in some years. What's your business with her?"

"Is she in town? The last time I saw her she was in Long Island, New York, but she said that she spent some part of the year down here."

"What's your name?" the little seated man asked.

"Joe. Joe Oliver."

"I'm Peter Southbrook." He stood and held out a hand for me to shake.

"Nice to meet you, Mr. Southbrook."

"You too, Mr. Oliver."

We stood there for an awkward moment, as if maybe the conversation was over.

"So," I said. "What about Mathilda Prim?"

"Well, Joe, I haven't seen Mattie in a few years. But that doesn't mean she's not here."

"She still have people in Peanut?"

"Most of them moved away some time after she did."

"Sounds like a migration," I said.

"They were a tough bunch," Peter informed. "Fightin',

drugs, and there was what you might call a looseness in their women."

Mr. Southbrook did not approve of the Prim Bunch, that much was sure. His dislike of them might have tinted my presence in his eyes.

"That hotel at the north end of the street," I said.

"Minerva's Inn? What about it?"

"That the only inn in town?"

"You're planning to stay?"

"I would like to find Mathilda. From what you tell me it might take a bit."

Peter Southbrook took a few moments to digest my plans.

Finally he said, "Minerva's is the only inn in twenty-two miles. But there's no businessmen in town around now. You should get a room pretty easy."

"Thank you, Mr. Southbrook. You've been very helpful."

"That's my job."

"You're the welcome wagon?"

"I'm the mayor of Peanut," he said proudly.

"Down here all by yourself. Is this some kind of holiday?"

He laughed. "No, sir, most of the municipal offices are upstairs. I sit down here alone so people can see what they voted for."

Minerva's Inn was walking distance from the town hall. It stood four stories and looked refurbished. The bricks were all neat, cleaned, and repointed. There was a flower box outside each window, all of them blooming with multicolored mums and daisies.

I wasn't so much aware of the stifling heat until I walked into the overlarge guesthouse.

It must've been thirty degrees cooler in there.

I counted fourteen paces from the front door to the reception desk. There sat a bronze-skinned round woman wearing a floral dress. She seemed to be bubbling with goodwill.

"Hello," she erupted. "I'm Wilma. Please, have a seat."

The chair was fashioned from dark wood and was upholstered with turquoise felt that matched the color of the thick carpeting.

I sat and said, "Nice to meet you, Wilma. My name is Joe."

It was then I saw it. The smiling hotelier was completely without empathy. I was nothing more than the cause for a brief, unpleasant performance. I think that she saw the revelation in my eyes.

"How can I help you, Joe?" she said, her brilliant smile having dimmed by half.

"I need a room for a night or two."

"Oh. I'm so sorry. We're booked for the next week."

"Doesn't look that busy."

"A group of technicians are coming in this evening."

"Technicians?"

"They come down here sometimes, to work at the Big Nickel."

"That metal building down the street?"

"Yes," she said, a little impatiently.

"What do they do there?"

"I wouldn't know. They built it two years ago and hired about eight hundred Peanutians." She pronounced the last word the way one would refer to the inhabitants of Venus.

"Some kind of science lab?"

"Is there anything else I can do for you, Joe?"

"Mayor Southbrook told me that there were lots of rooms available at Minerva's."

"Mayor Southbrook doesn't keep the reservations log."

The smile was gone.

Outside again I felt the heat. For the first time in a long while I wished I had a bigger car. The cramped seating of a Volkswagen Bug is not conducive to sleep. But that was the only place I had to rest. I was sure this was the place that would lead me to Mathilda Prim.

I'd spent a good deal of my adult life around the rich and powerful. As a cop I stood outside protecting their properties and their secrets. As a PI I went into those lives. In all those years I never felt much empathy for my *betters*. But Mathilda was different. I wanted her secure and adored the way millions felt about Jackie O and Princess Di. It was a powerful feeling. I don't believe I'd ever want anyone to feel that way about me.

"Mr. Oliver."

Walking on the hot pavement, I was transported as my grandmother sometimes was in church. I felt that if I found Quiller's widow I'd be saved or, at least, successful.

"Mr. Oliver! Yoo-hoo!"

The words were like a nagging thought you want to forget.

"Mr. Oliver!"

Wilma was running up the block in my direction. She wasn't built for that kind of locomotion. I stopped and then began to walk toward her. Relieved, she stopped completely, bending over almost far enough to touch her knees.

"What's the problem, Wilma?"

She had to take in six or seven sorely needed breaths before answering.

"I just realized that we have one vacant room. It's a room without a number and so it doesn't have a place on the computerized spreadsheet."

Taking in a deep breath, she stood up straight.

"I'm sorry if I was rude to you," she added. "It's been a long day."

32.

THE NUMBERLESS ROOM was a slender aisle, seven or eight feet wide but long, twenty, twenty-two feet. Above my head was a ceiling that I could reach up and touch. The bed was not quite queen-size and the floor, lacquered pine. There was a desk fashioned from pressboard and finished with a dark linoleum sheet. The chair was plastic and red and the window, not large enough to jump out of, looked out on Main Street.

It was warm on the fourth floor but not hot like out on the street. I sat on the red chair, didn't like the way it felt, and so went to sit on the bed. After a minute or so I went into the bathroom. It was equipped with toilet, sink on a stalk, a slender horizontal mirror that was like a slash across the wall, and a shower stall with no door or curtain.

I remember thinking that this was the future of working-class vacationing. Everything you could ask for but less.

I called Roger Ferris, only getting his voice on an answering service. I left him the hotel phone number, then called Aja.

"Hi, Daddy. Where are you?"

"In Black Appalachia."

"I thought Appalachia was all white."

"Wherever you got poor people, there's gonna be black skins somewhere."

"Okay."

"How you doin'?"

"I'm okay. Mama called. She said that she and Coleman are going back home to fix up the house. You think that's safe?"

"Yeah. I do."

"So he's not going to jail?"

"Naw. He'll turn state's evidence and they'll just file it away."

"Oliya's here. You wanna talk to her?"

"No. Not now."

"She's pretty wonderful. Taught me how to flip somebody if he grabs me and showed me the twelve exercises I need to be strong."

"You always needed a big sister, honey."

"I miss you. Come home soon."

"I will."

Somewhere around 10:00 the room phone rang. I didn't know I was asleep and so the old-fashioned ring startled me up to my feet. The bell sounded once more before I was sure enough to answer.

"Hello?"

"Joseph."

"Oh, Roger. Hey. Yeah. I left you the number. Right."

"You need to throw some water on your face?"

That sounded like a fine idea.

In the condensed bathroom I used the lime-colored

bowl-shaped sink to splash my face and neck. In the slit of a mirror I could see that I needed a shave. I had a razor somewhere. Where?

I dumped a double handful of water on my head.

"I'm back, Roger."

"You had something to tell me?"

"I went to see Quiller just a few hours before he died."

"He say anything useful?"

"I don't know, maybe. They told him that he was going to a federal supermax in Colorado."

"Okay. But him being dead means that's hardly a problem."

"Not for him, but how about for you?"

"I don't know what you're talking about. I already said for you to drop the investigation."

"I know. I only went there to see if there was anything I could do for the man."

"Why? He was a racist."

I was using the banter to gather my thoughts.

"Maybe," I allowed. "But I'm a professional. I went in and told him I was trying to prove whether he did something and if something was done to him. He was free to think what he wanted and I am too."

"Okay. I get you. Is there anything else you need to say?"

"Yeah. What is it you wanted out of this investigation?"

"I already told you that."

"No, man. No. You didn't put me on this job to protect the rights of the individual under the Constitution. Uh-uh."

"So what is it you think I'm after, Joe?"

That was the question, the only question that needed answering.

"When I got to my office last night your daughter and a couple of thugs were waiting for me."

"Cassandra?"

"You got any other daughters?"

"What did she want?"

"The helm of MDLT."

"And what did that have to do with you?"

I'm a student of human nature, not a master of it. But I knew the answer to that question would be like striking a match next to a vat of gasoline. Somebody was bound to get burned.

"She wants Quiller's blackmail file and also for me to ask you kindly to step down as CEO."

"Step down or what?"

"I think she thought you might be afraid of whatever Quiller had in his files," I said.

"What does she have to do with him?"

Instead of responding to that query I said, "If you refuse to stand down I am to put a bullet in your heart."

After a very long silence, Roger whispered, "She said that?"

"Yeah."

"And what did you tell her?"

"I asked how much. After she bowled me over with a number I told her, hell yeah."

I turned on the lamp set on a ledge beside the small bed. My long room looked shabbier under the stark white light.

"What does she want with the files?" Roger asked.

"I could ask you the same thing."

"What are you talking about?"

"Valeria Ursini."

The silence was intense.

"What about her?"

"Was she your girlfriend?"

"My wife was dead by then and it was only a brief affair."

"Your daughter thinks you had Valeria's boyfriend, George Laurel, murdered. She told me that Quiller's files prove it."

"No."

"Did you have Sola Prendergast kill George?"

"No. No, I did not."

"Definitely? You had nothing to do with it?"

"Yes, nothing."

"Then why's she so sure?"

"Joe, you have to believe me. I did not have that poor boy killed. Valeria and I had parted ways by the time she enrolled at Yale."

"But she got into Yale with your help."

"She was a straight-A student who had competed in the Olympics. My college fund simply recognized talent."

"Then why is Cassandra so certain?" I asked. "She doesn't seem like she's some kind of conspiracy theorist."

"Do you plan to kill me, Joe?"

"If I did I sure the fuck wouldn't warn you about it."

"You're down in Kentucky?"

"Uh-huh."

"If you get your hands on those files, I'd like to see them."

With those words he hung up.

I lay back on the mattress and fell right to sleep.

Before the Quiller Case I remembered very few dreams. And even then the great majority of the reveries were about running water or some such thing so that I'd wake up and go to the toilet.

That night I was lost in a deep forest, and someone, I didn't know who, was after me. I'd take a few steps and then stop, afraid that the sound of my footsteps would call down my enemy. That was the entirety of the dream; I'd take a few steps, get frightened by sounds of leaves rustling, then crouch down—naked and afraid.

The doorbell of the lean room was a double gong that reverberated a bit after sounding. I was sure that this was the horn of the men who were hunting me. I got so frightened that I sat up in the bed.

The red digits on the digital clock read 2:56.

The double gong sounded.

I was trying to think what kind of alarm it was when it sounded again.

"Who is it?"

"It is I, King Oliver."

I opened the door and there stood Mathilda Prim.

She was wearing a form-fitting stark-white silk dress with black ink splotches here and there. The hem was short but still presentable. In her right hand she held a fifth bottle with no label.

"Kentucky hooch," she said through a lovely smile.

"Come in."

The room was so narrow that I had to back away to give her space through which to enter.

"They gave you the smallest room in the house," she commented.

"So small it doesn't even rank a number."

She laughed and handed me the bottle.

"Did I wake you?"

"From a sleep that the whole world wants to come out of. Here, have a seat."

I pulled the red plastic chair up to the bottom edge of the bed. She sat on it and I took the mattress.

Once we were settled, the repartee temporarily evaporated.

"I don't think the man who designed this chair had much of a feeling for a woman's posterior," she said, trying to get comfortable on the uncomfortable chair.

"It's not really made for people," I observed. "We could change seats."

"No, it's okay."

Sometimes, when people get together and there's nothing to say, there are moments of quiet discomfort. We were still for a few moments, but somehow it felt . . . cozy.

I finally said, "I'm truly sorry about your husband."

"He gave you the code. I was happy to see that it was you. Also that you deciphered my little peanut sign."

That was the beginning of a longer silence. I got up and went to the bathroom to retrieve glasses wrapped in waxy paper. I brought these out and poured us both a shot and a half.

"Thank you," Mathilda said when I handed her glass over.

She took a sip. I did too. It felt a little like a forgotten ritual that had survived all of the species of humanity.

"What now?" I asked.

"You mean after . . . ?"

"Yeah."

We drank a little more.

"Alfie was dealing with so much. When I met him all he had was his mind and what he hated. And then, when he tried to change, it killed him."

"You think, I mean, you think he really killed himself?"

"One way or another."

She raised her head and gazed at me, deeply. Her dark lips were tinted red. The eyeshadow was mild luminescence without a specific color.

"Peanut is a hard town," she said. "And my family was the toughest nut in the bag. We came up fighting and drinking. I was in trouble since the age of fourteen."

"Yeah?"

She grinned, at my brevity, I think.

"Yeah," she agreed. "I got tired of it and left, burned the candle at both ends and found out that I was good in school. Real good. By the time I met Alfie I'd read my way through the library. He needed me, in his mind he needed me."

She took another sip, then moved from the chair to the bed.

With her back turned to me she said, "Hold me."

I wrapped my arms around her from behind. She leaned back and I felt a tremor, not knowing which of us it came from.

"I always carried a knife with me since I was eleven. My brothers taught me how to fight and Daddy taught me how to drink. Whenever I read a book, it was at the private library in Miss Donaldson's garage because the Prims thought reading was for punks."

"They'd beat you if you picked up a book?"

"Like an egg."

I held on a little tighter.

She lifted my hand and kissed it.

"Anyway, I left Peanut and went to Lexington. Up there I figured out that I had to get outta the South before I killed one'a them white men. I wasn't used to white people because my whole life was spent in a colored town. Up in Syracuse, around the university, I didn't get so mad and I hunkered down on an education."

I kissed the back of her neck and she leaned harder.

"By the time I met Alfie I was ready to say something. You know what I mean?"

"Yeah."

"And he was ready to listen. Up until that time I was either in my mind alone or just physically in the world. Even in school. But when I met Alfie, even though I hated things about him, we could hear each other and understand."

I pulled her even closer and breathed in the clean scent of her hair. We stayed quiet like that for five minutes at least.

"What can I do for you?" I asked.

"You're doin' it."

"Why did you send me that infinity symbol?"

"Isn't that funny? It's either infinity or a peanut."

"Yeah. I was happy to hear from you."

"Are you feelin' this?"

I nodded and she turned to me.

The bed was too small but we made it work. There was something very wrong about what we were doing, but we dropped the guilt to the floor along with our clothes.

We kept the light on and watched each other do everything like teenagers discovering the power of adult connection. It was a first for me and maybe for her.

Sleep never felt so good.

33.

STRONG SUNLIGHT ILLUMINATED the shaded window. I didn't remember opening my eyes.

"You awake?" she asked.

I turned and kissed her. She caressed my jawline with three gentle fingers.

"I hope I'm not pregnant."

I didn't have a reply.

"Don't you?" she asked.

I sat up and looked down on her. She grinned.

"You're a fool, King Oliver."

"That why you like me?"

She climbed out of the bed. I watched her long brown body sashay toward the bathroom and sighed, the venal forest surrounding Mel's country home a million miles away.

She came out of the bathroom and I went in. Then we reconvened on the bed, sitting in half lotus and facing each other.

"Is this what you came down here for?" Mathilda Prim asked.

"Hoping for this, but I had other intentions too."

"Like what?"

"The answers to a few questions."

"Let's get dressed and go down for breakfast."

"They serve this early?"

"For me they do."

The breakfast room had twelve round tables, each with four chairs. We were the only customers and so sat in the far corner next to a window overlooking a stand of dogwood trees.

The waitstaff, made up of two women servers and a cook, all called Mathilda Miss Prim with great reverence.

"You own this hotel?"

"Alfie did. Now, I guess, it falls to me."

"So you're the one who told Big Wilma to come runnin' after me?"

"She called the mayor because you mentioned him. Then she called me."

The fare was simple enough. Soft scrambled eggs, bacon, biscuits, and black coffee.

"So, King, what else did you want?"

"I called your assistant looking for you."

"And what did Minta have to say?"

"That you had disappeared and to tell her if I found you."

"You didn't, did you?"

"No. What's her story?"

"She'd been seduced by Alfie's earlier theories."

"The three-fifths rule?"

"Uh-huh. That's why she came to work for him. She's

much more on the side of the Men of Action than she is with me."

"Then why would you have her as an assistant?"

"Her self-appointed job was to guard me and to keep an open eye. It was easier to let her and hers think I was oblivious than to try and make it on my own."

"That's playin' a little close to the bone, ain't it?"

Mathilda flipped her right hand, dismissing my question.

"Alfie set up a plan for me to get away from them when I got the message you sent."

"How long ago did you come up with that?"

"When we were in Togo—"

"You were with him when he was running from the government?"

"We got together at least once a month."

"You were there when the guy tried to poison him?"

"Yes." Her expression turned hard, even unrelenting. "That white man was on the floor with the blood and buttermilk all over."

"Damn."

Mathilda had told me about her rough upbringing; this story cemented the tales.

"Okay," I said. "What about the Big Nickel?"

She sighed and reached across the table to hold my hand.

"I know we have to talk about these things, that you have a job to do. But it was really wonderful to have a smart boyfriend and not have to rip out my heart over it."

It was, I thought, a wonderful thing when, unbidden, a smile comes to your lips.

"I needed to be with you last night," she said as an

apology. "It's been hard bein' around those crazy hateful people hopin' they could set Alfie free."

"We can talk later if you want. I mean, my job was to find out why they had Alfred in stir. I haven't got the full story on that yet, but that's another thing. I just wanna know what's goin' on."

"Like what?"

"All kinds of things. That big building, for instance."

"The Big Nickel is a spider farm," she said.

"That thing about their webs replacing steel?"

"More than that. The strength of the webbing plus their light weight makes a material that could be the new plastic. Space-age stuff. When Alfie told me he was going to build a factory I said I wanted it in my town."

"I was under the impression that this town doesn't like you very much."

"Maybe not. But this is where I came from and so we built it here. Anything else?"

"I'm sorry I couldn't save your husband."

Mathilda's head reared back like a creature that felt threatened. Her eyes seemed to darken. There was definitely violence in that stare. And then, suddenly, it was gone. She smiled slightly and shook her head.

"We were living the kind of life that made about as much sense as an ostrich chick in a sparrow's nest," she said. "I mean, we were rich and knew all kinds of right-wing revolutionaries, bankers, and politicos. They didn't like me, but Alfie could do anything and they'd just have to grin and bear it."

"But all that changed," I supposed.

"One time he went to a rally that the Men of Action and

maybe half a dozen other groups held. I went. I mean, there was a smattering of Black and brown people there too. All of 'em thinkin' that the problem was what they called the Left and the Deep State. I listened for a while, and then, when Alfie was headed for the stage, I left. Went out to California and got a job at a diner in Venice usin' my cousin Bernice MacDaniels's ID and social security number. I didn't care about bein' rich and famous. I didn't need it if I had to listen to people bein' fools."

"What happened?"

"Two months went by. I met this car thief named Lido. We were seein' each other kinda and I was thinkin' about goin' back to school for a PhD in literature. Then one night, after Lido had gone, there was a knock on my door. Lido had given me a pistol and usually I would'a grabbed it, but for some reason I wasn't worried and opened up. Alfie was standin' there in a jean jacket and jeans. He'd given a private detective Bernice's name and finally found me.

"We talked for six hours. I told him that I will not suffer fools, that his people didn't understand a damn word of what they were sayin', that not one'a the people I heard onstage could'a passed his suffrage test. He knew it was true. He knew. When I told him that I wouldn't come back he said that if I would he'd change. Then he said that he'd change anyway and I wrote a good-bye note to Lido and went back with him."

"How long was that before he fled the country?"

"Six months, maybe seven. By then his friends had started to turn on him. They wanted to use his blackmail file and he said no, that some people didn't need their lives destroyed by a knife in the back."

"I thought they said that he ran because the government was on him about secrets he shared with the Russians?"

"Oh yeah, right. Uh. Can you imagine my Alfie givin' secrets to the Russians? But he didn't have any friends left. Bein' with me didn't cut the cord—it hacked it off."

"Speaking of birth, what about your son, Claxton Akim?"

"What about him?"

"Where is he?"

For the first time I felt suspicion coming from her. She had to swallow her maternal instincts before saying, "There's a woman I met in school who lives in Wyoming. Claxton is with her until he can be safe with me."

"Will that be soon?" I asked.

"With Alfie gone," she admitted sadly.

"And now you control everything that was his?"

"Yeah. Why?"

"I have something to ask you for."

"What?"

"Could I get the specs on the space cannon?"

"For what?"

I explained, in brief, about Antrobus, adding, "It's purely business and I'm quite sure that he won't give the secrets away."

"I trust you, King. But you'll have to do something for me."

"Of course."

"Alfie left me three things of value: a fortune in a Swiss bank account, our son, and a fat suitcase."

"What's in the suitcase?"

"A special-built computer attached to a ten-thousand-gigabyte memory drive."

"The blackmail file?"

"The password is Ten Thousand Things."

"Oh...kay."

"I want you to take the suitcase."

"And do what with it?"

"Destroy it, sell it, read about the people in it, condemning those you think deserve damnation."

"I thought I heard that Alfred had a guy that was going to release all the information to the world if something happened to him."

"There was a man," Mathilda said, nodding. "But he was from the way Alfie was before he met me. We were both pretty sure that he'd attack the Left and left-leaning people on the Right. At the end there we didn't even know what to do with the files."

"So does this guy expect you to turn over this database?"

"Years ago Alfie told him that there was an automatic code that would send him the files seventy-two hours after he was unable to cancel the delivery system."

"He was in jail more'n three days," I speculated.

"Yeah. But I'm pretty sure he had one of the guards making the call for him."

"But," I said, "I mean, wouldn't whoever had him in there have figured out what the guard was doing and either pay him off or monitor him or something?"

That was the one and only time that Mathilda had what I'd call a haughty look on her face.

"Alfie was a genius," she said. "He had the answer terminal send out a thousand random phone calls with the same abort message. Nobody would be able to find the guy that should get the message."

"So what happens now?"

"Doesn't matter. Alfie's man no longer has a connection to the real files. I'm the only one that has it."

It was a head scratcher, to say the least. But it really brought up only one important question.

"Who was it that had your husband captured and imprisoned here?"

Looking at me, Mathilda smiled.

"A while before things got crazy, Minta told me that she'd gotten a message from Alfie that he wanted me to meet someone. She drove me to a building on Seventh Avenue and brought me to an office. There Cassandra Ferris-Brathwaite was waiting."

"Whoa."

"You know her?"

"Yes, I do. What did she want?"

"She offered me one percent of MDLT stock if I would grant her access to Alfie's files."

"Eight billion dollars," I equated.

"I told her that my husband did not share that information with me. I said he had a man that was in charge of distributing that data."

"Did she believe you?"

"After that was when Alfie was hunted down and brought here. But I've had that suitcase over a year now. And when Alfie had you reach out to me, he was saying that you were the man that could handle it."

"How many files are on it?" I asked my temporary lover.

"I don't know exactly. Thousands. Tens of thousands."

"Where'd they all come from?"

"Official files from all around the world. You know Alfie never slept and his mind was always sharp, no matter how hard he was thinking. He broke computer codes in every nation, for dozens of police departments, government agencies, and databases of the rich. Then he'd hire individual agents to research the things he found."

"Knowledge is power," I said, more to myself than to her.

"When he told me about it I asked him how he would feel if somebody exposed him like that."

"I'm surprised he didn't ask that question himself."

"We had a special connection. It was like if we looked into each other we saw ourselves. I mean, just because I was with you last night don't mean I didn't love him. I did. I do."

It was what one might call an impossible moment. With the potential information on the giga-drive I could have built myself an empire—for good or evil. I could have become a modern-day Talleyrand. A puppet master.

"What do you say, Joe?"

"You wanna go upstairs and lie down for a while?"

We spent hours together in my tiny room. There was a good deal of temporary romance and erotic derring-do. But much of the time we spent talking and sharing little pieces of our lives that wouldn't matter to anyone, not even our solitary selves, unless they were there—with us.

By the time I fell asleep I couldn't have imagined anything, anywhere else in the world.

When I awoke again, at around 3:00 a.m., Mathilda was gone.

On the floor next to the bed was a fat brown suitcase. It didn't have a lock. What good would that have done? I set up the contrivance on the cheap desk and sat, naked, on the red plastic chair.

When I turned on the computer, the first screen asked for the password. I entered *Ten Thousand Things*. The second screen asked for search parameters.

In the morning I packed up my car and drove to the Blue Grass Airport. There I made a deal with the manager of the car rental service to buy the Volkswagen.

It was a sixteen-hour drive. I stopped twice for gas and food, and once to make a call to Melquarth.

"Hello?"

"Hey, Mel."

"Where are you?"

"Harrisburg, Pennsylvania."

"What can I do you for?"

"You in town?"

"Just about to leave for a watchmakers' convention in Chi."

"Mind if I stay at the place in Staten Island for a minute?"

"You know the codes. I kenneled the dogs so all you got to do is relax."

34.

OTHER THAN THE computer interface and the huge memory drive, there was a sleeve in the suitcase that contained a velvet sack filled with a good many seemingly flawless emeralds along with a system of key chains holding somewhere around a hundred individual keys. Folded into a cream-colored envelope was a twelve-page document concerning the Quiller Cannon. There was also a letter, scrawled on parchment, in what I suspected was Alfred Xavier Quiller's hand.

To whom it may concern,

My offerings to you are these files and 47 10-carat jewels. You have been bequeathed these curses in order that the knowledge might be known and subsequently wielded like an ax of truth. All of us have weaknesses. All of us have erred. These missteps don't matter much in the scheme of things. But some of us have sinned, that is — having committed an immoral act that is a transgression against divine law. Hopefully you, the person or persons who receive this trove of knowledge, will be, or become, wise enough to figure the right way to apply this knowledge in the pursuit of justice.

The key chain is for various safe-deposit boxes and storage spaces that may verify some of the claims that are made.

AX

I entered the name of a favorite political figure of mine. There was evidence that she helped a friend get away with an embezzlement. She was also involved in a hit-and-run accident. She was not behind the wheel, but neither had she gone to the police. The victim of the second transgression did not die but carried the memory of the event in his gait.

I sat back in the chair behind the desk that stood in place of the minister's podium overlooking the nave of the chapel. It was the proper place to preside over the countless indictments and downright sins that Quiller had collected when everybody else was asleep.

As a rule I am not the kind of man who is plagued by guilt or uncertainty. Like any other creature in the forest of the damned, I do what I have to in order to survive one more day. There's little guilt involved with fighting for one's life. But the incriminations of that device caused my heart to race and my mind to fill with undefinable guilt.

I typed in Roger Ferris's name. The machine was inactive for a full minute before presenting a list of damnations.

The headlines were: government overthrow, jury tampering, extortion, false witness, and murder.

I was only interested in one thing and so went there with some trepidation.

Reading about my grandmother's boyfriend, my employer, I felt empathy. I understood what he was going through and why he wanted a thumbs-up or thumbs-down on Quiller. It really was a moral quandary and not fear that drove him.

He'd told me the truth. He hadn't killed George Laurel, nor did he have the young man killed; at least that was the judgment of the Ten Thousand Things (TTT). But, regardless of his innocence, he was still involved with the murder, deeply so.

The software designed to search the memory banks of the TTT was simple but complete. It allowed the user to request information by name, transgression, political affiliation, gender, nationality, or race. You could ask who and how many of the residents of that drive had committed the crimes of murder, rape, sex trafficking, theft, betrayal, and more.

Many of the entries were achieved by investigation, interview, and subsequent research. Some crimes had files that provided convincing arguments, others had the locations of where the bodies or the contraband was buried. You could download specific files to a thumb drive in order to distribute a little information without revealing the rest of the trove.

The enormity of information, condemnations, and secrecy of the TTT was truly amazing. In order to gather and organize the events therein, Quiller would have had to have seven maids with seven mops working for a hundred years.

I thought that he probably used agents from institutions like Int-Op to collect data. He must have spent most of the millions of dollars he'd made combing through the billions of souls and their sins.

The last entry on the main menu was something called the dead file. This was a list of 219 individuals who had been killed, either by setup (i.e., sending information to the victims or, failing that, the authorities) or by literal assassination.

There was the feeling of hard-sweat obsessiveness to the data and its meaning. Quiller didn't only go after liberals and the Left. He wanted to show the world that it was rotten at the core.

After many hours of poring over the files, I decided to request a tally of all the inmates. I say *inmates* because the drive felt like a virtual prison even if those indicted didn't know it.

There were 10,364 individual sinners listed and indicted by Quiller.

I packed the device away in its suitcase and shoved it under the desk.

After that I sat for a very long time trying to make sense out of the predicament that had been laid upon my soul. The load was too much to bear and yet I couldn't just walk away from it. I didn't have the knowledge or wisdom, the courage or ambition, to undertake the task that Quiller's suitcase presented.

I didn't want the emeralds, not even for Aja. That wealth would have been a curse for anyone not willing and able to challenge the entire world.

In the end I decided to bury the device away, to hide it from others and also myself. Maybe one day I'd find someone who could see the use of the library of sins. Maybe.

It was dawn by the time I'd made my decision. Quiller was dead. Monica and Coleman were free, rutting like teenagers somewhere. I'd paid my psychic pound of flesh and survived, more or less intact. I'd loved and lost but that's just part of life. In a while, a few days or so, I'd be cautiously happy again.

After a few days and one last task.

"Hello," he answered on the first ring.

"You sleep even less than I do, Mr. Ferris."

"When you get as close to death as I am, son, you begin to feel like sleeping's a sin. What can I do for you?"

"I have it in mind to meet with you and your daughter."

"What for?"

"All I can tell you, sir, is that this is the only way to end your conflict with her."

"You want her brother there too?"

"No."

"Why not?"

"I don't think he's a player in this game."

"When?"

"Tomorrow. Midday. Anywhere you choose."

"What about the Obsidian Club?"

"Sounds posh."

"Are you sure about this, Joe?"

"More than I'd like to be."

"Okay. I'll set it up."

"How's my grandmother doing?"

"She's walking perfectly and if I ask her does it hurt she says, 'Roger, you got no reason to be askin' 'bout my butt.'"

That made me laugh.

"Okay, Joe. I'll set up the meeting for two thirty, teatime. Anything else?"

"Yeah. You'll have to be the one to reach out to Cassandra. You know how?"

"I know where she sleeps and the home addresses of Robert Billings and Ray Bears."

"See you then."

"Hello?"

"Olo."

"Joe. How are you?"

"Pretty good, considering. What's going on with you?"

"I quit Int-Op."

"Because of the dude Zyron bought out?"

"My mentor exposed him and he's out. But it's not that. I realized that I was too trusting. Hanging out with you and Melquarth, I remembered that the only ones I can trust are myself and the people I can see, and touch."

"Now, that is a fundamental fact. Where you gonna live?"

"New York's as good as anywhere. I'll take six months or so figuring out what to do next."

"And Mel?"

The contemplative silence had no pressure behind it. My question presented a lot to think about but little to say.

"He's kind of crazy," she said at last.

"That's like calling a hurricane a rainstorm."

She giggled. Giggled. I knew we would be good friends then.

"I don't usually worry about things like that," she said. "I've been around many crazy people. But your friend is different. I don't know."

"Well, whatever it is, it'll be nice to have you in town for a while. My daughter thinks you walk on water."

"She's a wonderful young woman. If I had a sister I would want her to be like Aja."

My bedroom at Melquarth's Staten Island shrine was a monastic cell on the third floor. The cot had a hard mattress and if you drew the shade it was black as night in there.

I slept well.

35.

MORNING AT MELQUARTH Frost's deconsecrated church was most certainly a religious experience. It honestly felt like being a penitent seeking forgiveness. The twelve stained glass windows that adorned the east and west walls of the nave were constructed in opposing pairs. On the eastern wall were the images of the saints: Matthew offering a few copper coins to a beggar woman in rags trying to care for her wretched children; Augustine sitting upon a humble bench in a green grove talking to a group of pious peasants in a way reminiscent of family; Pelagia, dressed as a nun from some bygone day, kneels down next to a prostrate man burning with fever and distress; Mary of Egypt, bathed in light, is standing in front of a cell, opening the barred door for a prisoner who sees his freedom in her; Olga is physically separating two men brandishing cudgels; and Dismas languishes on the cross, gazing to his left, from which a great radiance arises.

The western wall has: tax collector Matthew wielding a whip upon the back of a man with one hand while relieving the poor wretch of a small sack from which a gold coin falls; Augustine lies in a drunken stupor upon a plush divan being serviced in every way imaginable by prostitutes; Pelagia is a detail made large from the Augustine window, lifting his robe in a licentious manner; Mary of Egypt is urging a small boy to take the purse of a man who has his back turned; sword-wielding Princess Olga rides at the head of a troop of men slaughtering the innocent people of a small village; Dismas is holding a dagger at a child's throat, demanding that his mother hand over her necklace.

The tableaux and their pairings made up Melquarth's imagistic sermon. Sainthood, in his estimation, must exist not only in repentance but also in the acceptance of the evil within. Each window was designed by Mel himself and they were constructed by a centuries-old firm in Vatican City.

I never asked my friend about his money but I imagined that he wasn't interested in wealth and so squirreled away whatever he got from the extortions, heists, ransoms, and contract killings he engaged in before deciding to go, more or less, straight.

Taking the Staten Island train to St. George, I then boarded the ferry to Lower Manhattan. I was relaxed in a way that is related to deep exhaustion.

When I was standing at the back of the ferry staring into the water, someone said, "Hey, brother."

Turning, I saw a young Black man wearing black and very dark blue clothing. His skin was the color of palm wood, a mixture of light brown and gray. He wasn't dressed up or down, just modestly—that's what I thought.

"Hey," I answered.

"What you thinkin' 'bout?"

It seemed rude that someone I didn't know would just walk up and try to get in my head. I didn't utter this sentiment, but my face made clear these thoughts.

"Hold up, man," he said. "I saw you lookin' down in the water, way down, and I wondered if you were okay. That's all."

If you're in deep trouble, lifelines are almost always unexpected.

I'd been leaning against the waist-high wall and so straightened up.

"Um," I muttered. "I, uh, I been havin' a hard time, it's true. But I wasn't gonna jump or nuthin'."

"Wanna go sit down?" my new friend asked.

The benches were at the back of the sternward deck of the ferry, farthest away from the edge. I went with the young man because it pleased me that someone I didn't know showed concern about my well-being.

When we sat I asked, "What's your name?"

"Tremont Lewis. I live out in Staten Island."

"Joe Oliver. Brooklyn."

"So, what's goin' on with you, Joe?"

"You some kinda street preacher or somethin'?"

"Naw, man. You know. I had a sister killed herself. She was out in Saint Louis and they didn't even find her for six days."

"That's a mess."

"You know," he said, clasping his hands. "I always thought that if I was out there that maybe I could have noticed somethin' and asked her if I could help."

"That's the right thought to have. I mean, a lotta things

316

aren't our fault, but that doesn't mean we can't help out anyway."

"Yeah," Tremont Lewis said. He was looking out at the water now. "That's right."

For a good two minutes we sat there side by side looking out at the aquatic traffic between the two boroughs. Then the boat's engine shifted and the ferry lurched a little in the water.

"What you goin' to Manhattan for, Mr. Lewis?"

"Not gettin' off. I just take it back and forth a few times every week or so. Out here I seem to remember Melissa better."

The Obsidian Club is on Sixty-First Street a couple of blocks over on the eastern side of Fifth. There are no signs to tell you where it is. You have to know that it is lodged on the upper floors of a pretty modern office building. The business offices take up the first thirty-five floors or so. Past that, using a special elevator, are the four floors that make up the Obsidian Club.

In order to be offered membership, you have to be wealthy, an insider, and palatable to the membership at large. My grandmother once told me that Roger paid five hundred thousand dollars a year for his due. That included all food and drink.

"May I help you?"

The man standing behind the blue-white Carrara marble standing desk wore an immaculately understated suit. He was older than I but not more than a decade, and he was white like the golden sands of an inland desert.

"I'm a guest of Roger Ferris."

The maître d'hôtel had a slender face and a torso to go with it. His lip wanted a mustache but the Obsidian Club probably forbade it. The man looked at me for maybe six seconds. In times gone by, he might have told me about the servants' entrance or asked what my business was with Ferris.

The potential rejection was in his shoulders, but instead he said, "Take the hall behind me to the Promethean Room, about halfway to the Venus de Milo."

It wasn't the real Venus de Milo but it might have been. The wealth that inhabited those halls was beyond money. Obsidian's membership owned or controlled a significant portion of the Earth.

Big Billings and good-humored Ray were sitting on a stone bench across the way from the entrance to the Promethean Room. When they saw me turn toward the door they were a little surprised.

"I know," I said. "It's not often that the help gets a look inside."

I opened the door and was suddenly flooded by an effulgence of solar light.

The Promethean Room had a thirty-foot ceiling with an outer wall of glass that went all the way up. The long room was dominated by an ebony wood table that could seat at least thirty participants. But that day there were only two people there: Cassandra, who sat to the center right of the table, and Roger, who stood at the far window looking down on the east.

"Hello," I said with some volume. "Everybody waiting for me?"

Roger turned and began the thirty-pace stroll toward the center of the left side of the table. I met him at the chairs across from his daughter.

"Why is he here?" Cassandra asked the old man.

"Because I want him here."

"This is not his business."

"You wouldn't think so," I said jauntily. "But surprisingly enough I have something to say. You know, I'm a private dick and dicks do what they do."

"What's that supposed to mean?" Cassandra asked. And, before I could reply: "I'm done with you."

"I know," I said. "You wanted me to derail your father and clear the way for you and Alexander to take over MDLT. Derail or kill."

"I never asked you to kill anybody."

"Not in so many words. But that doesn't matter anyway because I delivered your message and decided that murder for hire wasn't my thing." I took that moment to sit.

Roger followed suit.

Cassandra wanted me obliterated from her sight. But if looks could kill I would have been dead long before the Quiller Case.

"You see," I said, "I was confused about what were the reasons I was hired to find out if Quiller was worthy of saving. I mean, who would care if a man like that lived or died, was free or caged?"

I glanced at my employer and he looked away.

"At first Quiller didn't even want me in the cell with him," I said to Cassandra. "He told me to leave but he finally, begrudgingly decided that I might be able to help him. At first I thought that he was somehow blackmailing your dad to get him out of Dutch. But your father said no and he was right...kinda. Quiller did have information that Roger didn't want divulged, but he wasn't protecting himself like you thought."

"No?" the daughter said on a sneer. "Then why was I told by Minta Kraft that that man Quiller had evidence that my father is a murderer?"

"That's where I got confused," I admitted.

"No," Roger said to me. "Don't."

"It's the only way, Rog," I told him. "You see," I then said to his daughter, "your father cares more about you and your brother than you think. My grandmother told me a long time ago that you were the stronger sibling, the one that looked after Alex. He's a weak man, given to dark moods and depression."

"There's a reason for that," she said, showing more humanity in those few words than I would have thought possible.

"Yes," I said. "He was broken over the murder of George Laurel."

"Joseph," Roger warned.

"Your brother met Valeria Ursini at the Olympics when your father was training the fencing team. Alexander fell in love with her, but she was infatuated with Roger."

"You always said that you gave us everything," daughter said to father, "but in reality you took it all."

"It seems like that," I said as Roger stood up and headed back for his post at the window.

"It is that," Cassandra said to the old man's back.

Roger stopped his escapist pilgrimage and settled onto a chair three seats down.

"Did you know that after Valeria started at Yale your father dropped her and Alex moved in?"

It gave me great pleasure to say something that Cassandra didn't know and that Roger didn't know that I had figured out.

"Yeah," I said. "He hooked up with her. He figured that there would be wedding bells and babies. But Ms. Ursini heard a different drum. She wanted a good time but no more. And when she got together with George Laurel, your brother couldn't take it. He offered Sola Prendergast enough money to pull his whole family out of poverty. That's why Sola hacked poor George to death."

"That's a lie!" the sister proclaimed.

"No," I said gently, and then I lied a little. "Quiller told me the story. When I asked him about your dad he told me that there was suspicion about George among the homicide cops of New Haven. They didn't have enough to go after a Ferris, so they let it drop. And then, years later, Quiller sent a lawyer in to offer Sola his services if he would tell him what really happened."

"Those are just words," Cassandra ejaculated, spittle popping from her lips. "Some story you made up to save that bastard's life."

"Sola signed a confession," I avowed solemnly.

Everything I said was true, only I hadn't heard it from Quiller directly. I read it in the TTT.

"That can't be," she said, aging in front of my eyes.

"Minta Kraft told you that Quiller had something on your father. You used her to set up Quiller. And she used you to bring him down."

"Please, Joseph," Roger pled.

"Your father's crime was to cover up your brother's paid-for butchery."

Cassandra turned her eyes to Roger. There was no mistaking the pain on both their faces. He wanted to deny everything and so did she.

"You should be happy," I said to Cassandra. "Your convoluted plan to destroy Quiller and get his blackmail file out in the world would have destroyed the only person you truly love."

There's little use for truth when it is the unwanted answer to a lifetime of hatred.

With great concentration Roger's only daughter was able to push against the tabletop and stand.

"Cassie," Roger said.

"Shut up!"

"I didn't know what to do," he continued. "I felt like you say, that it was all my fault. I wanted to save him. Save him."

Cassandra Ferris-Brathwaite turned away and stumbled the few steps to the wall. There she put out a hand to remain upright and walked to the door of the Promethean Room.

"You destroyed her," Roger Ferris said to me.

"She shot my grandmother by proxy. I gave her what she deserved face-to-face."

36.

"SO WHAT DID you do, Daddy?" Aja asked me months after the Quiller Case was closed.

"I gave the Ten Thousand Things file to someone I could trust and asked them to hide it . . . somewhere. Then I went on with my life."

"I mean about Mr. Ferris's son."

She was seated behind her reception desk while I sat in the same chair as when I talked to Roger's daughter.

"I retrieved the confession that Sola Prendergast wrote and the documentation that came with it," I said. "Then I turned it all over to Henri Tourneau."

"That's that nice police detective, right?"

"Uh-huh. Yeah."

"What'd he say?"

"That he'd call New Haven PD and see."

"And what'd they do?"

"Nothing."

The smile my daughter affected was filled with a kind of

sympathetic pain. Aja-Denise is a beautiful young woman. I know that, but when I look at her, all I see is my child.

"Did you tell Grandma B?"

"I wanted to, but hey, you know, she deserves a little happiness."

Aja smiled at me.

"What?" I asked her.

"How come you're tellin' me 'bout it?"

That was the right question. Aja almost always asked the hardest ones.

"Maybe two months after," I said, "after I thought it was through, I started waking up in the middle of the night."

"You were worried about it?"

"No, not worried. You know, honey, for a dozen years after I was in prison, I'd wake up in cold sweats."

"Yeah?"

"But I don't anymore. Ever since I saw Quiller in there, the fear is gone."

"That's good, right?"

"Yeah. It's good. But now those files have kind of like taken its place."

"You could give them to me," she offered.

"No. It's good enough that I share what I know with you. Now and then maybe I could think about it, and if there's something I need to talk out, I can call on you."

"Like I was your partner?"

"Maybe."

About the Author

WALTER MOSLEY is one of America's most celebrated writers. He was given the National Book Award's 2020 Medal for Distinguished Contribution to American Letters, named a Grand Master of the Mystery Writers of America, and honored with the Anisfield-Wolf Award, a Grammy, a PEN USA Lifetime Achievement Award, the Robert Kirsch Award, numerous Edgars, and several NAACP Image Awards. His work is translated into twenty-five languages. He has published fiction and nonfiction in *The New Yorker, Playboy,* and *The Nation.* As an executive producer, he adapted his novel *The Last Days of Ptolemy Grey* for Apple TV+, and he serves as a writer and executive producer for FX's *Snowfall.*